D1271324

FENZIG'S FORTUNE

FENZIG'S FORTUNE

JEAN RABE

FIVE STAR
An imprint of Thomson Gale, a part of The Thomson Corporation

THOMSON
™
GALE

Detroit • New York • San Francisco • New Haven, Conn. • Waterville, Maine • London

THOMSON

GALE

Copyright © 2007 by Jean Rabe.

Thomson Gale is part of The Thomson Corporation.

Thomson and Star Logo and Five Star are trademarks and Gale is a registered trademark used herein under license.

ALL RIGHTS RESERVED

This novel is a work of fiction. Names, characters, places, and incidents are either the product of the author's imagination, or, if real, used fictitiously.

No part of this book may be reproduced or transmitted in any form or by any electronic or mechanical means, including photocopying, recording or by any information storage and retrieval system, without the express written permission of the publisher, except where permitted by law.

Set in 11 pt. Plantin.

LIBRARY OF CONGRESS CATALOGING-IN-PUBLICATION DATA

Rabe, Jean.
    Fenzig's fortune / Jean Rabe.—1st ed.
      p. cm.
    ISBN-13: 978-1-59414-567-4 (hardcover : alk. paper)
    ISBN-10: 1-59414-567-9 (hardcover : alk. paper)
    1. Gnomes—Fiction. 2. Thieves—Fiction. 3. Middle Ages—Fiction. I. Title.
  PS3568.A232F46 2007
  813'.54—dc22
                                              2006034799

First Edition. First Printing: March 2007.

Published in 2007 in conjunction with Tekno Books and Ed Gorman.

Printed in the United States of America on permanent paper
10 9 8 7 6 5 4 3 2 1

This one's for John Helfers—
an exceptional editor and author,
but an even better friend.

CENTRAL ARKANSAS LIBRARY SYSTEM
JACKSONVILLE BRANCH
JACKSONVILLE, ARKANSAS

TREASURE HUNTER

An unpleasant odor clung to Fenzig's nostrils, reminding him of his grandfather's orchard at the end of the growing season, when all the ignored, misshapen apples fell to the ground and started to rot. But this smell was much, much stronger, and he more than didn't like it.

He tried to think about fresh-baked bread, which he dearly loved to smell—and eat. Fenzig's stomach rumbled, he licked his lips, and he breathed deeply—as he would over a table full of warm loaves just pulled from the oven. The faintest wisps of steam would be rising from them, and they would be all shiny from butter his Aunt Ermal always brushed across the tops. There would be an open jar of honey nearby, and perhaps a bowl of mashed strawberries or blackberries, a knife for cutting thick slices, fancy little dessert plates, and a pitcher of cold goat's milk.

"Heaven," Fenzig said, breathing deep again. "Simply h-h-h. . . ." He gagged and sputtered. His imagination was vivid, but it wasn't quite good enough to cover up the intense stench of this horrid place.

And it couldn't even come close to covering up the dirt.

This cell he'd been tossed in late last night hadn't been cleaned in who knew how long—years, he suspected, and a thick layer of grime covered everything. Something greasy coated the stone floor, the walls, and the mound of moldy old straw trying to pass itself off as a bed. In fact, something greasy covered everything.

Fenzig was quite the fastidious soul, and he couldn't stomach all the filth surrounding him.

But more than the dirt and the smell, he didn't like the darkness. The only light came from a feebly flickering torch outside in the hall. The small barred window high on his cell door didn't let much in—just enough to create a few shadows out of the blackness. Just enough so he could see the rats.

Fenzig didn't like rats. He spotted two on the far side of the small chamber, and that meant the darkest parts of the room undoubtedly hid more. The pair stared at him and wriggled their gleaming noses—the only things, Fenzig suspected, that weren't dirty in this horrible, horrible place.

He glared at the rats and stretched his short legs. A gnome, Fenzig was naturally short all over. Still, at three feet two inches he was practically towering for one of his diminutive race. A shock of dirty, sandy brown hair hung over his forehead. His once-light-gray trousers and tunic were now a darker shade of gray, and his bare feet were getting colder and dirtier as he padded across the stone floor toward the door—and also got wet as he stepped in something squishy that he was glad he couldn't see.

Fenzig, like most gnomes, didn't bother with shoes. They were too confining and didn't let the air circulate around his toes. The soles of his wide feet were tough, and the tops were covered with a curly mass of dark-brown hair that nearly matched the color of his eyes. He wouldn't have minded shoes now, however.

The rats squeaked at him as he came close, but they didn't run for cover. One defiantly reared up on its hind legs and sniffed the foul air.

They're hungry, Fenzig thought. *They're waiting for dinner. My dinner.*

"You can have all of it. Whatever 'it' is," he said glumly, ignoring his growling belly. "I'm hungry, too, but I'm not going to eat the slop they serve here. I'd rather starve first. Yes, indeed. I'd rather starve."

The two guards who had thrown the young gnome into the cell very late last night hadn't bothered to bring him a snack, and he'd refused to eat the small plate of breakfast someone slid under the door this morning. The lukewarm concoction had resembled nothing so much as a greenish brown cowpie, and he didn't much like eating things he couldn't quite identify. The meal might have been old eggs or spoiled oatmeal, but he wasn't about to taste it and find out.

The guards apparently didn't serve lunch here, or if they did they'd forgotten him. Or maybe he had slept through it, and the rats had gobbled it down. He suspected in either case he hadn't missed anything, and he certainly wasn't about to eat what might pass for dinner, which had to be coming soon—his grumbling stomach told him so.

"I *am* going to starve," he whimpered. Like most gnomes, Fenzig liked eating four or five generous meals a day, and sometimes a few sweets in between. He also liked living in a clean house that was warm and rat-free and pleasantly appointed. Thick cushions on padded chairs with padded hassocks to put his clean, bare feet on.

"I hate this place," he hissed. "Yes, indeed. I truly, truly hate this place."

"Get used to it, thief!" came a deep voice from beyond the door.

"You might as well get used to the food, too," called a second voice, this one high-pitched and angry-sounding. "You're going to be here for a while. A very long while. After all, you tried to steal from the king. You should be glad you're still alive. He could have had you killed instead of jailed."

9

The first voice chuckled, the laugh sounding evil to Fenzig. He pictured that guard as an ogre, one with warts and tusks and tangled hair that stuck out from under his armpits.

"But maybe the king'll change his mind and order the little thief hanged anyway. No use spending money to feed him for the rest of his miserable life."

"Hanged?" This from the higher-pitched guard. This one definitely not an ogre. "That'd be too good for him. Maybe the king'll have him tortured. Girond the Tormentor hasn't pulled off any legs for at least a month."

The guards laughed together then, loudly and much too long as far as Fenzig was concerned. Thoughts started churning in the gnome's head. *How long will I be here? Forever? Could the king really order me killed? I didn't hurt anyone. I've never ever in my short life hurt anyone.* He pursed his lips and suddenly felt much smaller than he really was, and more alone than he'd ever been before. More than hunger started burning in his belly— fear, the deep, intense kind that sent a shiver all the way through him and caused him to vomit.

Moments later the guards were chatting softly to themselves about hunting season starting soon. One of them tapped something against the wall, the way a bored man might tap his finger on a desk or against his temple. Fenzig suspected it was the haft of some long weapon being tapped, and his spirits sank even further.

The gnome craned his neck this way and that, still desperately trying to ignore the rancid smell of this place and trying to glance out the barred window—both attempts were futile. He jumped, his feet slapping the greasy stone floor. He jumped again and slipped, landing on his rump and sending the rats scampering into the darkest shadows. The window was about five feet up on the door. He could climb the wood; Fenzig knew he could climb practically anything. But why look out at the ugly mugs of the king's guards? Why not wait until they dozed off and then check things out? After all, they had to sleep some time.

There's got to be a way out of here. Yes, indeed, there just has to be. I'll find it. Indeed, I will. After all, despite Fenzig's state of utter despair, he considered himself resourceful. He'd gotten into the king's tower—no easy feat. He certainly should be able to get out of the king's dungeon.

Yeah, I'd gotten into the tower all right, he recalled. *Into the tower and right into trouble and into this very stinky, dirty hole.*

An Unfortunate
Recollection

Fenzig had picked a night when the sky was overcast and the fog that blanketed the ground was thick enough to cloak his presence. Dressed in tight-fitting, shadow-colored clothes, he made his way toward King Erlgrane's castle. He had smudged soot on his face and hands and on the tops of his toes so he could hide better in the darkness. And he breathed shallowly and stepped carefully so he would make no noise.

Stopping in the tall bushes at the perimeter of the manicured grounds, he listened to boots crunching across the gravel walkway. When he had memorized the sentries' dull and predictable routine, he slipped past them and started climbing the north tower's stone wall.

To the thief, climbing was virtually as easy as walking. His thin fingers found handholds that most people wouldn't think to use, wouldn't likely notice, and he was light enough that he could cling to vines and trellises that would buckle under the weight of human men.

Fenzig knew to go to this tower because the king's cleaning girls, whom he'd liberally plied with coins a few days ago in the marketplace, had revealed the location of the treasure vault. The thief, who relished money above all else, never objected to spending a few coins here and there when he was certain it would lead to making a lot more. Besides, the girls were pretty and smiled at Fenzig, chatted pleasantly with him—which was a change, as the humans of Burlengren tended to look askance at gnomes. Too, Fenzig knew from the girls' worn clothes that it was apparent the king wasn't paying them much. They were more than delighted by the coins he'd offered them.

Within moments he reached the top window. Just as the half-full moon edged out from behind a cloud, Fenzig squeezed inside. It was a narrow window, and a tight fit even for his lithe form. Perhaps at one time the window had served as a spot where archers stood and fired out at the enemy, he mused—when the kingdom was at war and the castle was under siege every year. Or perhaps it was merely a slit to allow a little light and fresh air into the fusty old place. The gods knew this place smelled musty enough even with a window.

The gods also knew, or so the thief believed, that King Erlgrane didn't need archers standing watch—out of this or any other window. Since the man inherited the land and the title from his childless uncle almost a decade ago, no one had seriously threatened the kingdom. Erlgrane, though not a just or fair ruler by any means, was known to be a shrewd one—negotiating peace with neighboring regions, enlarging his own territory through skillful political deals, and keeping a sizeable military force at the ready—as an implied threat.

But the kings before Erlgrane, ah, they must have had archers here, Fenzig suspected. He felt the smoothness of the stone just beyond the window, indicating many feet had shuffled about here at one time. He glanced out the slit, noticed the sentries strolling past on the grounds below, imagined, for the briefest of moments, that he had a bow and could expertly pick them off. He allowed himself a faint smile and also imagined, for slightly longer, that he was the king ordering the archers to find their targets and defend him from thieves who might try to steal his treasure—thieves who might possibly be small enough to fit through this window. King Fenzig!

Enough dreaming, he scolded himself. *Time to get to work.*

13

Indeed, it is.

Fenzig silently padded across a thickly carpeted landing toward a large, locked door—the entrance to the king's treasure chamber. It was the only door the thief could see, likely the only one on this level. Stairs descended from the landing and led to other rooms below—mysteries that might be unraveled during future expeditions.

There definitely will be future expeditions. Yes, indeed. Getting in was certainly easy enough. I'll just have to wait a few months or so before returning, just in case they actually put guards here for a while. Wait 'til the fuss dies down a bit.

If Fenzig were the foolish, overly greedy sort, he would explore the entire tower tonight. But while the thief took risks, he knew when to be cautious. This one room, this one very special treasure room, would be enough for this trip—he hadn't brought anyone with him to help carry the loot. There were limits to what he'd be able to haul out of here by himself.

King Erlgrane hadn't placed even one guard outside the treasure chamber door. They were stationed downstairs, the cleaning girls had said, where most burglars would be forced to enter. However, the thief noted that as insurance the king had installed half a dozen small bolts and locks on his treasure chamber door. They gleamed dimly in the light of a lantern that hung on the wall halfway down the stairwell. The thief touched the bolt at eye-level. "Why would you need guards anyway when you have these very fine locks?"

Fenzig knelt almost reverently in front of the door and reached into his pocket to retrieve a worn canvas pouch filled with thin metal picks. The gnome diligently set to work on the bottommost locks and was quite appreciative when one gave him a considerable amount of trouble.

His skills had not been challenged lately. *Indeed,* he thought, *it's been a long time since my talents had been put to any kind of a test.* It took him several minutes to get the clasp undone, then he moved onto the next bolt, and the next, and the top one that was nearly out of his reach. Finally, his stubby fingers wrapped around the handle.

The door creaked open, and he carefully inched his way into the room beyond. Light from the lantern spilled faintly into the chamber and danced like a cavorting ghost over mounds of heavily tarnished copper coins. There were a few piles of gold coins, too, and the thief's eyes locked onto these.

There were also a half-dozen chests that undoubtedly held gems, jewels, and strings of pearls—the thief was especially fond of the latter, as they could be fenced for considerable money farther to the north. And there were a few fancy jade figurines and beautiful ceramic pots that would also fetch some decent coin. A crystal vase that sparkled merrily in the scant light caught his eye. A nice piece, but a small one.

A good price for that vase, but not an outstanding one, the gnome thought after a moment.

All together, it was a respectable display, though he'd certainly expected King Erlgrane of Burlengren to have a bit more loot: some dazzling baubles and gilded statues, heavy mirrors with bejeweled gold frames, dozens upon dozens of ivory belt buckles—as the king was known to collect them—silver candlesticks, brass urns, ornamental daggers, and ancient swords dripping with eldritch enchantments. Treasures like that. Treasures he envisioned a king would own. Treasures that, provided he could carry them, he intended to take away.

This was a treasure, but not the treasure of a king.

Puzzled, but still moderately satisfied with what he would net tonight, Fenzig carefully picked his way among the coins, watchful of where he stepped. He, like practically everyone else in the kingdom, knew Erlgrane had an aging wizard under his royal thumb. The thief suspected the wizard had cast various protection spells about the place as an added precaution. The thief was wary of magic and didn't want to trigger any spells which might alert the guards, or worse—might alert the wizard. They might hold the gnome to the spot, turn him into a tiny lizard. Or . . . the gnome thought a moment . . . or *they might make an incredible horde of treasure look like only a modest one!* He'd heard that magic could do anything. Perhaps the king's treasure was far more valuable than it appeared. Why, a clever wizard could hide a fortune beneath an illusion of tarnished copper coins.

Fenzig knew not to step on any symbols scratched on the floor—he noticed two of these, which might or might not be active spells depending on how old they were. One could never be too careful where one stepped, he told himself. And he knew not to touch anything that glowed. Disturbing either could alert the castle occupants, and the thief wasn't armed—was never armed, and wasn't able to physically deal with any sentries. He leaned over a mound of gold coins, pulled a leather sack loose from his belt, and began stuffing it full. The soft clinking of the coins was music.

Odd, only the coins on top of this pile were gold. The ones underneath were iron, not worth nearly as much as even copper coins. He tested an iron coin with his fingers, then put it to his tongue. Definitely iron, definitely not a spell only making it look like iron.

Something is wrong with this treasure, the thief nearly said aloud. *I should get out of here.*

Fenzig quickly finished stuffing his bag with only the gold coins. It would be enough to let him live well for a while. The gnome would take a string of pearls or two while he was at it. Those would be light and could be carried around his neck. And then he would leave, as he suddenly had a very bad feeling about this place. He moved to the closest chest, examined the lock, retrieved his thinnest pick, and went to work. If there were pearls, they'd probably be in here. He took a deep breath, threw open the lid, and saw—

"Nothing," Fenzig whispered. "Empty. Something's definitely wrong."

"I'd say you're in the wrong, thief. Stay where you are!"

It was the first time in Fenzig's relatively lucrative career that he'd been caught, and he suspected he'd remember those words for the rest of his life—however short that life might now be. The gnome swallowed hard and turned toward the speaker.

"Guards, take this diminutive miscreant to the dungeon."

I'm dead, Fenzig thought. *Very, very dead.*

The speaker was Erlgrane's wizard, of course, an old human, nearly ancient, with stooped shoulders and a gray beard that hung below his waist. His skin was as pale and wrinkled as parchment, practically white—like it hadn't seen the sun in decades, and the fingers that edged past his voluminous sleeves were gnarled and bony and reminded the thief of a spider's legs.

"H-h-how?" the gnome stammered. "H-h-how did you know I was here?"

The wizard yawned and pointing at the treasure chamber's door. "Opening that set off a magical chime, waking me from a much-needed sleep. I summoned the guards. And here we all are." The wizard smiled self-righteously and yawned again, then steepled his spider-fingers beneath his chin. "It's been a long time since someone was foolish enough to try to steal from King Erlgrane."

Then the smile disappeared, and he glared at the gnome with rheumy blue eyes that looked out over wrinkled, dark circles. "You are very foolish, wee-one. Very, very foolish. This isn't even the real treasure chamber, *thief.* That treasure room is a great deal more difficult to find and much larger. It has many priceless riches inside. More wealth than the likes of you could possibly comprehend. This room contains nothing of any significant worth. Just as you are of no significant worth."

The thief swallowed hard.

"Valueless." The ancient man chuckled softly and gathered the folds of his dark robe in his spider-fingers.

With that, the wizard turned on his slippered heels and left, and the thief was roughly entrusted to the not-so-gentle care of the sentries. They turned him upside down and shook out every coin he had—including a few of his own that he'd come into the tower with. They confiscated his set of thieving picks and a small pouch filled with strips of dried venison (which he'd stolen from a merchant earlier). Then the tallest guard tossed the thief over a muscular shoulder, as if he were a sack of vegetables, and carried him roughly down several sets of stairs.

The second guard followed along behind, all the while berating the gnome for breaking into the castle and hinting that all manner of doom awaited him. Without pause, they unceremoniously threw Fenzig into this cell, locked the door, and left him with only the rats for company. The rats and the oppressive stink.

I've got to get out of here. Indeed, I must. Maybe I'll feign getting sick, he thought. *I'll double over when they bring me dinner, which has to be coming soon, and they'll open the cell door to see what's wrong. I could dash out, climb up the stairs, and run to freedom. Or maybe I could lie on the straw and pretend to be dead, and the guards will throw me out with the garbage. Or maybe I could climb the door and work the lock loose. Or maybe. . . .*

Fenzig's mind whirled with the possibilities—all of which seemed especially dismal on his very empty stomach.

"Oh, why did I try to steal from King Erlgrane?" he whispered as he whirled on the balls of his filthy, cold feet and strode toward the straw. "Why did I try such a stunt?" But he knew the answer. He had tried to steal from the king because the king was the richest man in all of Burlengren, the city nearest the gnome town of Graespeck.

He'd already stolen from most of the wealthy farmers in the area—not robbed them blind, mind you—just stole enough coins and pieces of jewelry to keep himself in food, clothes, and more than a few luxuries. He never took *everything* a person owned; he had some morals, after all. And he'd run various successful scams on travelers passing through, lining his pockets with their gold and getting away before they were the wiser.

It wasn't that the gnome didn't like to work, for he considered thieving very hard work. He just didn't like the kind of work that was the same thing every day, physical work that was overly strenuous and made him sweat. Why labor hard for a few coins a week when he could steal as much as he needed—and then some? A steady job was for those who were not as creative, skilled, or clever as he.

So Fenzig had tried to steal from King Erlgrane because the king was rich and the gnome wanted a share of it. *And I should have gotten away with it,* he fumed. *I am an expert thief and I shouldn't have been caught.*

"I hate this place." Fenzig sat listlessly on the straw. He pursed his lips and glowered at the rats. "I hate you. Indeed, I hate the smell. And I hate the fact that I was caught." Grimly, the gnome realized he had only himself to blame for his predicament. "I shouldn't have tried to steal from King Erlgrane. I should've stuck to stealing from farmers. Not as much money. But they don't have wizards and guards, and indeed they can't hang you in the public square or hand you over to someone named Girond the Tormentor."

His stomach rumbled more loudly, and he briefly wondered what was keeping the rubbish they'd serve for dinner. Maybe he'd try just a little. Just enough to keep up his strength so he could formulate a plan of escape. He was still muttering to himself when the door creaked open.

The same gruff guards who'd brought him here last night were illuminated in the torchlight.

"King Erlgrane will see you now," the tallest sneered.

The second grinned maliciously and slowly drew his index finger across his neck.

A chill raced down Fenzig's short spine.

A Grim Proposition

The gnome felt himself being lifted as a guard on either side hoisted him by the armpits. They were holding him so tight that he couldn't wriggle free. Occasionally one would "accidentally" jab him in the ribs, as the other maneuvered around to scrape him along a rough section of wall.

I'm going to die, Fenzig thought sadly. *I'm so terribly young, and I'm going to die before I really get to live. How will they do it? A rope? An axe? Maybe these oafs will drop me down the stairs so I break my neck. I wonder if it will hurt? Of course it will hurt. But I wonder how much it will hurt. How long will it take? Will anybody tell my father? Probably not,* Fenzig decided after being carried up two flights of stairs. *Nobody even asked my name.*

Fenzig survived being manhandled up the interminably long staircase and expected to be taken to a torture chamber or a courtyard with a gallows where King Erlgrane would pass sentence without so much as a trial and solemnly watch the execution. Or maybe his death would be handled someplace more public, where he'd be made an example to young people, showing them the penalty for a life of crime. Maybe he'd be hanged in front of the entire town and his body left to rot to feed the crows. People in Burlengren didn't much care for gnomes anyway.

"At least the air is better here," he whispered. He was breathing deeper, clearing the stench that had settled in his lungs.

"Finer still where you're being taken," one of the guards offered.

Fenzig hadn't expected to be brought into King Erlgrane's audience chamber and set down at a long marble-topped table filled with steaming food: bowls brimming with delicious-looking sugar beets, plates piled high with mouth-watering vegetables, tureens of soup, dishes of candied fruit, loaves of just-baked bread—and little bowls to wash your fingers in.

The room was almost larger than the gnome's home town. White marble pillars, festooned with carvings of plump cherubs edged in gold trim lined the sides and supported the heavy roof that was oh-so-high above the gnome's head. There was a large mural on the ceiling that had elegantly dressed humans dancing across it, and the floor was covered with a thick rug shot through with threads of silver and woven in an intricate pattern. Everything in the room had a pattern in it, but Fenzig wasn't paying a lot of attention to the details. He was too busy eyeing the huge roast turkey in the center of the table and the bowl of boiled potatoes sitting near a container of thick, savory gravy. The scents of the food were helping him forget the odors of his cell and even raising his spirits a little.

I wonder if this is my last meal? I heard condemned prisoners always get a last meal, he thought. *This certainly would be a fine last meal. Especially if there is dessert.* He stretched forward and dangled his fingers into his water bowl, then wiped them dry on his pantleg.

He wondered if he should dig in or if he needed some kind of permission. He judged the distance to the turkey and to the roast. The table was large—human-sized, not gnome-sized—and he wouldn't be able to reach the meat without standing on his chair. The guards were posted behind him, hovering to make sure he stayed put, though one briefly moved out of the way so a serving girl could pour him a glass of juice. It smelled of raspberries, sweet and inviting.

"King Erlgrane will join you soon," she said, then whispered, "Don't eat or drink anything until he arrives. It's not polite."

Fenzig fidgeted nervously and looked around. He coughed to cover up the sounds of his rumbling stomach, and he tried to concentrate on the polished silver candlesticks on the table, anything to keep his mind off the food. It had been far too long since he'd eaten.

The napkins were made of silk, so fine-looking he'd been afraid to dry his fingers on them, and the plush chairs that ringed the room were worth a small fortune. The knives and forks and spoons were made of real silver, not wood or steel like common families used. Fenzig's own family was not well-off, and until he'd "procured" a set of silver for his mother's birthday two years back, there hadn't been enough knives and forks for everyone at the table.

I should have broken into this room instead, he thought. *I could have made off with the candlesticks and a dozen spoons, and I'll bet the wizard wouldn't have known. Who'd cast protection or warning spells in a dining room?*

Trumpets blared just beyond the chamber, and, as the refrain died, twin mahogany doors slowly opened to reveal the glistening brass instruments and the trumpeters who, dressed uniformly, also stepped back uniformly. King Erlgrane strode in between them. He was attired in dark velvets—navy, violet, and forest green, all trimmed with pearls and beads. Fenzig guessed the outfit was worth more than all the coins in the fake treasure room.

King Erlgrane reminded Fenzig of a hawk, with a narrow beaklike nose too long for his fleshy face and dark beady eyes that seemed to regard the gnome as prey. The king's hands fluttered like a bird's wings, and his long neck bobbed forward as he glided farther into the room.

Fenzig's mouth dropped open as the king selected a chair at the end of the table. The gnome had been so engrossed with the impending meal that he hadn't noticed *that* chair. Well, to be fair, the chair was a good distance from the gnome and couldn't be seen well until he turned his head so his chin touched his shoulder. Besides, it wasn't exactly a chair, Fenzig decided. It was more like a throne. It was high-backed and made of burnished brass and some dark wood that gleamed warmly in the light of the candles. Its padded back and sides were covered with an expensive brocade material, and embedded into the wood along the top and at the handrests were plum-sized rubies and jacinths. Fenzig surmised that any one of those stones could buy enough food to feed every gnome in his town for several months, maybe a year—even given the gnomes' voracious appetites.

King Erlgrane was wearing even larger gems, the gnome noticed as the monarch reached for his wine glass. Each manicured finger, including his thumb, was bedecked with at least one ring set with a big, glittering stone.

How can one man have so much wealth? Fenzig wondered. *And what would have been so bad about me taking just a little of it? How can he move his fingers wearing all of that? How can he lift his hands?*

"Good evening, *thief*," the king said. His voice was deep and musical, and the gnome thought he might have enjoyed listening to it under other circumstances.

The king swished the juice about in the crystal goblet, never spilling a drop, held it to his nose, and his lips edged upward into a slight smile. Then he swallowed only a little of it and motioned to a serving girl.

She quickly sliced the turkey, releasing even more scents to tantalize the gnome. Fenzig could barely contain himself while she filled the king's plate and buttered his bread. Finally, the king nodded toward the gnome, indicating he could eat.

For a moment Fenzig forgot all about his imminent doom and stretched forward. His hand closed about the lip of a bowl of jellied cranberries, and he tugged it closer. The serving girls put on his plate the things he couldn't reach—which was almost everything on the table—and he filled his plate and emptied it thrice before he noticed quite a bit of time had passed. Embarrassed, he looked up at King Erlgrane. The monarch had apparently long since finished his meal and was leaning back in the throne-like chair, coolly regarding the stuffed gnome.

Fenzig reluctantly finished his last bite of turkey, pretended to wipe his mouth on the silk napkin, then shoved the napkin in his trouser pocket, where two others and a crystal salt shaker were already nested.

Now he's going to tell me how I will die, he thought nervously. The gnome started to sweat and took a quick glance around, noticing six guards—all stationed by the room's exits, and all with swords drawn. *No way out,* he decided. *I'm done for. At least I'll go out with a full belly.*

"I could have you killed. *Should* have you killed, wee-one." The king used the somewhat derogatory nickname the humans of the area had given the gnome race. "Stealing from me is punishable by death. Are you aware of that?"

Of course I'm aware of that, Fenzig answered to himself. *Yes, indeed, now I am aware of that. What do you think the prison guards told me—repeatedly? What do you think I'm so nervous about? Why are my knuckles so white? And my very full stomach isn't doing flip-flops because of the food. The food was great by the way, thank you,* the gnome added, wondering if he should compliment the king out loud.

King Erlgrane clapped his hands, and the serving girls began to clear the table. "Stand up, wee-one. I want to get a good look at this *master thief* who had the gall to break into my castle."

Fenzig slid out of the chair and reluctantly padded toward King Erlgrane. The king leaned back in his throne and angled his lean form so he faced away from the table and could better view the gnome. The monarch's change in posture also let Fenzig see even more jewels. A sapphire-encrusted dagger stuck out of a sheath in the king's right boot. His belt buckle was hammered gold—the image of a unicorn with diamond eyes—and he wore wrist bracers set with shimmering black opals.

He wears a fortune, Fenzig thought, his mouth watering ever so slightly. *More wealth than. . . .*

"You're quite thin for a wee-one, though I daresay if you keep eating like that you won't be," he began. "Won't have to worry about you fitting through my tower windows." He drew his lips into a thin line. "I've heard you're a rather accomplished burglar. My wizard, who was not at all pleased that you roused him last night, cast a few spells to learn about you—Fenzighan Wiznagrik, isn't it? Well, it seems, *little Fenzighan,* that you've been lightening the purses of travelers in my realm, not to mention stealing from my farmers."

My *wizard,* my *realm,* my *farmers. Do you think everything is yours?* Fenzig nervously shifted his weight back and forth on his feet, but he managed to meet King Erlgrane's steady gaze.

"You don't deny any of this, do you, wee-one?"

The gnome shook his head. "No. I am a thief. But I never hurt anybody, your majesty, ever. And, indeed, I never took *everything* anybody had. And I don't think I should die."

"Everybody dies eventually, my little thief." The king rubbed his chin and eyed the gnome stonily. He let the silence in the room become ponderous before breaking it again. "No one lives forever, Fenzighan Wiznagrik. But if you're as good a thief as my wizard thinks you are, perhaps you could outlive this day. Maybe live a good, long time, or in any event as long as wee-ones tend to live. Perhaps we could strike a deal. I'll overlook your past transgressions if you perform a little errand for me. Interested? One small errand in exchange for your one small life?"

The gnome had not expected to be offered a way out of his predicament.

"An errand?"

King Erlgrane nodded. "Nothing too complex. I need you to pick up something for me a few miles north of here."

"I'm to go someplace and get something for you?" Fenzig briefly wondered why King Erlgrane didn't send one of his guards or servants. "That's it?"

"Yes," he replied silkily. "But you'll need to use your skills. You'll have to steal what I want."

Fenzig gulped. Stealing had gotten him into his current pickle. Could stealing get him out? Would stealing for King Erlgrane really be illegal, since the king made all the rules? Maybe it wouldn't be stealing at all. Maybe it would just be appropriating something by royal decree. The gnome looked at the floor and at his dirty bare feet.

King Erlgrane eased out of the thronelike chair and stood, towering over the gnome. Fenzig looked up.

"Well, wee-one? Steal *for* me, and I will forget you tried to steal *from* me." The king idly drummed his fingers on the table. "What is your answer?"

"Wh-wh-what do you want stolen?" Fenzig stammered.

"Three gems," the king replied. "Three beautiful emeralds all the same size. Nothing too complex and nothing difficult to carry."

"Who do I have to steal them from?"

"The duke of K'Nosha. Duke Rehmir."

"The duke? His manor is not just a few miles from here. It's close to a hundred miles. And that's not going to be easy. He controls a lot of land and an army. Why, if he caught me. . . ."

"He'd kill you. Of course, if you don't try, I'll kill you," King Erlgrane said evenly. "In any event, it should be easier than stealing from me, and you thought you could do that. Your answer, thief?"

Dozens of questions continued to swirl in Fenzig's head, but he was afraid to ask them. Why didn't the king just *ask* the duke for the gems? Or buy them?

"Do you know where he keeps them?" Fenzig finally risked. "Are they well guarded?"

"My friends tell me Duke Rehmir keeps them in his study, on the mantel of his fireplace where he can easily admire them. I would assume he has guards. After all, the gems are quite valuable."

"And that's why you want them? Because they're valuable?" Fenzig hadn't meant to ask those questions aloud, and the king's perturbed expression was evidence he should have kept them to himself.

"I adore gems," King Erlgrane replied. There was more of an edge to his voice, as if he was losing patience with his prisoner. "They fascinate me." He waggled his bejeweled fingers for effect.

I can see that, Fenzig thought. *You're wearing enough gems for a couple dozen people. What do you need with three more?* "Why. . . ."

"I want these particular gems because they are perfect, flawless. They would be the pinnacles of my collection. With them in my possession, I would be able to bargain with Duke Rehmir for something I want even more than the emeralds. And I *will* have the emeralds, thief. Either you can steal them and live, or I will have you slowly and very painfully drawn and quartered and get some other skilled individual to perform the task. Your answer?"

"Yes," Fenzig said quietly. "I'll steal them for you."

King Erlgrane exhaled slowly and allowed himself a broad

smile. "Good. Sleep well tonight, Fenzighan Wiznagrik, for you'll want to get an early start in the morning. A pony will be provided for you, and several days' worth of food. Beyond that, you'll have to fend for yourself. I'll even give you a few enchanted items to help in your endeavor."

King Erlgrane looked to the far end of the room, and two guards came forward, flanking a comely human woman who carried a gleaming short sword on a velvet pillow.

"This weapon is magical," the king said. "It will aid you in the event the duke's guards are armored fighting men."

"I don't know how to use a sword," Fenzig offered. "In fact, I've never used any kind of weapon. I've never had to fight before, only dreamt about it, and. . . ."

"Then hopefully you won't need it."

Next, the woman removed a plain silver ring from the pillow. It looked much too big for Fenzig's small fingers, but when she bent over and placed it on his index finger, it glittered like a firefly and instantly shrank to fit.

"The enchantment in this ring will bend rays of light around you, rendering you invisible to most eyes. It will work only three times before the magic fades, and it will work for only several minutes at a time. So use it wisely," the king suggested.

"And don't try to use it in this castle as a means of escape." The voice was the old wizard's.

Fenzig hadn't seen him enter the room, but there he was, standing inches away from the king. The wizard looked more rested, and the black circles beneath his eyes were nearly gone, making the wrinkles even more prominent. He was still stooping, a function of age, not lack of sleep, and he still looked sullen. He was dressed in a heavy black robe that trailed on the floor behind him and contrasted sharply with his beard and what few strands of hair were left on his head.

"I'm not going to try anything," Fenzig said. *But as soon as I get out of this place I'm going to disappear—turn invisible with this ring—and run so fast no one will catch me,* he told himself silently. *Why, I'll go to a new country, sell the sword for some starting money, never steal again, and. . . .*

"And I'll put a stop to any notions you might have about fleeing the moment King Erlgrane lets you out of the castle," the wizard said.

The guards clamped their meaty hands on Fenzig's shoulders, painfully holding him in place. The king and the girl with the pillow slowly backed away, and the wizard began mumbling and edging closer.

The gnome couldn't make out exactly what the ancient man was saying, though he could tell there were words of some sort. They sounded almost melodic, despite the wizard's scratchy voice. As the unknown words grew louder the wizard started wiggling his spider-leg fingers, spinning them in the air like a woman would use knitting needles. His fingernails glowed a pale blue; then the glow intensified and stretched out to engulf the gnome.

Fenzig felt like his stomach was rising into his throat.

The glow darkened to a rich sapphire color, and it made the gnome tingle all over as if a hundred mosquitos were nipping at his skin. He felt flushed, but he wasn't sure if that was a sensation of the magic or because he was so nervous. Maybe something he ate was starting to disagree with him.

Before he could ponder the situation further, the glow dimmed and fled down his limbs, disappearing all but around his left hand. The glow stayed there, like a glove. Beneath the blue haze he saw a mark appear. He squinted to make it out, and as the image came into focus, the glow vanished entirely.

A bright blue heart, roughly the size of a grape, remained on the center of the back of his hand, the tip pointed toward his wrist. As he stared at it he could almost swear it was pulsing, as if it were beating. Fenzig's mouth gaped open as a faint line edged outward from the tip of the heart and grew to touch his wrist.

"There. The spell is finished," the wizard announced smugly.

"W-w-what? What's finished? W-w-what spell?" Fenzig stammered.

"The homing spell," the wizard replied. "Each day that line will grow a little longer, and when it moves over your shoulder and reaches your neck, it will kill you. It's a simple enchantment, really, but it is very effective."

The gnome rubbed furiously at the back of his hand, trying to wipe away the heart. "You said I'd live!" he cried at the king. "You said if I agreed to steal the emeralds, you'd let me live."

"Only I can remove the heart," the wizard continued. "When you bring King Erlgrane's emeralds here, and he is satisfied they are the correct ones, I will cancel the spell. And then you will most certainly live."

Fenzig paled. "How long do I have?"

The wizard looked at him quizzically.

"How long do I have before the line reaches my throat?"

"Two weeks, maybe a little more," he replied. "But maybe a little less. Magic is often not precise, and I've never used this spell on a gnome. Of course, two weeks should be plenty of time. Five days there, the same amount back, and a couple of days to steal the emeralds. Plenty of time."

"But if it takes longer than that?"

"It obviously has taken some thieves longer," King Erlgrane calmly informed him. "You're not the first thief I've sent on this mission. The first was nearly five years ago, after I became interested in the gems—after other avenues of getting what I truly wanted were closed to me. Another thief was sent . . . oh, two or three years ago I think. The affairs of state in the intervening years, and acquiring land to the south. . . . Well, all of that has kept me so preoccupied I hadn't time to think about the gems."

"But now you're thinking about them again?"

The king nodded. "Yes, now I am again thinking about them."

"The other thieves you sent?" Fenzig prompted.

"Let's hope you're more skilled than they. Let's hope you're as good as your reputation indicates."

Fenzig looked from the wrinkled face of the wizard to the regal face of the king. "I'll get your emeralds," he said simply.

"Good," the king said. "Guards, take our prisoner back to his cell for the evening. He needs to get some rest. He's got a big day ahead of him tomorrow, and I'm sure he'll want to start early."

Very early, Fenzig thought as he glanced at the pulsing blue heart on the back of his hand. *Very, very early.*

VICTUALS AND RUMINATIONS

Fenzig rode out of Burlengren's gates just after dawn. He'd been given his choice of ponies from King Erlgrane's royal stables, and he selected the only white one. It was tall for a pony, nearly fourteen hands high, and the gnome had more than a little difficulty hoisting himself into the saddle. Perhaps the healthiest of the bunch, its coat glistened in the early morning sun, and its eyes were a rich blue and looked to be full of intelligence.

At first Fenzig considered the beast a fine pick, as it was certainly the handsomest mount available and was undoubtedly worth a handful of gold coins. The latter factor was the true reason he selected the pony. If King Erlgrane allowed him to keep it after all of this was done, he could sell it for a tidy sum.

But after an hour on the trail to Duke Rehmir's, Fenzig realized he might have made an error. A common-looking pony, chestnut or dun in color, even black, probably would have been better, for it would not be as likely to be noticed or remembered. There weren't many white ones, especially one as fine and large as this. The pony would make him stand out in virtually any crowd.

"Did anyone see who robbed the duke?" Fenzig pictured a guard asking. "Well, sir, I didn't get a real good look at him, but he was very short, had hairy feet, and he was mounted on the most beautiful white pony. I saw him ride in that direction."

Wonderful, Fenzig thought. *Thieves need to blend in with a crowd, not stick out like a swollen thumb. If I'd gotten more sleep I would have been thinking straight at the stables and made a different choice. But maybe if I'm lucky I can trade this pony for another before I reach the duke's estate.*

Still, the pony was good-natured and had a quick gait, and that was some consolation. Speed was important, the gnome mused as he looked at the blue heart on the back of his hand. The line was just over his wrist.

"Mistake," Fenzig pronounced. "I'll call you Mistake, my fine white pony. That's what my life has been, one big mistake going on for about three days now—ever since I got the brilliant notion to steal from King Erlgrane."

He dug his heels into the pony's sides to urge it to go a little faster, then he leaned forward in the saddle and patted its neck in praise and let his fingers comb through its soft hair. It had a striking wheat-colored mane and tail, the latter of which it constantly swished to chase away the flies, occasionally swatting the gnome as well. The saddlebags across its rump were filled with dried meats and fruits, enough for at least two days and maybe three.

Enough for a human, Fenzig mentally corrected. *Unless I exercise a lot of willpower, it will be all gone by nightfall. And then what will I do?* A plump waterskin hung from the saddle's horn, and a smaller one filled with raspberry juice was draped on a cord around the gnome's shoulder.

As a gesture of sympathy, Fenzig had also been given three silver coins from the stable master. "In case the hunting's not good," he'd been told.

Just one of those silver coins, and the crystal salt shaker still hidden in his pocket, could buy a fair amount of vegetables, though nothing fancy and certainly not anything like roast beef or turkey, and any accommodations the remaining coins could purchase would not be especially good—but would certainly be better than a rat-filled cell. He'd had more coins in his pockets when he broke into the king's tower. In any event, the three coins made Fenzig feel not quite broke. He would have felt a lot better, however, if he didn't have to steal three particular emeralds from Duke Rehmir just to stay alive.

The miles seemed to melt beneath the pony's hooves, and Fenzig wondered if he truly was making good time. It was far past breakfast and within a few hours of lunch, so he stopped and let the pony rest and graze, and he prudently picked through his rations. He was careful not to eat too much, despite his argumentative stomach. When he was finished, he fished a carefully folded parchment from one of the bags and spread it on the ground. His finger traced the road out of Burlengren.

Though Fenzig had an extensive vocabulary, he couldn't read a single word scrawled on the map. He had never taken well to formal schooling, as he'd put more effort into stealing from the teacher than in learning from her. As a consequence, he'd been thrown out of school—two years past on his thirteenth birthday—and had never learned to read. Still, he could interpret signs well enough. A tankard over a word or two symbolized a tavern, a horse painted on a plank indicated a stable, and a plate of food on a sign above a doorway meant there were victuals to be had inside.

He hadn't, as of yet, needed to know more than that, and he reckoned he could understand this map well enough. The sketch of a castle at the south end, where the road originated, was Burlengren. The gnome town of Graespeck was a little to the northwest, though it wasn't indicated. There were other side roads, smaller and twisting, that led to villages he wasn't interested in. The crude drawing of a clump of trees to the northeast, coupled with the skull sketched in the middle of them, indicated what the people of Burlengren referred to as the Haunted Woods.

There were lots of words on the parchment, but Fenzig shrugged them off. He could see where the road went on its twisty, curvy way around the low hills, and he could see where it passed by K'Nosha, the town adjacent to the duke's estate. In fact, he probably didn't need the map at all, as he'd been to K'Nosha a few years ago and had seen Duke Rehmir's very imposing manor house in the distance. Still, he thought he'd look at the various landmarks as he went so he could tell how much progress he was making.

And it's time to make some progress now, he decided. *Time and my life are a-wasting.*

Shortly after Fenzig resumed his trek, he passed a family heading into Burlengren—two adults and two children crowded into a small wagon. The children pointed at him and laughed.

"Never seen a gnome before?" he called at them angrily. It wasn't the first time ignorant human children had poked fun at him.

"Never such a dirty one," the little boy called back.

His sister stuck out her tongue. "And never such a dirty one on such a pretty pony."

Oh, no, Fenzig thought, looking down at his chest. *My horse is spotless, my gear is clean, and I look like a pig—worse than a pig because of the king's dungeon.*

He'd been so worried about the king's mission and the magical heart the wizard had put on him that he'd forgotten all about his state of dress—and his smell.

"Talk about you standing out, Mistake. Look at me," Fenzig muttered half under his breath. Then he whistled. "And look at that."

His view strayed a couple hundred yards to the right, where a small brick farmhouse and a weather-beaten barn sat off to the side of the road. A thickset woman was hanging laundry on a lengthy piece of clothesline. Several of the garments looked as if they belonged to children, and from this distance, they also looked conveniently Fenzig-sized.

"I'll bet I can find something clean to wear there," he whispered as he urged Mistake closer.

He hid the pony behind the barn and then dawdled in the late morning shadows until the woman went inside. He didn't see anyone else, and from the intoxicating scents wafting across the yard, the gnome guessed everyone was inside eating an early lunch.

Slithering as silently as a cat on the hunt, he hid behind a large oak tree, then rushed to hide behind a barrel, all the while getting nearer to the clothes. He poked his head out and ogled the selection on the line. Greens, grays, browns. *Perfect,* he thought. *I can put together something presentable and that won't stand out, common colors that won't catch anyone's eye.*

Creeping behind some wind-tossed bed sheets, the gnome made his way to an old tree stump that rested directly under the clothesline. He took one more glance at the farmhouse before he hopped up on the stump and started making his selections.

Better take a couple of changes of clothes, he thought, *in case it takes me a few tries to get something that fits.*

His damp merchandise in hand, he jumped off the stump and turned to make his way back to Mistake when an especially pleasing odor caught his attention. He took a last look at the house and his eyes locked onto an apple pie cooling on the windowsill.

The gnome's common sense warred with his appetite. He knew he should leave now, before he was discovered. But the pie smelled very good—so very, very good. In the end, his appetite won, and he carefully laid the clothes on the stump and dashed toward the house.

"Mama! Mama, mama, I'm going out to play."

Fenzig heard the child just as he wrapped his small fingers around the rim of the warm pie plate. Then he heard the house's front door open and little feet beating across the plank porch.

The child turned the corner and stared at Fenzig. The little boy was cute, and the gnome grinned at him.

The wide-eyed youngster returned Fenzig's smile, then called, "Mama, there's a funny-looking little man stealing our pie."

So much for cute, Fenzig thought as he whirled on his bare feet and dashed across the yard, pie balanced precariously in both hands.

"Mama!" the child bellowed loudly. "Maammaa. Maaammmaaa!"

The gnome was running so fast he almost passed by the stump. He skidded to a brief stop—only long enough to balance the pie on his right palm and to use his left hand to grab the clothes and stuff them under his arm. He resumed his tight hold on the apple masterpiece and took off.

"Get him, Papa!" the child squealed.

Papa?

Fenzig risked a glance over his shoulder and saw a big man trundle out of the house, cursing and gesturing wildly. The man jumped off the porch and started after Fenzig, a none-too-pleased look on his bearded face. Fenzig churned his little legs even faster.

Never steal in broad daylight, he lectured himself. *You know better than that, Fenzighan Wiznagrik. One mistake after another. Maybe one mistake too many. Only steal when there are plenty of shadows. Steal in the dark. Gods! I hope I'm faster than he is. If he catches me....*

"Stop, thief!" the man shouted. "Stop or I'll kill you!"

Well, that answers the question of what he'll do to me, Fenzig whimpered silently. He pumped his short legs harder, until his side ached from the exertion, and still he heard the pounding of the man's feet behind him, pounding in time with his small heart. *He's gaining on me,* the gnome thought. *In another moment he's going to.* . . .

Then the gnome's mouth dropped open in pleasant surprise as Mistake cantered around the side of the barn toward him. Whether instinctively drawn by the gnome's hopeless situation or because of the approach of the fragrant pie, Fenzig couldn't say—and didn't care. Pony and gnome ran toward each other, and when he was close enough, Fenzig jumped up and set the pie between the saddlebags. Still clutching the clothes under his arm, he grabbed the reins, leaped to thrust his foot into the stirrup, and heaved himself into the saddle.

"I'll kill you!" the farmer yelled loudly.

"Impressive vocabulary," Fenzig muttered. "Don't you know any other words?"

"Come back here!"

"Right," Fenzig cursed. "You think I'd be dumb enough to do that?"

He stuffed the damp clothes in front of him, stretched behind him to grab the pie, and cradled it to his chest. "Move, Mistake!" he barked.

The pony complied, taking off at a brisk trot and showering the approaching farmer with dirt.

I amaze myself sometimes, Fenzig thought as he nudged Mistake in the ribs to get just a little more speed from the pony. "Thanks for your help," he added aloud to the pony.

Mistake assumed an easy canter, and Fenzig concentrated on keeping the pie and the clothes from tumbling onto the road. It was a difficult balancing act, but he wasn't about to give up his hard-won prizes.

"Let's put a little distance between us and the house," the gnome said. "Then I'll share some of this luscious dessert with you. I think you've earned a few bites."

The farm fell out of sight as the road started to twist by the Haunted Woods. Fenzig began whistling a complex, perky tune while he thought about eating the pie and trying on his new-found clothes. The melody was one he had learned as a young child, and it worked well with the rhythmic clopping of Mistake's hooves.

But suddenly the tune didn't fit well with the pounding of the horse's hooves behind him.

Now what? Fenzig wondered. Curious, he glanced over his shoulder and bit his lower lip in consternation. The farmer was on a big black plow horse, which was rapidly gaining on the much smaller pony. The farmer obviously wasn't about to give up and let the gnome go.

"Hurry!" Fenzig snapped. He kicked his heels into his pony's sides, and Mistake took off at a fast gallop. Dirt churned up, some of it flying in the slight breeze and nesting in the gnome's eyes.

Can my situation possibly get worse? He shook his head in a futile attempt to clear his eyes. They stung horribly.

"I . . . will . . . kill . . . you . . . gnome!"

We're not going to make it, Fenzig thought, as he risked another look back and saw that the farmer was holding his horse's reins in one hand and a sharp-tined pitchfork in the other. *He's going to catch me. He's going to skewer me. It's just a pie and some old clothes. I didn't steal anything valuable. I didn't take any coins. Nothing to kill me over. Nothing. . . .*

"Of course!" Thinking quickly, Fenzig steered Mistake into the trees. The pony moved swiftly, but managed to carefully pick its way through the underbrush so it wouldn't stumble. Within moments, the gnome and his mount were surrounded by forest. The farmer's cries of "I'll kill you!" and "Come back here, wee-one," were muffled by the surrounding vegetation.

"Shhh!" Fenzig cautioned Mistake. "He can't see us where

we are, but let's go in a little deeper, just in case he tries to follow us." The gnome slipped from the pony's back, holding the reins in one hand and the pie in the other. Carefully, slowly, he led Mistake. "I know this forest isn't really haunted," he told the pony. "It's just named the Haunted Woods because a wagonful of travelers disappeared in it about a dozen or so years ago. Brigands most likely were to blame, or so the word was around town. And the thieves' guilds spread enough rumors about dead creatures that prowl this place. The farmer will think about the dead and will stay away. Humans can be pretty gullible sometimes."

The gnome had skirted the edges of enough thieves' guilds to know that some of their members often hid out in these woods. The Burlengren Watch wasn't about to come in here after them—the guilds had circulated enough fear-filled stories to give even the burliest of warriors pause. Too, the occasional disappearance of people expected in town helped. The locals figured whatever lived in these woods got them.

If Fenzig ran into brigands or thieves, he was certain he could talk his way out of any trouble. He was one of them, after all. And he didn't have anything valuable to steal. Except Mistake. He swallowed hard. If the thieves took his pony, he'd never make it to Duke Rehmir's in time.

A thrashing noise intruded on Fenzig's thoughts. The gnome suspected the farmer was whacking the foliage with his pitchfork. But the farmer didn't come in quite deep enough, and he never saw the gnome and pony hiding behind a tall, thick bush. After several long minutes, the man cursed loudly and gave up.

Breathing a sigh of relief, Fenzig spied a small pond. "C'mon," he whispered, still wary that the farmer might be within earshot. He led the pony toward the cool, inviting water. "Time for a snack."

Sitting with his back propped up against an old elm, Fenzig dug into the pie with his fingers, letting the sticky fruit juice run down his hand and chin. He'd finished a little more than half of it when he glanced up and saw Mistake looking sadly at him. "Want some?" He held out the plate, and the pony perked up and quickly gobbled down the rest. Then the gnome wiped his hands and face with one of the silk napkins he'd taken from King Erlgrane's dinner table.

"You're okay for a pony," Fenzig said as he got to his feet and started taking off his filthy clothes. "Even though you're white, I'm going to keep you and take good care of you. And if we get out of this, I'm going to change your name to something much more noble. What would you like? Ivory? Fleetfoot? Fortune? How about King Erlgrane?" He added the last selection with a hint of sarcasm.

Fenzig stuffed his dirty clothes under a bush, deciding they were hopelessly ruined and not worth washing. Then he spread the stolen garments over low-hanging tree limbs to help them dry. He inspected them more closely. One of the shirts he had grabbed by accident was man-sized. The gnome wondered if it would make a good nightshirt. It was practically new, and it was made of expensive material, not the kind of thing a farmer would normally wear. There were tiny green leaves embroidered about the cuffs and the collar. Someone had put a lot of care into making it.

"I'll bet this was his best shirt," Fenzig said glumly. "Probably wore it to socials, parties, perhaps even funerals. No wonder he charged after me. This probably cost him more than the rest of all his clothes put together, or maybe it was a present from his mother and had a lot of sentimental value. Maybe his wife made it for him. It would mean a lot to me if I had something like this. I probably shouldn't keep it."

The gnome wasn't usually saddened by a successful theft and

had never had second thoughts over one before. He usually felt elated, proud that he was able to accomplish another heist and happy to have gained some booty without getting caught. Of course, he'd never actually seen the reaction of a victim before. He was usually well away before they discovered their belongings missing.

"Just one mistake after another," he mumbled, wondering for an instant if all his victims were always that upset. "Well, maybe I can rectify this one mistake." Fenzig vowed to take good care of the shirt and to return it after he gave King Erlgrane the emeralds he was going to steal. "I'd return it right now if I didn't think the farmer'd skewer me. Or if I didn't think it would lose me too much time."

Washing himself quickly and thoroughly in the cool pond, the gnome was determined to make himself presentable. The pony drank its fill while Fenzig dried himself in the sun and decided what to wear. "Gray pants, green shirt," he told the pony. "Though the pant legs are a might too long, and I'm a might too tired. Let's take a quick nap and then be on our way. You could do with a little rest, I'm sure. You ran pretty hard from that farmer."

These woods are safe enough, the gnome convinced himself. *After all, judging by the position of the sun, it's perhaps noon or a little past. The road is not far away, just beyond that big willow over there. If we sleep for an hour, we'll be rested enough to travel until a little past sunset. I know this homing spell will keep moving. But I can spare an hour. Just one.*

That decided, Fenzig quickly plunged into a deep slumber.

He awoke to the persistent hoot of an owl and the incessant chirping of crickets.

Fenzig rubbed his eyes and slowly opened them. At first he thought he was only dreaming about opening his eyes, because if he'd really opened them, the world wouldn't be pitch-black—not if he'd only slept an hour. He felt his face and discovered that indeed his eyes were open, and that indeed he was awake.

He shook his head and heard the owl hoot again. "No!" he shouted angrily, startling the owl, which must have been on a branch somewhere above his head. It flew off into the darkness.

Fenzig slammed his fist into the ground. As his eyes grew accustomed to the darkness, he made out the shapes of trees and of his pony nearby. Faint starlight filtered down through the leafy canopy overhead, and there were chirping and buzzing insects everywhere. Though Fenzig never cared for the dark, his gnomish eyes let him see reasonably well in it.

I meant to sleep only an hour, the exasperated gnome scolded himself. *Instead I've slept the whole day away. I wonder what time it is? I wonder where the line is on my arm?* It was too dark for him to see the wizard's mark.

Grumbling, he rose and stretched. Although he was angry at himself and worried that his nap had cost him precious hours, he had to admit that for the first time in three days he felt rested.

"Mistake, let's get out of here," he said. The pony pricked up its ears and started toward the gnome.

Fenzig folded the farmer's precious shirt, then gathered the other remaining pilfered garments—a tunic, a shirt, and a pair of pants. Good for two changes of clothes, he decided.

He turned to put them in one of the pony's saddlebags, but stopped when he heard a sharp crack. Then a snap.

The crickets quieted, and Fenzig shivered.

He wasn't alone in the Haunted Woods.

FENZIG'S MISTAKE

Maybe it's just a raccoon or a ground squirrel making the noise, Fenzig thought. *No use getting worried over nothing. Maybe it's one of those thieves from the city, just wandering around. No. A good thief wouldn't make so much noise. It's probably a small deer.*

But after a few more twigs snapped, the gnome grabbed the short sword, just in case the animal out there wasn't so small or if—*gulp*—it was something other than an animal. He belted on the scabbard, pulled the blade from it, and gasped as the metal of the sword glowed pale blue, illuminating his surroundings.

Who needs a torch with this thing? I knew the sword was magical, King Erlgrane said it was, he mused. *But it didn't light up like this inside the castle. Of course, it wasn't dark inside the castle. Well, it was dark in my cell, but I never bothered to look at the sword then. Wonder if I'll get to keep it after I steal the emeralds? Erlgrane might forget all about the sword after he has the gems. He seems to want those emeralds very badly. He'll be thinking only about the gems, not about me or the sword or the pony or. . . .*

A low growl stopped his musings. Mistake whinnied nervously and pawed at the ground.

"Whatever you are, go away!" Fenzig spat, praying that it wasn't a ghost, that the woods weren't truly haunted, and that this was somehow all a bad dream. He lowered his voice and tried to sound large. "Leave us alone and I won't have to kill you." He waved the blade for effect, then quickly stepped back toward the elm as a catlike creature poked its head out from behind a bush.

The gnome breathed a small sigh of relief, knowing that what he faced was natural, not supernatural. Judging by its head, it was a big cat, probably a panther. And although Fenzig knew panthers were dangerous, or so the tales around his village claimed, he suspected it wouldn't attack someone with a glowing sword. He gritted his teeth, bravely flourished the blade again, then gulped as the creature slowly emerged all the way out of the bushes.

The creature looked *mostly* like a panther. It had a graceful, lanky frame and sleek blue-black fur that practically shimmered. Its pointed panther ears—two pairs of them—were laid back against its head, its cat-yellow eyes were fixed on the gnome, and it wriggled its whiskers and sniffed the air. What it also had—and what a panther didn't—was an extra pair of legs, giving it six, and two long, snakelike tails that undulated almost hypnotically in the still night air. At the end of each tail was a leaf-shaped appendage.

Fenzig stared slack-jawed at the creature as it drew back its upper lip and snarled, revealing a double row of glistening white, pointed teeth. Saliva dripped from its lower lip and landed hissing, like acid, on the ground.

Fenzig trembled. He'd never seen the like of this creature before, but he knew what it was. The gnome hunters in his hometown, who'd cut short their expeditions whenever they spotted one of these, gave pretty vivid descriptions. Those descriptions matched what Fenzig was staring at. And the gnome hunters had given the beast a name.

"A craven cat," he whispered. "You wouldn't like to eat me or Mistake," he informed the creature, hoping it might understand him, "but in my pony's pack I have some dried beef that you might like. I can even salt it for you. Stay right there, and I'll get it. Stay. Stay."

The beast growled, but didn't move. It watched intently as the gnome groped around in the saddlebags, finally coming up with a fistful of meat. Fenzig hurled the dried beef at the animal, which immediately fell to devouring it. At the same time, the gnome gripped the short sword more tightly and grabbed Mistake's reins with his free hand. He started creeping backward, away from the feasting animal.

However, he hadn't taken more than a dozen steps when the craven cat finished its meal and looked up for more. It growled menacingly and padded forward, its tentacle-tails waving and striking the ferns.

Terrific, Fenzig thought. *I gave you all the meat I had. I've got some dried fruit left, but you don't look like the fruit-eating type. You look like the pony- and gnome-eating type. Why can't you just go back to whatever nightmare spawned you?*

"Why don't you leave us alone? I don't have any more. Go bother somebody else." Fenzig continued to chatter nervously as he backed up, and the beast continued to follow. It matched him step for step, six sinewy legs in time with the gnome's short, stubby ones. It looked like it was difficult for the cat to walk so slowly.

"You're not going to go away, are you?"

The catlike beast snarled and bared its fangs in answer. A strand of saliva spilled over its lower lip and hit the ground, hissing. The grass there shriveled and died in a heartbeat.

The gnome gulped. "No. You're not going away on your own. I guess I'll have to make you." With a show of bravery that surprised him, Fenzig dropped Mistake's reins and dashed toward the creature, waving the glowing sword and yelling. The gnome knew he didn't understand the proper techniques of wielding a blade, but he'd watched enough staged fights in the marketplace to get a general idea of how it was done. Gritting his teeth and returning the animal's snarl, he swept the magical short sword in wide arcs that caused the pale blue light to dance and shimmer in the air and reflect wildly off the cat's slick coat.

The beast turned and bolted on its six legs, jumping over a low bush and melting quickly into the darkness.

"Well, guess I showed it, right Mistake?" Fenzig said, puffing out his nervous chest with pride and returning to the pony. "Now, how about you and I get out of the woods and back on the road. Traveling at night is certainly better than sitting here and being bait for . . . more?"

His path toward the road was blocked by three of the snarling, catlike creatures—only this time their tentacle-tails were curled forward over their backs, snaking toward him, the leaflike appendages at the ends snapping hungrily and revealing more rows of teeth.

"Now where did you come from?" Fenzig started brandishing his sword again, as he had to frighten off the first one. But these fellows didn't seem as easily cowed.

Strength in numbers, the gnome mused. *Maybe I should hop on Mistake and ride right through them. Or maybe I could. . . .*

Another snarl sounded from behind him. Glancing over his shoulder, the gnome saw still more of the beasts. He counted noses—five behind him, plus three in front—and one in the front group was pretty big. The hunters in his hometown ran from only one, he recalled, and there are eight here. The odds were definitely against him.

The largest beast growled fiercely, flexing its half-dozen paws and clawing at the ground. Its tentacle-tails coiled like snakes about to strike; then its eyes met Fenzig's and held his gaze for the space of a horror-filled moment. The great beast sniffed the air, and a rumble erupted from deep in its throat—a resonant sound that cut through the clearing and was quickly echoed by the rest of the pack. The sound grew, seemed deafening.

Almost as one, they started slowly advancing, their acidic

saliva dropping on the ground and making sickening hissing sounds as the grass died beneath them.

The gnome trembled in fear, and Mistake reared back and bolted.

"No!" Fenzig called after the pony, but it fled in panic, veering to the left of the group of five beasts. They turned and sprinted after it, snarling and snapping, their tails lashing out to brush against the pony's rear legs. "Leave Mistake alone!"

Fenzig bravely chased after them, his small feet stumbling over the uneven ground. He waved the glowing sword and hollered, praying the beasts would scatter and not harm the pony. But in his concern for Mistake, he'd forgotten about the three behind him.

They charged the running gnome, and the largest leapt through the air and struck him squarely on the back, sending him flying to meet the forest floor. Its twin tails whipped at his neck, and the leaf-like appendages burned like coals where they struck Fenzig's exposed flesh. Their tiny, thornlike teeth dug in.

The wind rushed from his lungs, and his face and chest hit hard against the damp earth. The glowing short sword flew from his fingers, and he felt himself slipping into unconsciousness.

Fight it! Fenzig's mind screamed. *If I drift off, I'm a dead gnome. They'll eat me for a late-night snack. And if I die, what about Mistake? And if Mistake dies, what about me?*

He shook his head and tried to get up, but he discovered a heavy weight on his back. Craning his neck as far around as it would go, he spied the large beast, its front legs planted squarely on him. The creature's eyes glowed malevolently, and in that instant they looked like the eyes of a man, not of a cat creature. Indeed, for a heartbeat he saw the visage of a man. He shivered, and it snarled, and the gnome watched in fear and disgust as gobs of saliva fell on his borrowed clothes and sizzled and popped as they started to eat through the cloth. Suddenly, his skin felt like it was on fire.

Fenzig whipped his head the other way and spotted his short sword a little more than two yards in front of him, resting in a bed of ferns well out of his reach. One of the other catlike beasts was sniffing it and pawing at the pommel. Deciding the sword couldn't be eaten, it turned its attention to Fenzig and grunted.

Where's the third? Fenzig wondered.

His question was quickly answered when the creature in question padded by him and looked right into his face. Its maw was inches from his nose, and the smell of its strong, fetid breath made the gnome gag. The craven cat sniffed him, then opened its mouth and snapped at him. The gnome immediately pulled his head in toward his shoulders like a turtle, causing the animal to barely miss sinking its teeth into his cheek. In its eyes he'd seen yet another human visage. Were these beasts born of sorcery? Were they witches or changelings?

"I'll not die to the likes of you!" Fenzig screamed as he summoned all his strength and thrust up with his arms, as if he were doing pushups. He dislodged the creature on his back and surged forward in a fast crawl, hitting the one in front of him with his shoulder. Caught by surprise, it backed up, and Fenzig capitalized on the moment by jumping to his feet and rushing toward his sword.

The cat near the weapon stood its ground and flicked its snapping tails menacingly, but Fenzig wasn't about to be turned away. He kicked his right leg forward, intent on striking the cat-like creature in the side and knocking it off balance. His aim was true, and his foot connected, but he didn't have the strength to phase the beast. His teeth chattered as a wave of frigid cold raced up his foot and settled in his chest. Then he swallowed hard when it turned to face him.

"Gods! What *are* you?" The gnome leapt to the beast's side, narrowly avoiding a snapping tail. He kicked out again, aiming for a spot just behind the creature's rump. His foot connected again, with ribs from the feel of it, and the catlike thing growled in anger and stepped back. Again, the blast of cold shot up his body from where he connected with the cat.

He slammed his teeth together, trying to blot out the sensation, and Fenzig used the precious seconds he gained to dive on his sword. His fingers closed on the pommel, and he rolled into the ferns to distance himself from the closest beast. Then he sprang to his feet and backed up until he felt the trunk of a thick tree against him.

At least they can't get at my behind now, he thought. The three craven cats grouped together to form a line. Standing practically shoulder to shoulder, the motion of their intertwining tails difficult to follow, they snapped and snarled but kept their distance. The gnome was glad they were giving him pause right now. *Maybe they're worried because I struck one,* Fenzig thought. *Maybe I hurt it. Or maybe they're keeping back because of the sword.*

They probably think I know how to use it, the gnome mused. *Let them keep thinking that. Maybe they don't like the light. It doesn't matter. I've got to figure a way out of this and find Mistake.*

For several minutes it seemed like a standoff. Every so often the craven cats would growl menacingly and take a cautious step forward, their center pair of feet pawing at the ground. Fenzig would yell, flourish the sword, and they would take a step back. But they wouldn't run away, and they wouldn't present him with an opportunity to leave the tree and head for the road.

At last, the largest beast separated itself from the group and padded toward the gnome. The other two kept their distance but watched the gnome and their pack leader closely. The big creature started circling the tree, bringing the loop in closer and closer with each circuit, its twin tails flicking toward the gnome, their tiny mouths snapping. Fenzig warily kept his eyes on its questing tentacle-tails. The spots on his neck where the leafy appendages had hit him before still burned. The gnome shifted the grip on his sword. As the creature tightened its circle, he stepped forward and lashed out.

Though his swing was unpracticed, Fenzig managed to slice through the air—and a tail in the process. The snakelike black thing fell to the ground and writhed, oozing an acidic ichor that hissed and burned the grass and sent an acrid stench into the air. The craven cat yowled in pain.

The gnome expected the beast to jump back and lick its wound, but it took another tactic entirely. It darted in toward Fenzig, and the gnome was hard pressed to bring his weapon up in time to defend himself. The beast lunged at him again, and the gnome blindly struck out with the blade. He heard a faint hum in the air as the sword arced toward the beast, a hum that seemed to intensify when the magic blade sank into the beast's underbelly.

But the momentum of the creature carried it forward to impact with the gnome's chest. Though dying, the beast snapped at Fenzig, spitting an acidlike substance that burned his skin. He felt the beast's claws rake through his clothing and slash his left arm. The gnome grimaced and shoved the animal away, careful to keep hold of his sword.

The other two craven cats growled loudly as they watched the death spasms of their leader. As they moved up to sniff the dying animal, Fenzig edged away from the tree. He crept as silently as he could toward where he believed the road was. He thought he might have gotten turned around a little, but when he checked the position of the stars, he was pleased he was heading in the right direction.

Now to find my pony, Fenzig mused. *And then I'll ride hard*

and fast away from this place. I've got a lot of time to make up.
He guessed he'd made it about halfway to the road when he heard the two beasts come up behind him. The animals themselves were silent, but the sizzle of their saliva hitting the ground gave them away.

"Don't you ever quit?" he asked as he whirled to face them. He brandished his sword and shouted, hoping that would be enough to drive them off. He didn't like the idea of having to kill another one. They didn't move, and in a moment they were joined by their five panting and slavering friends.

"Well, at least Mistake got away. Too fast for you, wasn't he?" Then Fenzig looked at the beasts a little more closely and shuddered. The light of the sword was just bright enough to let the gnome see their heads. Their jaws were dripping blood, and from one appendaged tail hung a clump of white hair.

"Mistake," he whispered. "You got my pony." His heart sank. Not only had he just lost his mode of transportation to K'Nosha and the duke's estate—dooming himself because he'd never make the king's deadline, he'd just lost a friend.

Fenzig considered charging the pack, eking out retribution for his pony's death—since he was no doubt going to die to the wizard's homing spell. Why not end it all now?

But then . . . he knew that there were always possibilities, that a way to K'Nosha might somehow still present itself. Swallowing his pride and any desire for a quick death he might have entertained, the gnome wheeled on the balls of his feet and dashed in the direction of the road. The yowling and growling behind him, coupled with the rhythmic thudding of their paws against the ground and the hissing of their acidic saliva, told him he had only seconds before they'd be on him.

Crouching and springing, Fenzig leapt at a low-hanging branch, barely grabbing onto it with his free hand. A craven cat jumped at the gnome's dangling bare feet, and Fenzig felt a burning-hot tentacle brush against his soles. Swinging like a monkey, the gnome pulled himself up to the branch and held on tight. Below him, in an uneven ring around the base of the trunk, were the horrid beasts.

"Mistake wasn't enough for you, huh? Still hungry? Eat magic steel!" he cried as he leaned forward and stabbed at one that was leaping up. The blade only nicked the beast, but the threat was apparently enough to keep it from jumping up again. The creature snarled and glared at him invidiously.

"Yeah! You gawk at me all you want!" he sputtered. "With those eyes you could probably see me if I was at the top of this tree. See me. Waitaminute! My ring! I forgot all about it. I can use the ring to turn invisible and then sneak out of here." Below him, the beasts sniffed the air and snarled practically in unison, and Fenzig quickly rethought his plan. "You'd smell me, though, even if you couldn't see me. And even if I was invisible, I'd still move branches and ferns. It wouldn't take a genius to find me. Wonder what god thought you up? One having a decidedly nasty day, I'd guess." The pack paced around the tree and rumbled at the gnome, and Fenzig continued talking to himself as he climbed to a higher branch. "What am I going to do? Sit here until you leave?"

In the end, that's what the gnome settled on, sitting in the tree until morning. He knew he couldn't defeat the craven cats. Morning wasn't far off, he discovered, and when it arrived the woods came alive with the sounds of birds and insects and all manner of life. The beasts slunk away, whether because they didn't like the daytime or because they'd gotten tired of waiting for the gnome to come down.

When they were out of sight, Fenzig skittered down the trunk and assessed his situation. His spare clothes, including the farmer's fine shirt, were deeper in the woods.

And they're going to stay there, he thought. *No sense chancing a run-in with more craven cats—or worse. Mistake is dead, my dried meat is in the belly of an acid-drooling creature, and I'm certainly not going to waste what time I have left searching for my skin of raspberry juice.*

Fenzig crept toward the road and started shuffling toward K'Nosha.

"Of course," he grumbled to himself, "without my pony I won't make it to Duke Rehmir's on time anyway. Unless some miracle comes along."

He glanced at the back of his hand. The blue line snaked outward from the tip of the heart and passed his wrist by at least an inch.

ON THE WRONG FOOT

"What do I do now?" The gnome continued on the road to K'Nosha. The sun climbed higher in the sky, heading toward its lunchtime position. But Fenzig didn't need the sun to tell him what time it was; his stomach was capable of that. He stopped and looked down at his complaining belly, then patted it. "You're probably not going to get anything to eat today, or maybe the day after. So you might as well stop growling," he lectured it. "You've got to realize that finding something to eat is the least of our worries right now. Food got me into this mess, after all. If I hadn't wanted that apple pie so badly, Mistake and I would've never ended up in the woods. Mistake would still be alive. And I'd be much closer to K'Nosha, thank you."

He stared at the road in front of him. It connected K'Nosha to Burlengren, and to the gnome it seemed impossibly long. "I have no food. I have no transportation. No map, not that I needed it. But I still have this cursed homing spell—and I certainly don't need that." He looked at the back of his hand. He stomped his thick-soled heels into the dirt in frustration and scowled. The sun had warmed the road, and the dirt felt wonderful against the bottoms of his tired feet. But even that pleasant sensation couldn't raise Fenzig's falling spirits. Without Mistake, he wouldn't be able to get to Duke Rehmir's manor house, steal the emeralds, and make it back to King Erlgrane's castle before the magical blue line reached his neck and killed him.

I could go back to Burlengren and ask the wizard to stop his spell, Fenzig thought. *Maybe he would do it if I asked him real nice. Then I could get another pony out of the king's stables and try again.*

But Fenzig remembered the look on the wizard's face when he was awakened during the failed robbery. And he remembered how pleased the wizard seemed over the gnome's predicament and current mission. And he remembered that the king mentioned other thieves not making the assignment in the given time frame.

No, the wizard isn't about to stop his spell. In fact, I'll bet he wants me to fail, just as the other thieves failed, Fenzig decided. *He probably likes killing thieves with his homing spell.* So going back to King Erlgrane's without the gems wasn't an option. But giving up and dying wasn't exactly a palatable solution either.

I've just got to think of something, he mused as he continued to walk and occasionally stomp. *Perhaps I could sneak back to the farm, the one that had that delicious apple pie.*

Fenzig had visions of poking through the barn to see if the family might have any ponies or donkeys—something small enough for him to ride. But what if the farmer caught him? "I'll kill you," Fenzig remembered the farmer yelling. No, going to the farmer's was not the best choice either.

Besides, he thought, *I don't have that fancy shirt to give back as a peace offering. It's probably in pieces now, lining the den of some little animal or lining the stomach of a craven cat.*

The gnome pursed his lips, scratched his head, then picked up his pace. He'd look for a different farm with a barn fairly close to the road. He'd quietly enter, select a mount, and release the other animals so the angry farmer would have to catch a horse before he could give chase. And by then the gnome would be long gone. Yes, that was a reasonable plan.

Fenzig stayed toward the center of the road, where there seemed to be fewer rocks. Wagon ruts were worn to either side of him, and he could make out the tracks of lots of horses' hooves. He tried to count the hoofprints to help keep his mind off his situation.

He was on eight hundred and seventy-four when he spotted a farm in the distance and heard the pounding of hooves behind him. The gnome whirled and saw a pair of black and white horses bearing down on him, pulling a garish red boxlike wagon driven by a thin man in equally garish clothing. Fenzig waved frantically.

"Stop!" the gnome yelled in as loud a voice as he could muster. Though the farm ahead fit into his plans, the wagon was closer. "A blackbird in the hand . . . ," his mother always used to say. "Please stop!"

The wagon did, though not before the horses came within a few feet of the little thief. Fenzig could tell they'd been running hard. There was a thin sheen of sweat on their heaving sides, and they snorted loudly. Perhaps something had spooked them, like a snake in the road. Or perhaps the driver was simply in a hurry to get somewhere. He liked the idea of the driver being in the mood to get somewhere fast.

"You there," the driver called in a reedy tenor voice. He stood and dangled the reins in his right hand; his left hand was on his hip. The pose made him look annoyed—which Fenzig judged he was. His expression was stern, and his voice matched it. "You can't just walk down the center of the road blocking traffic. It's not polite. And I'm in a hurry. Move, little boy. Didn't your parents teach you any manners?"

"Of course they did." Fenzig offered the driver a weak smile. "But I'm not a little boy. I'm a gnome."

"A gnome?"

"Gnome," Fenzig replied. "One of the small people. We don't get any bigger than this. As a matter of fact, I'm taller than most gnomes."

"Oh, I see. I've heard of your kind, but I never saw one this close. Never had a gnome for a customer before."

"Well, we're all over this land," Fenzig added, "but most of us stay in our own town, leaving human cities to humans."

"I see. Probably a good idea. So why don't you go back to your tiny town and get out of the middle of the road."

"How about a ride?" Fenzig put on his best face.

"How about buying some hair-removal tonic for your feet? I'm a salesman, and I have a few jars in the wagon. I'll sell them to you at a discount. Then we'll talk about a ride."

"No thanks. Gnomes are supposed to have hairy feet."

"Hmm. Then how about some hair-growth tonic? Guaranteed to produce thick, luxurious, curly locks to keep your feet warm on those cold winter nights."

"It's a long time until winter," Fenzig replied. "But I might buy some if I had any money." The gnome's mind began churning, concocting a tale that quickly tumbled from his lips. "I had lots of money, enough to buy dozens of jars of your tonic, but I was robbed by bandits on the side of the road several miles back, near the Haunted Woods. I'm surprised they didn't try to rob you, too. They killed my pony, roughed me up, and took all my coins—everything but my old sword. I was on my way to K'Nosha to visit my favorite aunt. She's very sick and might not live much longer. Now that I'm without transportation, I might not get there before it's too late." The gnome shed a few tears for effect.

The driver's expression softened. "I'm not planning on going into K'Nosha. It's a big city, and I'm not fond of those. I prefer small, friendly villages. I was just going to stop at some of the farms nearby, sell some of my wares. Maybe I'll stop at the village a few miles south of K'Nosha."

"Could I get a ride part of the way?"

The driver sighed.

"It would get me closer to my aunt. She's a real sweet lady."

The driver sighed again and nodded, leaned out of the wagon, and extended a gloved hand to help the gnome up. "All right. I don't suppose you'll take up much space."

As Fenzig climbed in, he spotted words painted on the wagon's side. In bright purple, yellow, blue, and green paint, they covered nearly every inch of the wagon's side and proclaimed:

Carmen the Magnificent
Healer of Ills
Dispenser of Pills
Scriber of Wills
and Provider of Thrills

In smaller dark-blue letters were the words:

HAIR-GROWTH TONIC, VITAMINS, SKIN CREAMS, FOOT POWDERS, DIGESTIVE AIDS, INSECT REPELLENTS, HAIR DETANGLERS, WART ELIMINATORS, SNAKE-BITE OILS, BUNION ERASERS, WRINKLE DISSOLVERS, HAIR-REMOVAL LOTIONS, TOOTHACHE TABLETS, COLD TONICS, SORE-THROAT SOOTHERS, LOVE POTIONS, HANGNAIL DETACH-ERS, TENSION RELIEVERS, PERFUMES, FLU REMEDIES, AND SCENTED MUSTACHE WAX.

Additional words revealed that:

Carmen is an excellent calligrapher and will gladly pen bills and wills, decrees and degrees, letters for lovers, petitions to politicians, and more—all for a truly very modest fee. The best

showman in the land, Carmen gives free performances daily at
dusk. Your one-stop shop to cure what ails you and to be heart-
ily entertained!

Fenzig wondered how Carmen was able to fit all that on the
wagon, though the gnome supposed anyone who claimed to be
an excellent calligrapher could do almost anything with words.
Words? Wait a minute, Fenzig's mind screamed. *I can't read!
Well, I can't read anything other than my own name. How can I
read what's on the wagon?*
The gnome took a perch next to the driver and craned his
neck around to study the side of the wagon more closely. His
leaning and twisting almost made him fall off the bench seat.
"How—" Fenzig started as he caught himself.
"How is it that the sign on my wagon is written in your gnomish tongue?" Carmen asked.
Gnome? Fenzig thought. *I don't think I could tell the difference
between human and gnome words. It all looks like chicken-scratches
to me—except for the words on the wagon.* "Yes," he answered out
loud. "How is it that the words are written in gnome? Especially
when you've never had a gnome for a customer."
"I used several jars of a special magical paint that I bought in
some old town a few years ago. The words always appear in the
viewer's native language. Supposedly, even illiterate scoundrels
who never got an education and can't read a single syllable can
understand my sign. It sort of mentally tells them my message.
Clever, huh? And best of all, the paint will never wear off. So if
I want to change occupations or paint my wagon a different
color, I'll have to find some more of the magical paint—a lot
more. I don't think I have more than a beakerful of the purple
color left. By the way, I'm Carmen the Magnificent, Sage
Supreme of the High Reaches, Wordsmith Extraordinaire of the
World, and Maestro of Mirage for the entire northern part of
the continent. Who are you?"

"Fenzig," the gnome replied.

"Your name's small because you're small?"

"No. I'm not small for a gnome. Not at all. Fenzig's just a short version of Fenzighan. Kinda like Rob is short for Robert or Carm would be short for Carmen."

"Oh. So Fenzig the what?"

"Just Fenzig. We don't bother with titles."

"Oh," the peddler said again. "I see." The words sounded tinged with disappointment, as if Carmen were expecting some grand appellation to spew from the gnome's lips. "Well, we've got to get moving, eh? Never can tell if there are dissatisfied customers on your tail." Carmen rose slightly from his seat, glanced around the corner of the wagon and back down the road, then flicked the reins and urged the horses into a quick gait.

The gnome ogled his unusual-looking benefactor. Carmen was small for a human, not much more than five feet and a few inches tall.

Perhaps he's got a big name to make up for it, Fenzig thought. *He lets all his titles puff out his chest for him.*

Carmen was on the slight side, though his voluminous clothing made him look a little bigger. He was dressed in bright red pants, of a design like a pirate would wear. Snug around the waist and tied just above the ankles, they billowed in satiny folds around his legs. His leather boots were dyed green and sported brass bells and buckles that tinkled and sparkled respectively. A black sash trimmed in violet and gold thread was tied around his waist, and a flashy gold-and-coral medallion swung from his neck. A puffy-sleeved, ruffled shirt that was striped orange, yellow, and lime green nearly made the gnome dizzy just looking at it and competed with everything else the human was wearing.

Carmen wore a thigh-length cloak of bright turquoise, lined

in a light gray silk that looked like liquid silver. Atop his head was a broad-brimmed black hat with a long maroon feather stuck in the band. His long hair was styled loose about his shoulders. It was a pale blond, almost white, the same color as his thin, drooping mustache that hung a few inches below his chin. It looked to Fenzig as if Carmen didn't bother to use any of his scented waxes on it.

"Like my outfit?" Carmen quipped. "I noticed you giving me the once-over. I had it specially made. You can't find clothes like this just anywhere."

"It's very, very. . . ." Fenzig found himself at an unaccustomed loss for words.

"It's very noticeable," Carmen finished. "I like to stand out in a crowd, attract attention—be the center of attention, in fact. Look larger than I actually am. That's important in my business. Looking large and attracting a crowd."

Not in mine, the gnome thought. He'd just gone from losing a beautiful pony that he thought was a might too noticeable to being perched on a wagon that might blind anyone looking at it for too long.

Stand out in a crowd? Fenzig pondered. *No. Carmen wouldn't stand out in a crowd. He'd definitely draw one—a pretty big one.*

"It's very nice," the gnome said. "My own clothes are in rather bad shape. The bandits were none too kind."

"Well, we can fix that. Climb back into the wagon. Third shelf on the right. You'll find a little wicker basket filled with needles and thread. You can mend your shirt in no time and patch the rip in those breeches. There're also a couple of jugs of water back there. The brown jugs. You can wash up a little bit. You wouldn't want to be seen in my company looking like you do now, would you?" As Carmen said the last, he pointed up and down at the gnome.

Fenzig nodded, and Carmen drew back a curtain behind the

bench. It opened to the inside of the wagon, and the gnome dutifully clambered back and headed toward the jugs. The inside was warm and stuffy, and it smelled like dozens of different things: spices, flowers, cedar, and more. First the gnome quenched his thirst, then he started to scrub off the grime, all the while whiffing in the wonderful aromas.

Wonder if he's got any food in here? I think I smelled apricots, Fenzig thought. *Of course he has to have food in here; it's just a matter of finding it.*

He glanced about the cramped surroundings as he continued to clean up. There were shelves to his left and right, and the wicker basket was easy to spot. Everything else on the shelves consisted of various-sized glass bottles and vials and ceramic jars and bowls—all labeled and nicely lettered and filled with a rainbow-colored assortment of liquids and powders. But Carmen hadn't used magic paint or enchanted ink on the containers, so Fenzig couldn't make out a word to identify any of it. There were crates piled here and there, and very little room to move between them—even for someone the gnome's size.

Good thing Carmen is on the thin side, the gnome mused, *or he wouldn't be able to get to his wares. Wonder where the food is? Maybe in one of the crates. I don't think I want to take my chances with eating anything in one of those bowls.*

"Find the sewing basket?" Carmen was peering into the wagon, while still guiding the wagon.

"Found it," Fenzig announced, temporarily abandoning his idea for a food hunt. He stretched on his toes and grabbed the basket, then made his way back to the wagon seat. The gnome could tell that Carmen had slowed the horses' pace. *Probably no sight of dissatisfied customers,* he guessed.

"Thanks for your hospitality," the gnome said. "I really was down on my luck." He took off his shirt and inspected the tears. The breeze tickled his bare skin as he set to work. Fenzig wasn't very proficient with a needle and thread, and he stuck himself three times before Carmen "tsk tsk-ed" and passed him the reins.

"I hope you know how to drive a team better than you can sew," the human said glumly. "What's that?" Carmen was pointing at the blue heart and line on Fenzig's left hand. It was closing in on three inches past his wrist.

"A tattoo," the gnome said quickly.

"Looks like a homing spell," Carmen stated.

"A what?" Fenzig feigned surprise.

"A homing spell, an enchantment that keeps a person on a leash, so to speak. It's a nasty spell and often a deadly one, usually used on people bound to a task."

"Good thing this is just a tattoo," Fenzig replied. *No need to tell a stranger about my predicament,* he thought. *My situation is none of his business.* "Got it in Burlengren. I thought my aunt might like it."

"Most people wear their hearts on their sleeves, not on their hands," Carmen joked.

Fenzig was glad the peddler was rather fast with a needle and thread. Within minutes the gnome had his stolen shirt back on and was pulling down the sleeve to cover up as much of the "tattoo" as possible. "Do you know much about magic?" the gnome asked as he passed the reins to Carmen and took off his breeches. He accepted the reins again as the peddler went to work on the ripped pant leg. "Magic and spells and such have always fascinated me. You have magical paint and love potions. Anything else?" *Anything that might get rid of this homing spell?* he added to himself.

"No. I'm not one to put much faith in magic," Carmen replied. "One of my sisters, on the other hand, claims to be a fledgling wizard."

"Does she live around here?"

"I don't know," the human answered distantly. "I don't see her all that often. She's not looked on with favor by our family and friends. Instead of concentrating on spellcraft, she concentrates on stealing. She's nothing more than a common thief. My family has no use for thieves. And not a lot of use for peddlers." The last he added quietly.

"And I suppose you don't like thieves either."

"Thieves should be hanged," Carmen said. "Or worse."

The next several hours were passed in silence. The countryside looked idyllic. Oaks and maples grew near the road and provided a wind block for a great field of wheat that swayed like a dancer in the soft breeze. The robins and blackbirds perched on the highest branches sang melodious songs. The sun started its path toward the horizon, and the gnome's stomach softly growled. Fenzig snuck an occasional peek at the line on his arm and each time noticed it was a smidgen longer than it had been when he looked at it before. He wondered how far away the village Carmen had mentioned was. He hoped K'Nosha wasn't much beyond that. As the miles continued to pass, and Carmen and he took turns handling the reins, the gnome started scheming.

It's too bad Carmen's not going all the way into K'Nosha, Fenzig thought. *Despite his malice toward thieves, he's an all right sort. I don't want to steal from people I like. And I don't really want to steal from Carmen. But he's not going all the way to K'Nosha, so I guess I'm just going to have to steal his wagon. What choice do I have? I might not find another ride in time.*

There're plenty of large bowls and jars back there, he thought. *We'll have to stop someplace for the night, and when Carmen's busy with something I can hit him over the head with a heavy bowl and knock him out. Then I'll tie him up with his clothes and steal his wagon and horses. I'll stick him behind a tree, where it will be more difficult for someone to spot him from the road. He'll be able to work himself free—eventually. Or he'll be rescued—eventually. He just won't be able to catch up with me until I've made off with Duke Rehmir's emeralds and am safely back at King Erlgrane's palace.*

Fenzig's plot included selling the horses and wagon, probably in the small village just south of K'Nosha. He didn't want to take the gaudy thing into town. With the money, he'd buy plenty of food, another change of clothes, and a nondescript pony. Then he'd ride to the duke's, steal the emeralds, and make it back to King Erlgrane's before the blue line ended his life.

Perfect, the gnome thought. *Things will work out after all.*

"You know," Carmen said, finally breaking the silence, "I'm glad I found you along the road. You're good company, and an honest man—not at all like my sister and some of the other folks I've run into. I was a little leery of letting you have a ride. You can never be too careful picking up strangers. You might offer them friendship, while they'll offer you a dagger in the back. You just never know what they'll try to do."

Fenzig nodded and smiled weakly.

"Hungry?" Carmen asked. "It'll be sunset soon, so we might as well set up camp for the night. I've got a good-sized tent back there that I'm willing to share. And I've got some dried venison and lots of vegetables. I make a pretty mean stew."

"That sounds wonderful," Fenzig replied. "It's been a long while since I've eaten."

The gnome continued to scheme as a few more miles drifted by, his plans churning more rapidly with the thought of getting something to eat. Finally Carmen guided the wagon and horses next to a large willow tree a little way off the road. The tent was pitched while the stew simmered over a small fire, and Fenzig's mouth watered in anticipation. *I'll wait until after dinner before I knock him out,* the gnome decided. *No use expending energy on tying someone up on an empty stomach.*

Carmen dipped a ladle into the steaming mass of meat and

carrots and fixed the gnome a big bowlful. It was accompanied by sweet, hot herbal tea. *This is heavenly,* Fenzig thought as he dug in. *This is simply delicious. Very tasty. And I am so very tired.*

His eyelids drooped shut, and he was aware of nothing else until he awoke to a breakfast of bacon and eggs. The tent was already packed, and Carmen passed him a plate.

"Hungry?" the human asked again.

The baffled gnome accepted the plate and quickly downed the eggs and bacon. They were filling and warm and were followed by three biscuits generously topped with raspberry jam.

THE ROAD TO K'NOSHA

"What happened?" Fenzig didn't bother to hide his puzzlement.

"Beg your pardon?"

"What happened? I just ate supper and now I just finished breakfast—both of which were delicious, thank you. Where did the time go?" He furtively glanced at his arm. The blue line that extended from the heart on the back of his hand was halfway up to his elbow. He shuddered and pushed his sleeve down to his wrist, registering with satisfaction that the peddler hadn't noticed.

"Well, you ate an awful lot of my stew last night, drank a few cups of herbal tea, and drifted off to sleep. I put you in the tent with me. I didn't want you sleeping out in the open in case it rained. Couldn't have you catching a cold on top of everything else that's happened to you—the bandits and all." Carmen's tone was cheerful. "I guess I should have warned you that my tea is very relaxing. It can put you right to sleep if you're not careful."

Fenzig nodded glumly. He noticed Carmen had changed into a new set of clothes that were even more garish than what he'd had on yesterday. Bright pink warred with purple and fought with green, vermillion, and ocher. His cloak had a rainbow design of dark blue, lemon yellow, violet, and olive, and his high leather boots were glistening black trimmed in scarlet with green clovers painted on the cuffs. The gnome blinked and looked at the ground.

"Still hungry?"

"I'm always *still* hungry. It goes with being a gnome," Fenzig replied as he accepted the second plate filled with three more biscuits. The jam was sweet, and it quickly found its way to his stomach to join the rest of breakfast.

The peddler passed him the last biscuit on the cookplate, scraped the last of the jam onto it, and smiled.

"You're not like other people," Fenzig said between bites.

Carmen looked at him quizzically.

"Well, I mean not like other humans. You're being nice to me. Awfully nice. A lot of humans, they don't seem to care for gnomes. Call us wee-ones."

"I think you're kinda cute. Are female gnomes as cute as you?"

The gnome scowled. "Yeah, cute."

"Wee-ones doesn't sound so bad. It sounds cute, too."

"Cute." He shuddered. "No? Not bad? But they usually follow it up with wee-brains or endless-stomachs or some such other insult. We tend to stick to ourselves 'cause we don't quite fit in with you humans."

"But your aunt . . . you said she lives in K'Nosha. That's a human town."

"There're exceptions." The gnome paused to finish the last of his bacon. "See, she and I are exceptions, not the rule."

"So, you live in a human town? Burlengren?"

"I travel around a lot. Don't call any place home. Not really. I haven't been to Graespeck, my home town, for quite some time, been visiting human communities, the marketplaces. I like the human marketplaces."

"So do I."

Fenzig swept his gaze up to Carmen's face and squinted, noted that the human had wrapped an orange-sequined scarf around his hat.

"But you don't like humans?" the peddler asked politely. "Just their trappings?"

The gnome shrugged. "I try to like everybody. But humans are . . . well, their furniture is too large, the spoons too big for our mouths, their music sounds funny, and their humor doesn't make a lot of sense."

"So you gnomes tend to avoid us?"

"Most. Most of us keep to ourselves, like I said. Makes life easier. Even when I'm in human cities, I keep to myself."

"Must be lonely."

He nodded.

"Which is maybe why people are suspicious of gnomes or don't care for them," the peddler offered. "Being different can frighten some people. And setting yourselves apart from the rest of the world can't help."

The gnome shrugged again. "You're different."

The peddler cocked his head. "I'm not sure if that's a compliment." He adjusted his broad-brimmed hat and stretched toward a kettle. "Care for some tea?"

"Not this morning." *I've had enough sleep, thank you,* the gnome added to himself. *I need my wits about me if I'm to take your wagon and horses in broad daylight.*

Carmen picked up the last of the dishes and scrubbed them in a small tub of water. He put out the fire by dumping over the tub. "Ready?" he asked. "We've got to get on the road."

Fenzig jumped to his feet. He had to admit that despite the creeping line on his arm he felt good and was ready to travel again. His belly was full, he'd had a good night's rest—better than he'd had in several days—and nothing untoward had happened to him. Of course, he still had to figure out how and when to clobber Carmen the Magnificent so he could steal the wagon and horses.

"I was thinking last night," Carmen began as he took a seat

on the bench and grabbed the reins. "I know how important family is. And I can imagine what my family would be going through if something were to happen to me."

For an instant Carmen's voice sounded sarcastic, but Fenzig dismissed it. "I need to see my aunt before she dies," was all the gnome said.

"I understand," Carmen replied softly. "Family is important." He flicked the reins, and the horses began to move forward at a steady, plodding pace. Then he turned to regard the gnome. "And because family is so important I've decided to go into K'Nosha after all. Why bother with peddling my wondrous wares in a small village when I can hawk to a much larger crowd in a city bursting with life? Besides, that way I can get you all the way to your aunt's. Not to her door, mind you, I've no interest in seeing a withered old gnome woman, cute though she might be, who probably doesn't like humans. No offense. Can you find her place on your own once we get to town?"

Fenzig nodded yes and quickly dismissed all thoughts of thumping Carmen on the head. *I've no need to resort to violence when I'm getting what I want anyway,* he thought.

"Of course," Carmen added, "I'd appreciate a favor in return."

"Name it."

"Help me sell some of this stuff. It won't take long, a couple of hours at most. You can visit your aunt first, then help me. When we're done for the evening you can go back and spend more time with her. Consider it payment for the ride and the food."

"That's the least I can do," Fenzig agreed, though he had no intention of keeping up his end of the bargain.

The pair soon fell into the routine of taking turns at the reins. The gnome seemed to have an aptitude for driving the team, and he liked sitting up high on the wagon, looking at the world from a different perspective.

Farmland unfolded before them, and the gnome admiringly eyed the field hands weeding the crops. He respected them for being able to labor long hours like that, getting the skin on their hands cracked and dirty, but he felt sorry for them at the same time. They weren't as smart as he was, or else they'd steal and swindle for a living. He guessed that in some respects Carmen and he were a lot alike. The gnome doubted that all those containers in the wagon were really filled with medicine to cure stomachaches, rashes, and whatnot. But he bet people paid good money for the concoctions regardless. The bottles looked nice.

As the hours went by, they passed a few people on horseback. Carmen stopped the ones who were well dressed, which indicated they had some money about them.

The peddler treated Fenzig to a bag of dried figs while he busied himself selling to a trio of fancily attired travelers. The older man, who was wearing a fine black coat and matching trousers, stared hard at the side of the wagon.

"I have a wart on my finger," he said, extending his hand so Carmen could see. "I've had it for years, and I can't seem to get rid of it."

"It's a good thing you passed by," Carmen said, rising and doffing his hat with a grand flourish. "I have just the thing." The peddler excused himself and ducked into the back of the wagon.

Fenzig munched on the figs as he listened to Carmen rummage around among the crates and bins. The peddler returned a few moments later with a blue glass jar stoppered with a green cork.

"Wart remover," Carmen announced, pointing at a label that Fenzig couldn't read.

"I'll take it," the man said. "How much?"

"Only one gold coin," Carmen announced.

"That's expensive," the man returned.

"Consider it a bargain 'cause it'll get rid of your wart."

The man fished around inside his coat pocket and produced a shiny gold coin.

"Do you have any hand cream?" The young woman who spoke looked as if she could be the older man's daughter. She was pretty for a human, and her smile was warm.

"Four pieces of silver, dear lady," Carmen said as he once again disappeared into the wagon, returning a moment later with a small jar.

"How about insect repellent?" asked the other member of the trio, a young man who could have been either the gentleman's son or the girl's husband. "Do you have any insect repellent that works? Really works? I don't like all these insects. And I don't want to buy something if it's not going to work. You're not some snake oil salesman, are you?"

"Everything I sell works, and I don't sell snake oil," Carmen spouted. "I offer only the finest medicinal treatments. Use them according to the directions on the label and you'll be amazed at the results."

The gnome admired Carmen's glib tongue and persuasive spiels, and he took mental notes of how the peddler dealt with strangers. *Maybe I'll get enough money to buy my own wagon and start an operation like this,* Fenzig mused as Carmen handed a vial of insect repellent to the young man and collected four more silver coins. The peddler bowed and doffed his hat to the young lady.

"Does the stuff *really* work?" the gnome asked as they rode out of earshot of the trio.

"My wares?"

Fenzig nodded.

"Of course the stuff works. Everything works, though I'll

admit that some concoctions work better than others. I brew all the elixirs myself."

"Are they hard to make?"

"No, my dear gnome. I'm Carmen the Magnificent. Nothing is difficult for me."

When they rounded a bend in the road, Fenzig's heart started beating faster. A small village came into view, and in the distance he could see the spires of K'Nosha. They were getting close. Nightfall would find him inside Duke Rehmir's imposing manor house, searching for the emeralds. By dawn, he would be back on the road toward Burlengren. He'd stop and steal a pony from this village, and then he'd have time to spare before this cursed homing spell could do him in.

"What are you smiling about?" Carmen broke in on Fenzig's pleasant musings.

"I was thinking about my aunt."

It had been several years since the gnome had visited K'Nosha—he was nine or ten or eleven and with his mother, and he'd forgotten just how impressive it was. A high stone wall circled the city, and when they rode through the gate they passed between tall stone barbicans manned by sentries. Carmen nodded to the guards, and the gnome was amused to see their gaping expressions over the peddler's mode of dress.

"Just let me off here," Fenzig quipped. "I'll find my aunt's place."

Carmen slowed the wagon, and the gnome climbed off.

"Meet me in the center of town in a couple of hours," Carmen instructed. "Show up as a curious customer and answer 'yes' to all of my questions."

"Huh?"

"Not 'huh.' *Yes.* You'll understand," the peddler added.

"Yes," Fenzig said as he waved and quickly lost himself in the throng of people moving to and from shops. A few stopped in their tracks to glance at him, muttering "wee-one" just loud enough so he could hear. Others smiled and nodded as he passed by. The latter's seeming acceptance of him made him feel a little better about humans. Not all of them were prejudiced.

It was lunchtime, but for a change he wasn't thinking about food. He practically skipped over the cobblestone streets, he was so happy to be near the duke's home on schedule—if not a little ahead of it.

The wagon certainly made better time than poor Mistake would have, he thought. He passed by the shops of armorers, woodworkers, scribes, tailors, glassblowers, and grocers. A weaver displayed a beautiful green-and-yellow quilt in the window, which Fenzig decided his aunt—his real and very healthy aunt back in his hometown—would like. If he stole enough items of his own from the duke's manor house—after taking the emeralds, of course—he might stop and buy this for her on his way out of the city. He'd also have to buy a pony, or a horse and a plain-looking wagon, if he decided not to steal one, so he made a point of looking for the stables on his way out the other side of the city and toward Duke Rehmir's estate.

Where the city ended on its northern boundary, the duke's property began. The gnome marveled at the manicured lawn that went on for acres and acres and acres. The trees were all neatly trimmed, giving them a sculpted look, and in the distance Fenzig spied a magnificent garden filled with white, yellow, scarlet, violet, and bright pink flowers. The blooms were planted so that each complemented the others. Hundreds of butterflies flitted about them and drew the gnome's attention for several minutes.

Carmen could have taken a lesson in color from the gardeners, the gnome said to himself as he slipped behind a spruce and peered through the branches for a better look. He wanted to make sure he had the lay of the land during daylight, because he'd be back when it was dark, and he didn't want any surprises like unexpected low spots in the lawn that might trip him up. He mentally charted his course from tree to tree, to large rock, to a statue of four women kneeling in the garden, right up to the manor house wall. The less time he had to spend running across open ground the better. He couldn't afford to get caught by the duke's guards.

He moved closer, finding another spruce to hide behind, and ogled the manor house. The wall surrounding it was made of natural stones and stood roughly five gnomes high. Fenzig suspected he would have little trouble climbing it, and the spikes on top were placed about a foot apart, so he'd be able to squeeze easily between them. Beyond was a massive structure made of white stone that Fenzig guessed to be five stories tall—the first hidden by the wall, the other four extending above it. It was trimmed with gray-blue slate and looked every bit as impressive as King Erlgrane's castle, though this building was quite a little bit smaller.

Its black slate roof was steeply pitched, and at intervals along the base of the roof were places for sentries to stand. The gnome counted eight sentries on this side, meaning there were likely an equal number on the other side, plus a few patrolling the grounds. An impressive army barracks was beyond the manor house, and more of the duke's property extended beyond that.

"Nothing too difficult," Fenzig whispered. "There can't be more than sixty or seventy rooms in the whole place. Finding the study won't be that hard." The gnome knew he could automatically eliminate the top and bottom stories. The first floor probably consisted of audience chambers, servants' quarters, a kitchen, and dining room, maybe a ballroom if the duke was into throwing parties. The study likely would be on the second or third floor. Studies were often-used rooms, Fenzig judged, and an often-used room would not be on the topmost floors where a person would have to climb a lot of stairs to get there.

A place like this must have lots of expensive knickknacks, he thought, deciding he might as well take a few crystal vases or expensive odds and ends as well as the emeralds—just some small, yet valuable things so he could show some reasonable profit from all of this.

I'll come back later tonight, the gnome thought. *I'll slip over the wall, climb to the second or third floor, find the study, grab the emeralds, and leave. If the search takes me a while, until morning, I'll get that quilt for my aunt on the way out of town. King Erlgrane will be happy, end of homing spell, last I'll see of that old wizard, and I'll be alive.*

He glanced at his arm as he turned and started back toward K'Nosha. The blue line was definitely headed toward his elbow.

By the time he made his way to the center of town, it was late afternoon. A crowd had gathered near the fountain, and Fenzig instinctively knew what was in the center of all those people. The crowd was too deep, and he was too short, to see over their heads, so he started squeezing between them and making his way toward the main attraction—which had to be Carmen the Magnificent. He had no intention of helping out the peddler, had no intention of keeping his promise. He just wanted a closer look. Out of gnomish curiosity.

Just a little closer, he thought. *But not too close or he'll see me. Maybe I want him to see me. Oh, why am I doing this? I suppose I owe Carmen something for the food and the ride, but I'd really rather just stay quietly in the background, out of sight and out of mind. That's it, I'm not going any closer. In fact, I'll turn back and. . . .* The gnome had just about convinced himself to abandon the peddler and find some shady alley to doze in, when he froze in his tracks.

78

"You! Gnome!" Carmen called.

Fenzig cringed. He had unwittingly made his way to nearly the front of the crowd, and he was being pointed at by the gaudily attired peddler.

"Yes?" Fenzig remembered his line perfectly.

"I'll bet you'd love something to keep your feet warm on those cold winter nights!"

"Yes."

"I've got just the thing—hair-growth tonic. Just spread some on the top of your feet, wait a little while, and you'll have even more hair—a thick, curly mass to keep out the chill. Would you like to try some before buying?"

"Yes."

"Then step right up and spread some of this on the tops of your feet." Carmen winked at Fenzig and passed him a bottle of thick blue cream.

As the gnome started spreading it on his feet—registering that it smelled horrible—he listened to the peddler continue his pitch. "You there with the bald head. I'll bet you'd like to have a great mass of curly hair when you wake up in the morning."

"I guess I would," the fellow agreed, embarrassed at having been singled out, but hopeful nonetheless.

"Well, all you have to do is buy a bottle of my tonic, spread a little on before going to bed, and in the morning you'll be the delighted recipient of women's admiration. Your barber will be amazed. Your friends won't recognize you!"

"How do I know it'll work?" the bald man asked, a hint of skepticism lacing his voice.

"Let's ask our gnome demonstrator," Carmen said. "Well, gnome. Do you have more hair on your feet? Did the tonic work?"

"Yes."

"Would you like to buy a bottle and recommend it to all of

your friends?"

"Yes."

"And would you say it's the finest hair tonic that can be had anywhere in the land?"

"Yes."

"I'll buy a bottle!" the bald man cried.

"Give me two bottles," called another.

"I'll take three!"

"And let's not forget some of my other fine products," Carmen added as he took in gold and silver pieces and handed out bottles filled with the noxious-smelling cream. "How about my fabulous wrinkle remover? Maybe our gnome friend would be willing to demonstrate that one, too. Do you have wrinkles, gnome? Age spots?"

"Yes."

"Would you like them to go away?"

"Yes."

"Put on some of this," Carmen barked as he thrust a red ceramic jar into Fenzig's small hands. "That's it; just smear the stuff anywhere you have wrinkles."

The gnome sighed and started smoothing the salve on his face and hands.

"It'll take a few minutes to work, ladies and gentlemen," Carmen continued to babble. "In the meantime, step right up and procure your hair-growth tonic. I have only a limited number of bottles of this fabulous miracle concoction left to sell."

Fenzig stood there looking at his hands while people pressed closer to the wagon and shelled out their hard-earned coins.

I don't have wrinkles or age spots, he grumbled to himself. *I'm not old enough to have wrinkles or age spots. I'm only fifteen. I want out of here. I want to hide until it's dark, then be on my way to Duke Rehmir's manor house.*

"Well, gnome?" Carmen quipped just as Fenzig turned to

leave. "Did the cream work?"

"Yes."

"Did it get rid of all your wrinkles?"

"Yes."

"I want some!" a woman called. "And I want two jars for my sister!"

"It's only a gold piece a jar—a small price to pay for beauty," Carmen gushed. "The more wrinkles you have, the longer it will take for them to go away. But in most cases, if you apply the cream tonight, by morning your skin will be as soft and wrinkle-free as a baby's bottom."

"I'll take a jar!"

Fenzig slipped back through the crowd. *If I had any money I'd spend it on a hot bath so I could get this stinky stuff off me,* he thought. *Who knows where I lost those three silver pieces and that crystal salt shaker? Probably left them for the craven cats in the Haunted Woods.* He settled for splashing in the nearby fountain and scrubbing furiously. Afterward, he dried his face and hands on the cape of a tall man caught up in Carmen's sales pitch.

"I have an abundance of ointments for all kinds of ailments," Carmen proclaimed. "And as a thank you for your patronage, I will perform a magic show for you in just a few hours. Right after dinner, and right before dusk. But first, let me show you some more of my unique and fabulous unguents and balms."

"Do you have anything for rashes?" Fenzig heard the tall man say.

"Of course I do!" Carmen replied. "Step right up, sir, I'll be glad to demonstrate."

The gnome ran from the courtyard before he could be singled out to "demonstrate" anything else. He found a nearby alley and clung to the shadows. Selecting a crate that was relatively clean, the gnome sat on it and watched the audience grow and Carmen's supply of miracle cures dwindle. He rested for a time, and headed toward the duke's estate just as the peddler started his magic act.

A Gem of a Plan

"We're a lot alike, Carmen and I," Fenzig muttered. "He steals from people, too. He's just more upfront about it than I am. He takes their gold in exchange for worthless concoctions that smell bad. I, on the other hand, just take their gold. I don't suppose either approach is very honorable. But at least I'm not cheating anyone to their face. And I'm not lying to them."

But I'm not being fair to them either. All right, stealing might be wrong, he admitted to himself, *and maybe King Erlgrane had a right to punish me. But to punish me by making me commit another crime? That's not right either. Two wrongs never ever made the proverbial right in anyone's life. If I get through all of this in one piece, I think I'll have a long talk with my father. Maybe he needs some help with his woodcarving business. I could give it a try anyway. Again. It might not be so bad this time. Maybe I'll even go back to school.*

At the moment, however, the gnome knew he didn't have any choice but to steal from Duke Rehmir—not if he wanted to live. And it was only three emeralds, he kept telling himself. Just three gems. Someone as rich as the duke might not miss them.

No. He won't miss them at all.

It was not yet so dark that Fenzig couldn't see the line on his arm, so he risked a glance. The end of it was just at his elbow, meaning tomorrow it would start toward his shoulder. *The line is moving faster than the wizard estimated it would,* Fenzig thought. Too fast. But perhaps the wizard's estimate was based on a human, who would naturally have longer limbs. Seven more days at best, the gnome judged, seven more days that he had to live. Six at the minimum, eight and a half at the outside. And he knew it would take at least three days to get back to King Erlgrane's, probably four.

"I'm still doing all right," he whispered, attempting to bolster his sagging spirits. "I'm on schedule, but not as much ahead as I hoped I'd be." His stomach growled, reminding him he hadn't eaten since the breakfast Carmen had made for him. "I'll take care of you later," he said, giving it a soft swat.

The gnome reached the edge of the duke's estate by sunset. On his way out of town he'd "appropriated" a leather sack and a belt that had a couple of pouches attached to it—things he'd need for hauling away other things, namely things that glittered and sparkled. He vowed to take enough wealth with him to buy a means of transportation to Burlengren. If not, he'd have to steal a pony from the nearby village, though he didn't like to perform back-to-back thefts. He considered it tempting fate.

He followed the route he'd visualized earlier in the day, moving quickly over the relatively flat landscape and using the trees and bushes for cover. He hovered amid the evergreens in the garden outside the stone wall until dusk overtook the land. Then he slid quietly from shadow to deepening shadow and scaled the wall.

As he squeezed between the spikes on top and looked toward the manor house, he swallowed hard. The duke's home was much larger than he'd thought, and searching for a study that displayed three emeralds could take longer than he'd originally anticipated. Although the land surrounding the garden and outer wall was flat, the grounds that lay beyond the wall and that directly surrounded the manor were in a bowl-like depression. It effectively hid much of the place from view—until one was directly upon it. The bulk of the manor house was actually eight stories tall, not five as the gnome had guessed earlier. And it was more spread out than he'd first thought.

Fenzig whistled softly. This is a palace, not a manor house. *And it's huge, bigger than King Erlgrane's castle even—maybe one hundred and fifty rooms, give or take a dozen. It's a good thing this is in another country and not under the king's jurisdiction,* the gnome said to himself. *If it were on the king's lands, he'd claim it. The property is very defensible, perfect for a monarch. The duke would be homeless, and the king would be moving in his furniture tomorrow. Searching this place is going to take a while.*

He dashed toward the building. There wasn't much cover in the depression, just a few ornamental shrubs. *Good thing I'm a gnome,* Fenzig mused as he nimbly leapt over a patch of mud. *If I were any taller those sentries on the parapets would spot me. Of course, if I weren't a gnome, I wouldn't have fit through the window in King Erlgrane's tower, and I wouldn't be in this mess.*

Within moments he was at the base of the immense palace. Selecting a wall practically covered by ivy, he started his climb. The thick vines smelled strongly of musk. Their scent was almost overpowering, but they did make climbing easier. The odor clung to his nostrils and reminded him of Carmen's delicious tea. He yawned, and his eyelids felt heavy. The tips of his fingers were becoming numb.

Concentrate, you idiot, he scolded himself. *These vines are probably supposed to discourage thieves and put them to sleep before they can get inside. But they can't discourage me. I'm not going to fall for it.* Fenzig bit his lower lip. The pain helped him to focus his attention on climbing. The white stones of the manor felt cool against the palms of his hands, and his fingers fit perfectly in the cracks between the stones. *Higher, higher, that's it,* he coaxed. *I'm just about to the second floor. Let's try for the third.*

He stifled a yawn, closed his eyes, felt his fingers relax, and he bit down harder on his lip. A warm trickle of blood ran down his chin, and his eyes snapped open. *No wonder there aren't many sentries,* he thought. *If you get too close to the building, you'll take a nap. All the sentries have to do is come by and scoop you up. Come on, that's it. I'm almost there.*

The gnome passed by a second-story window, and though he was groggy and yawning and having visions about a soft feather bed, he made it to the third floor. He sat on the outside window ledge for a moment and shook his head in an attempt to clear his senses. This vantage point put him almost even with the base of the wall that circled the manor. Satisfied he would remain awake and alert, he rubbed his sleeve across his mouth to wipe away the blood, then set to work on the window. It was latched from the inside, but to a thief of Fenzig's skill it presented little challenge. He eased the frame back and forth and up and down just a fraction of an inch. Still, it was enough to jimmy the latch. He slid open the window and entered the hallway beyond. His scabbarded sword thunked up against the sill, and he flinched.

No one hear me, he pleaded silently. *Please, no one hear me. I promise I'll try to go straight if no one notices me. My father can teach me the woodworking trade. I'll make window frames, not break into them. No one hear me.*

It seemed no one had, as no one came out to investigate. Satisfied that everything was proceeding smoothly, Fenzig looked into the first doorway. "Wow," he whispered. "Too bad everything's glass, or I'd take a couple of pieces with me." The room contained an exquisite collection: clear, blue, and green vases, cups, goblets, and bowls. A chandelier in the center of the room caused light to dance off every piece, dazzling the gnome and causing him to stand transfixed for several moments.

"Next room," Fenzig murmured, reluctantly pulling his eyes away from the colors. He crept like a cat a few more feet and narrowly avoided a glowing spot low on the wall. *Hmm.* A magical alarm, he guessed. *Well, you didn't catch me. I'm too clever. No one is going to catch Fenzig the Dashing, Fenzig the Fabulous, Thief Extraordinaire. Ha! There, I gave myself a title Carmen would approve of. This is the real reason I chose this profession,* he inwardly crowed. *Overcoming obstacles, bypassing locks and tricks and traps, avoiding guards. The challenge. The thrill. The. . . . Uh-oh.*

Fenzig ducked and hid in the shadows inside a door frame. He watched as a half-dozen men in uniform exited a room a few yards away, turned in unison, and retreated down the hall.

Sentries, the gnome surmised, *though these are dressed a little better than the ones on the grounds and on the roof. Maybe these guys are better, or maybe different clothes mean they're from different units. Doesn't matter, I can avoid all of them.*

When they were out of sight, he stepped from the shadows and stretched. His head was still a little foggy from the odd ivy, but his senses were growing sharper. The air in here smelled better, too. It smelled of cedar, which was what the doors and floor were made off. The boards were well polished and glowed faintly in the light from a sconce halfway down the hall. As he padded forward, he heard regular and multiple footsteps above him.

Probably the guard force prowling upstairs now, the gnome inferred. *Guess you can't be too careful when you're a duke and have lots of valuables to protect. Too bad your sentries aren't sharp enough, though, Duke Rehmir, and too bad your ivy isn't potent enough. Too bad for you. Too good for me.*

His confidence growing, and all thoughts of woodworking with his father evaporating, he smiled slyly and glided several more steps, looking in rooms to his right and left where the doors were open. He'd look behind the closed doors later, he decided. No use opening them now and risking squeaking hinges and clicking latches. He'd eliminate the open rooms first.

The next three rooms he passed contained little furniture: a few chairs, a couch, low tables filled with knickknacks that didn't look particularly valuable. The next room was a library, poised just at the edge of a staircase that twisted up into more shadows and curled downward to the level below. Fenzig paused to look at the shelves that covered every wall and stretched to the ceiling. The room smelled like leather from all the dyed bindings on the tomes and the upholstery on the chairs. For a moment the gnome regretted not knowing how to read.

There must be something to the skill, he sadly mused as he moved toward the steps. *Maybe if someday they write everything in magical ink, like Carmen's paint. . . .*

Heavy footsteps ascending interrupted his thoughts, and he slid into the library. The footsteps came closer and were unevenly paced, indicating these probably weren't guards. Fenzig scooted into the niche under a desk just in time to see an old gentleman in a uniform similar to those worn by the sentries—though more ostentatious—and a portly middle-aged man in a robe and sleeping gown enter the room. The gnome nervously fidgeted with his fingernails as he hoped neither one of them would come close enough to see him. He breathed a sigh of relief when they stayed near the doorway, each selecting a well-padded chair. From the gnome's vantage point, he could see only the older man, but he could hear both clearly.

"I just don't know, Ketterhagen." It was the portly man speaking. Fenzig saw that the older man offered a sympathetic smile. "King Erlgrane is marshaling his forces. I suspect he's going to try a raid on my manor—as if he hasn't done enough to me already. Why this blasted land is so important to him is beyond me."

"He's obsessed with it. Perhaps he's gone mad because of it, sir," the aged sentry replied. "Your army is large, and under my command Erlgrane cannot defeat it—not in a fair, straight-up fight. You have more property than he does, and it is in a better location. So defensible. And valuable. From here, he could strike out against the Northern Kingdoms if he's a mind to. He's already acquired land to the south, all the way to the sea. But you mustn't give in to him, no matter what. My forces are at their finest. King Erlgrane knows he doesn't have the men to overrun your estate. That's why he's tried so many different strategies on and off through the past few years. I suspect he's just marshaling his men to worry you, sir."

"It's working, my old friend. I am worried. I've refused his every offer for him to come to my estate and discuss matters. I don't want him here. I don't trust him. I'm a stubborn man, I'll admit, my dear general. This land has been in my family for centuries. And since King Erlgrane refuses to undo the terrible thing he has wrought, why should I even consider dealing with him?"

"Indeed, sir!"

The gnome stopped fidgeting and listened more closely. The portly man must be Duke Rehmir. If he could follow the pair out of here, perhaps he might follow them right to the study. *Please let them go to the study. It's a better place to chat than a library,* he thought.

"He's already taken practically everything I value. Why should I give him this?"

"That's the spirit, sir!"

He doesn't have your emeralds, Fenzig thought. *Not yet, anyway. But I'll be taking them to him shortly, thank you very much, sir. Besides, you have plenty of expensive vases. Just one of those vases is worth enough to feed all the gnomes in my town for a month.*

"But that spirit won't mend my heart," the duke added sadly. "The king has sundered that. Perhaps I could fall on his mercy and beg once more that he make things right."

"I doubt begging would work, sir. It didn't years ago."

Jean Rabe

You're a smart man, General Ketterhagen, the gnome mused. *Erlgrane's not the pitying kind. He'd rather show people the inside of his dungeon than grant them any mercy. And I'll wager neither you nor the duke would like the dungeon after living here.*

"Well, no use worrying about politics tonight," the duke concluded. "I think I'll retire for the evening—after a smoke in the study."

The study! That's it! Fenzig's mind screamed. *Yes! Yes! Yes! I am such a lucky little thief. Let's go to the study!*

"See you in the morning, Ketterhagen."

"Good night, sir."

Fenzig heard the heavy footsteps leave the room, and he was about to dart out from under the desk when he noticed the old general was still sitting in the chair. *Leave!* the gnome mentally urged him. *Get out of here so I can follow the duke! It will save me lots of time. Leave! Leave! Leave! It will. . . .*

The old general closed his eyes and tapped his foot. "Oh, bother," he grumbled. "I do wish there were something I could do to make the duke happy. It's been five years now since King Erlgrane—"

"Sir!" A new voice intruded on the scene.

Fenzig scowled and tried to relax. *It looks as if I'm going to be here for a while,* he thought glumly. *I could care less what the king did to the duke or what the duke did to the king. It couldn't have been any worse than what Erlgrane had his wizard do to me. And I don't care who ends up with this estate. I just want those emeralds!*

"Sir?"

"Yes, Sergeant Rogan. I'm in here."

"General Ketterhagen, we discovered footprints in the outer yards in a patch of mud. The prints were pointed toward the house. We think there is an intruder on the grounds. Small, like that of a child or a woman."

Try a gnome, Fenzig scowled.

90

"Perhaps a thief."

You're right there.

"We've considered that, General Ketterhagen, sir."

"Well, snap to it then! Find your intruder. It will give you something to do this night. Probably just one of the children from town, out here on a dare. That's what it was the last time. But just in case it is a thief. . . ."

Rats! Fenzig cursed. *I thought I was being careful to avoid any patches of dirt where I might leave footprints. I must have missed a step. Better hurry. Now, Ketterhagen, move! I've got to get to the study, and then I've got to get out of here.*

"In fact, I'll go outside with you, Sergeant. A walk would do these old bones some good."

"Very well, sir."

Yes, very well indeed, thank you, the gnome added. *Leave! Leave!* He waited almost a full minute after the old man had exited the room, then he padded toward the stairway. *Up or down? Second floor or fourth,* he wondered. *Up or down? Which way did the duke go?* His eyes narrowed when he spotted depressed nap on the stairway leading up. His fingers ruffled the carpet. *Someone's walked this way recently. I'll try up.*

The stairs were steep for someone Fenzig's size, and because the ceilings were so tall it was a long way to the next floor. By the time he reached the fourth-floor landing he was huffing and clutching his side. *Climbing a wall is easier than this,* he scowled. *Now to smell for tobacco.*

He spent the next several minutes silently racing from doorway to doorway, sniffing for the scent of a pipe or cigar. That floor finished, he climbed another flight of stairs as fast as his short legs would take him, cursing the duke for breaking with tradition and putting his study on the fifth floor or higher. He rounded the corner of the landing and almost slid into the duke, who was leaving a room, smoldering pipe in one hand

and pouch of tobacco in the other.

The gnome's heart thundered in his chest, and he dropped to the floor and rolled to the side. Still prone, he reached for his magical short sword and was about to pull it from the scabbard, but instead watched in amazement as the duke walked right past him and started down the stairs.

The man is muttering to himself, Fenzig thought. *No, he's not muttering, he's sobbing. And whatever he's upset about has made him pretty well oblivious to his surroundings. Lucky for me. Fighting the duke wasn't part of my bargain with King Erlgrane, thank you.* The gnome took a deep breath, steadied his frazzled nerves, and waited until the top of the duke's head bobbed out of sight.

Two more deep breaths and Fenzig darted to the door the duke had closed behind him. *Locked! Well, of course he'd lock it if he keeps emeralds on the mantel.*

The gnome eyed the keyhole and jiggled the knob. *I've nothing to pick it with,* he cursed to himself. *Wait!* Fenzig grinned and unclasped the belt that held his sword scabbard. Using the prong, he worked the lock open and stepped inside. *I am so very, very clever!* The room was lit by a thick candle on a table; its flame provided just enough light so Fenzig could make out the place's most impressive features. The room smelled strongly of sweet pipe smoke, the scent having nowhere to go with the only window closed. The lingering traces of smoke tickled the gnome's senses. Fenzig enjoyed a good pipe now and then, as did most gnomes.

Later, he told himself. *After I'm done here. This place looks more like a museum than a study, a look-but-don't-touch kind of place.*

Two suits of polished, ornamental plate mail flanked a fireplace that hadn't been used in months. A long sword rested in the right glove of one, and a gleaming halberd in the left glove of the other.

Definitely museum pieces, the gnome noted. *The suits have to be a hundred years old or more, judging by their designs and faceplates. And I'll bet they're worth a lot. Too heavy to carry out with me, though. Good thing King Erlgrane didn't want those.*

Richly colored shields and pennants from various countries were draped on the walls, and across from the gnome hung a massive tapestry embroidered with unicorns and other mythical beasts and shot through with gold and silver thread. He guessed the tapestry was worth a small fortune. There was only one chair, a high-backed, overstuffed one that was worn on the arms and the seat. *A favorite, comfortable chair,* Fenzig thought. *It faces the fireplace where you can warm your feet and admire the . . . emeralds.*

The gnome padded all the way into the room, closing and locking the door behind him so anyone outside would not realize there was something amiss. Standing in front of the fireplace, he looked up. Set in a crystal case with a black velvet lining, the gems were tilted so that the person sitting in the chair could admire them. Each was as big as Fenzig's fist and gleamed warmly in the room's meager light. The gnome knew quite a bit about gems, and he didn't need a jeweler's lens to tell him these were cut perfectly.

My gods! the gnome thought to himself. *They're worth more than I could imagine. If I had but one of those I could buy my own castle and furnish it well. I wonder what they'd look like under a brighter light. Light? The duke didn't snuff out the candle. That means he's probably coming back, and that means I'd better get out of here fast.*

The gnome stood on his tiptoes and reached for the gems, but they were just out of reach. Muttering under his breath, he turned and strode toward the chair, intending to tug it closer to the fireplace and use it to climb up on. His small hands were on the chair's worn arms when he heard a *clink* behind him. Glancing over his shoulder, he saw that one of the suits of plate mail had lifted up its visor, revealing the weathered face of a man underneath.

"I'd say you're not supposed to be here, wee-one. Wouldn't you, Drollo?"

The other suit flipped up its faceplate, showing the visage of a darker-skinned man with tight black curls plastered across his forehead. "Oh, I can guarantee you he's not supposed to be here."

"Shall we have at him, then, Drollo my friend?" the first guard quipped. He raised his long sword in a mock salute to the gnome. "Never much cared for gnomes."

"I could use a bit of sport," the other replied. "I was getting tired of just standing here. This is the most boring guard duty in all of the duke's holdings."

They're going to kill me! Fenzig's mind screamed. He drew his short sword and cringed as the guards laughed. Their longer weapons could let them stand out of his reach while still fighting him.

"C-c-couldn't we talk this over?" Fenzig stammered. "I could leave."

"You will leave, thief, in a box—dead," the darker man said. With that, he stepped forward and swung the halberd. The weapon consisted of an axe-like blade at the end of a long metal pole and looked entirely too formidable to Fenzig.

The gnome fell flat to the floor and felt a rush of air as the blade swished above him. "I'm going to die," he gushed.

"Yes, you are," the other guard agreed as he raised his long sword and brought it down. "And I will not lose any sleep in killing you."

Fenzig rolled to the side and heard a sickening *thunk*. Jumping to his feet he saw that the blade had sunk deep into the polished floor. The guard effortlessly pulled it free in a heartbeat and advanced on the trembling gnome. This time the sword

94

sliced through the air on a course for Fenzig's neck. The gnome ducked and watched in horror as a clump of his brown curls fell to the floor, neatly severed by the guard's blade.

"Stand still and we'll make this painless!" the guard with the halberd barked.

"Not a chance!" Fenzig spat back. In that instant the gnome remembered his ring. Concentrating, he felt his skin tingle, as if he'd just stepped out of a warm bath into chill air. Goosebumps raced up and down his arms and legs, then his arms—and his whole body—seemed to blink out of existence. He grinned with delight when he watched the guards glance about the room, looking for their quarry. *Why didn't I use this before?* he wondered. *I could have waltzed in without anybody spotting me. I guess I'm not used to having nifty magical maguffins at my disposal.*

"Where'd he go?" The guard with the long sword, the one named Drollo, seemed furious. "He was right here!"

"You stand by the door to make sure he doesn't leave. I'll start searching." The guard held his halberd cautiously out in front of him. "We'll get him—even if there's sorcery at work! I hate wizards!"

So do I. Fenzig ducked behind the leather chair and snickered.

"I heard him!"

The gnome gulped as the chair was shoved backward, knocking him on his rump. His short sword flew from his grasp and skittered across the floor, instantly becoming visible.

"Indeed it is sorcery! Start swinging at the air, you might connect with him!" Drollo barked. The guard took a step away from the door, bending to retrieve Fenzig's blade. "Gnomes! Distrustful little people. I'll bet they're all thieves!"

I can't be defenseless! the gnome scolded himself. *I can't let him get that weapon.* Without another thought, Fenzig launched himself forward, his belly struck the polished floor, and he slid the few feet to his weapon. As he grasped the hilt it became invisible again, and he instinctively brought it up to parry the thrust of the long sword. As the two blades connected, a flash of bright green light filled the room. When the glow vanished, the stunned guard held a thoroughly rusted sword. Within a few heartbeats more, it fell to pieces.

"Amazing," Fenzig whispered. "The king told me this was magical, but not what it did."

"I hear him!" The guard with the halberd was persistent. Despite what had happened to his companion's blade, he swung the poleaxe, and the gnome had to jump back to avoid being sliced through the middle. "He's nearby! I can hear him breathing!"

As Fenzig dodged a second blow, his short sword accidentally touched the armor of his previous victim, who was moving up behind him. Another flash of light followed, and the man was howling in rage and standing there in a quilted outfit that had served as padding for the armor.

"Get back!" Fenzig sneered at the remaining armored guard. "Keep your distance, or I'll rust your weapon and armor too! That's it, back away some more."

The guard paused for an instant, looking about for some sign of the invisible intruder, and in that quiet moment the gnome heard the pounding of feet coming up the stairs. *More guards will be here any second,* he thought. *I've got to get those emeralds and get out of here.*

He whirled on the guard holding the halberd and urged him toward the tapestry. The gnome kept his back to the fireplace so he could also see the unarmored guard to his left by the door. "Drop the weapon, or I'll rust it and your friend!" Fenzig doubted the blade would rust people, as it hadn't rusted any of the craven cats. But he made the threat sound forceful, and the guard complied. "Now, if you two want to live, walk over to the mantel and take down the emeralds."

"That won't be necessary." The voice was sultry and feminine and came from behind him. "*I'm* taking them."

Fenzig glanced over his shoulder, and his mouth fell open in surprise. A lithe woman clad in a tight black tunic and leggings was already absconding with the emeralds and their glass case. Her short-cropped hair was as dark as midnight, and her brilliant blue eyes flashed mischievously, seeming to lock onto the gnome's gaze—even though he was still invisible. She had black powder or soot smeared on her face and hands. About the only thing that wasn't black was a gold-and-coral necklace that she'd likely lifted from another room in the duke's manor.

Something's familiar about her, Fenzig thought. *The way she moves . . . so catlike. An expert thief.*

She backed toward the window, which Fenzig noticed was now open. "Those emeralds are mine!" the gnome howled. "Mine! You've got no right to them!" His bare feet slammed on the wood, closing the distance between himself and the competing thief.

He was nearly on her when the door to the study burst open, and a half-dozen sentries poured in. To complicate matters, the guard with the halberd was leaping at the gnome. Though Fenzig could not be seen, his footsteps could be heard, and the guard's flailing arms managed to strike the side of the gnome's head.

The impact sent Fenzig down. The other thief dashed out through the window. And the armorless guard finally bellowed, "Intruder! Summon the duke!"

Fenzig scrambled to his feet. At the same time, the guard who'd struck him flailed about again and grabbed a handful of shirt. The gnome brought the short sword around, touching it to the guard's armor, and in a flash the surprised man was left in padded clothes.

The gnome heard the gasps and curses of the six sentries,

and he uttered a few curses of his own as the persistent, near-naked guard refused to let go of his shirt. Not wanting to hurt the man, but desperate to be after the other thief, Fenzig balled his free hand and smacked it backward, connecting with the guard's face.

The man yelped in pain and relaxed his grip, just enough for the gnome to tug free. Again he darted toward the window. But this time his path was blocked by the first guard—who slammed down the pane and latched it. "You're not getting out of here, ghost!" he barked. "Whatever foul manner of creature or wizard you are, you'll not get away from us."

"What's going on here?" The portly duke stomped into the room, which was in a bit of disarray because of the struggle. "My jewels! Someone will die for this, I swear it! Where are the emeralds?"

Several guards started talking at once, and words such as "thief," "sorcerer," and "ghost" were spoken the loudest. Fenzig tried to use the confusion to slip away.

As the duke strode forward into the room, with more guards behind him, the gnome padded softly toward the door. The window was blocked off, so he'd have to leave by a different exit to pursue the female thief. He sheathed his sword and slid past the angry duke.

"I can't believe you let someone steal my jewels!" the duke's voice boomed. "Some guards you are! Bumbling idiots!"

I might feel sorry for you, sir, Fenzig thought as he neared the door frame. *But right now I've myself to think about. If I don't get those emeralds, I'll be. . . .* "What?"

Just as the gnome's right foot stretched out into the hallway, blackness enveloped him. It was a smothering darkness, heavy and thick and all-enveloping. *A rug? No, it's the unicorn tapestry,* Fenzig's mind wailed. The gnome realized the guards had tossed it, hoping it would connect with something unseen—which it had. Several pairs of hands fumbled about the tapestry, closing it in even more tightly around the frightened thief.

"I've got him, sir," the gnome heard one guard proclaim.

"He's a little fellow!" another shouted. "A child!"

"He feels awfully solid for a ghost!"

"Be careful! He's got a weapon that rusts metal."

The gnome felt himself being lifted. He struggled to reach the scabbard where the sword rested. *If I can just get to it,* he huffed, *I can cut myself free, rust the rest of the sentries' weapons, and get out of here. If I can just. . . .*

The guards were holding him so tightly he was having difficulty breathing, so tightly he couldn't maneuver his arm down to his waist where the weapon was tied. When he struggled to find an opening so he could get more air, someone struck him on the back of the head. His senses reeled, and blackness claimed him.

ANOTHER PROPOSITION

"I've got him, sir! He's not going anywhere." The voice belonged to the guard named Drollo. "Shall I cut off his head, sir? I'm sure we can figure out where it is. We beheaded the last thief!"

As Fenzig regained his senses, he tried to shout "No!" But they were holding him so tightly that the only thing escaping his lips and coming through the folds of the tapestry was a muffled gurgling sound.

Leave my head alone, you incompetent excuses for fighting men! he fumed. *If you were real men you wouldn't hit people over the head from behind. You'd fight them fairly. Of course,* he added, *I wasn't exactly being fair with the invisibility ring, but then I wasn't trying to fight anyone.*

The gnome wriggled an arm upward and gingerly probed at a growing bump on the back of his head, cursing himself for getting caught. Vowing to regain his freedom, he struggled like a fly caught in a spiderweb. Eventually he figured out this tactic was futile and decided it would be better to conserve his strength for when the guards relaxed their grip on the tapestry, affording him a better opportunity to escape.

They're certainly incompetent enough to present me an opportunity, he thought. *And when they do I'll grab my sword and rust the weapons and armor of all of them!*

"Shall I run him through perhaps?" The guard holding the tapestry was bloodthirsty and persistent. "Maybe we should burn him—outside, of course. Or we could string him up from one of the big trees behind the palace. I suppose we could even draw and quarter him, though that's not done much anymore."

"Don't kill him yet." The gnome recognized the duke's voice and breathed a sigh of relief at his commuted death sentence. "I want the jewels back first."

Fenzig felt part of the tapestry being pulled away from him. His captors were in effect fashioning a bag out of the material and were gathering it about his neck. Only his aching head was freed, while the rest of his body sweltered amid the thick bunched-up material. He gasped for air and cursed as he felt someone tug on his hair and yank on his ears.

"Here, sir, here's his face. If you feel about here and here, you can. . . ."

"Oh, my eye!" Fenzig sputtered.

"He feels very small, as if he's a child. Perhaps, sir. . . ."

"Let go of my nose!"

"He certainly doesn't sound like a child." This came from the duke.

One of the sentries had a firm hold on the gnome's ears and was holding his head in a viselike grip. The duke knelt until his face was even with Fenzig's, and the gnome could smell the hint of sweet tobacco on the portly man's breath.

"Scoundrel," the duke began evenly, "you will return those emeralds to me now, or I will give the order for the beginning of your demise. My guards will make sure your death is slow and painful. You will have hours, perhaps even days, to contemplate the folly of stealing from me before you finally expire."

"I don't have the emeralds," Fenzig gulped. Before he could offer any further explanation, the guard holding his ears jostled him hard. "Hey, cut it out!"

"I'll cut out your tongue!" the guard spat. "You . . . you . . . you're a gnome?"

Fenzig watched the duke back away. "Yes. He is a gnome. A wee-one," the duke said. "A fairly young one from the looks of him. He's not a ghost or a sorcerer, despite what some of you claimed, though I'll wager he was employing some type of magic to make himself unseen. But whatever would possess a gnome to steal from me? I've done nothing untoward concerning the wee-ones and their land. I treat the wee-ones employed in the kitchen most fairly and pay them well. I've done no ill to the gnomes."

Fenzig saw that all eyes in the room were fixed on him. *I'm not invisible anymore,* he realized with dismay. *Now they can see me. Everyone can see me. Even if I get away they'll know who to look for. My description will be ingrained in the minds of every guard and bounty hunter in the land.*

"Sir," one of the guards cut in, "the gnome wasn't working alone. He had an accomplice. While he kept us busy and rusted poor Roderick's and Drollo's weapons and armor, his accomplice crept in the window and made off with your gems. They had the caper rather well timed."

"I *was* working alone!" Fenzig moaned. "I always work alone."

"No use trying to defend your partner, thief," another guard said. "She'll not be free long. By the way, sir, his partner isn't a gnome. She's a human—and a nice-looking young one at that."

"She was working alone, too!" Fenzig continued. "It was a coincidence we were both trying to steal the emeralds at the same time. I never saw her before tonight. Honest!"

"Honest? Ha! I've never met an honest thief," the duke said sadly. "Search him. I want those emeralds."

Fenzig's arms were grabbed; the guards' fingers dug harshly into his flesh as the tapestry dropped free around him. He felt humiliated as the guards pulled off all his clothes and turned them inside out, searching pockets and hems and ripping apart a few of the seams. To the gnome, their efforts seemed to take an eternity. Only when they were satisfied that the gems were nowhere to be found did they allow him to dress. As he put on his shirt, Fenzig glanced anxiously at his arm. The line extended from the heart on his hand to a few inches past his elbow and was heading toward his shoulder. The line was speeding up, just as his heart had been speeding along since he was caught.

Fenzig straightened his clothes and tried to make himself presentable as he watched the duke examine his short sword. The guards kept him at weaponspoint, not allowing him to move more than a foot in any direction.

"Tell us where your accomplice can be found, and perhaps, just perhaps, I will spare your life," the duke intoned evenly. He set the short sword on the mantel and strode toward the gnome. "I'm a reasonable man. If I get my emeralds back, I will show you some amount of mercy. Where is she, thief?"

"Please believe me!" Fenzig implored. "I don't know where she is. I don't know who she is! But whoever she is and wherever she is—she has your emeralds. Not me. And the longer we talk about it, the more time she has to get away. She's not going to stick around K'Nosha. She'd be a fool to stay!"

One of the guards stepped forward. "I got a real good look at her, sir. She was young, with unusually short hair for a woman. It was black like the night sky. She had a build as slender and graceful as a dancer's, and she had beautiful eyes that sparkled like sapphires—the only thing about her that wasn't black. And . . . sir . . . she was wearing the necklace, the one your wife always wore."

The duke rubbed his chin. His shoulders visibly sagged, and he mouthed a word the gnome could not make out. He turned away from Fenzig and rubbed his eyes; then after several long moments, he pivoted to face the gnome again, then began pacing.

"Few people know of those jewels, thief. Too few for such a

coincidence as tonight to occur. I think you're lying. I think you were working with her. I think she told you where to find the jewels, and I think she set you up. You were her diversion so she could make off with them. Though what would prompt her to steal from me—to steal those particular gems—I can't imagine. In any event, maybe a few days in my dungeon will help your tongue utter the truth about where I can find her. I will have those emeralds back, or you will most certainly die."

Fenzig shivered. "I really don't have anything to do with the woman who stole your gems. I. . . . Oh, what does it matter? I'm going to die anyway," Fenzig whispered. "King Erlgrane has seen to that."

"Erlgrane?"

The gnome had the duke's full attention now. *I might as well tell him the entire story,* Fenzig mused. *If I'm going to die, I might as well die with a clear conscience.*

The tale tumbled from Fenzig's lips—about his failed theft from Erlgrane's castle, his capture by the wizard, his time in the horrid cell, and his reprieve from death in exchange for stealing Duke Rehmir's emeralds. He embellished the story with the homing spell, and he pulled up the sleeve of his shirt to show the line. Then he finished the tale by detailing how he had slipped into the manor and watched in horror as the other thief took the gems before he could get them.

"So I've no reason to lie to you," Fenzig concluded. "I was working alone. And now that your emeralds are gone, I have nothing to give King Erlgrane, and I will die. I figure I've got six or seven days left, maybe eight if I'm lucky. But luck hasn't been on my side lately."

The duke began to pace. "Then you'd best make good use of those days."

Fenzig looked at him quizzically. *Is the duke going to let me go free?* he wondered. *Maybe he won't throw me in his dungeon now that he knows I'm telling the truth. He wouldn't imprison a dying man, would he? Maybe he'll let me live my last few days however I want. I always heard he was a much fairer ruler than Erlgrane.*

"I can have the homing spell negated," the duke said, interrupting Fenzig's thoughts. "I can have your worthless life saved."

Saved? I'll live!

"Great!" the gnome gushed aloud as his face broke into a broad grin. "Oh, that's great. You're the most wonderful human I've ever met, thank you. Why. . . ."

The duke's scowl cut Fenzig off. He cleared his throat and continued. "But to save you, first you'll have to bring me the emeralds—and the female thief who stole them—all unharmed. That's the price of my saving your life." The duke balled one of his hands into a fist and slammed it against an open palm for emphasis. "If indeed you have only six days left, you won't have time to recover the gems and make it back to King Erlgrane's. You'll have to come back here. Even if you had eight days left and could locate the gems quickly, you might not reach Erlgrane's in time. I am still the safer bet. Besides, if you returned to King Erlgrane with the gems, I suspect he would order you killed anyway. It would tie up loose ends and your potentially loose lips. I am your only safe way out of your predicament."

The gnome gulped, and his wide eyes met Duke Rehmir's icy stare.

"Do you agree to my terms, thief?" The duke's tone seemed challenging. "Or do you want to simply curl up and die? Take the easy way out of life?"

That's not much of a choice, Fenzig thought. *It seems I'm to be a puppet again, following the orders of some potentate in pursuit of three gems. If I ever get out of this, I think I'll definitely try my hand at woodworking. I doubt anyone would have a homing spell cast on you 'cause they didn't like a chair you fashioned. I'm done being a thief. I want to be my own man. I'm tired of people pulling my strings.*

"I agree to your terms," the gnome stated finally. "Though since I've never seen that thief before tonight, locating her could be difficult."

"Her name's Carmella." The duke's tone softened. "She wears a gold-and-coral necklace that my wife favored. She's worn it for the past few years. I suspect she won't take it off."

"So she's been here before? Stole from you before?" Fenzig was curious. "And your wife would like the necklace back, too, while I'm at it—right?"

The duke shook his head. "I don't care about the necklace. My wife died long years ago, so it matters little that someone else wears it now. All I care about is getting those gems back."

"All right." Fenzig puffed out his chest. "I'll find this Carmella for you, sir. Carmella? Carmen?" His eyes popped wide.

The necklace the thief wore looked the same as the one Carmen wore. In fact, he'd seen Carmen move gracefully about the wagon—just as gracefully as the thief did. *No wonder there was a familiarity about the thief,* he thought.

Are Carmen and Carmella one and the same? Was Carmen coming to K'Nosha all along, planning to steal the emeralds? Was he—she—still in town with his—her—peddler routine? Was. . . .

". . . so be careful," the duke added. Fenzig had missed part of what the man said, so engrossed was the gnome with thoughts of the gaudily dressed peddler. "The necklace allows her to read the thoughts of others, but not while she's talking or doing anything strenuous. She has to concentrate to pick through another's thoughts. So be wary. Approach her when she's busy—otherwise she'll know you're coming."

So that's how he—she—knew I was going to steal the emeralds, Fenzig thought. *That's probably why I was given the sleepy-time tea. He—she—knew I was going to clobber him—her—and steal the horses and wagon.*

"When did this Carmella steal the necklace from your wife?" Fenzig's curiosity got the better of him again. The gnome wondered why the duke didn't have better security if his manor house had been robbed before. "What has she taken besides the necklace?"

The duke pointedly avoided the questions. "My wife loved the necklace because of its beauty. She wore it at every state function so others would admire it and so she could tell if any nearby dignitaries were thinking ill thoughts toward me."

Fenzig was rudely shoved from behind. "Don't you think you'd better be going?" It was the guard in the padded clothes. "Time is wasting, and Carmella's getting farther away."

"I'll find Carmella," the gnome promised. *She might even still be in town, if I'm lucky. It can't be that hard to find her, especially since I know she's dressed as a man, not a woman, wearing colors that clash, and hawking elixirs and the like from a cherry-red wagon.*

"Find her and the gems quickly," the duke urged. "You must bring both to me if you want that homing spell lifted."

"What about my sword?"

"You won't be needing it."

CARMEN'S TRUTH

The pony wasn't nearly as pretty as the one Fenzig had selected from King Erlgrane's stables just a few days ago. In fact, Fenzig wasn't allowed to select his own mount this time—he was given one and had no choice in the matter. Still, the pony was brown, a color he preferred. It seemed healthy and strong, but was not in as good a condition as Mistake had been, he noted, or rather, not in as good a condition as Mistake had been before the unfortunate incident in the Haunted Woods. It was not as large, and it lacked that clever gleam in its eyes.

The animal was saddled and waiting for him shortly after dawn. The gnome had spent the few intervening hours—between his capture and now—in the duke's dungeon. The accommodations were similar to his cell in King Erlgrane's castle, and Fenzig wondered if all rich men used the same malicious and unimaginative architect for their prisons and populated them with hungry rats to worry their prisoners.

"Hello, my name is Puppet," Fenzig told the pony as he climbed into the saddle and prodded it toward K'Nosha. "The duke is pulling my strings today, so we'd better be off. I'm not going to name you. I don't intend to be in your company long enough to get friendly. This is simply a business arrangement between you and me. We're going after Carmen—or Carmella—or whoever he—or she—is. Who knows? Maybe there's two of them and one hides in the crates in the wagon. And then when we're done, you're going back to Duke Rehmir's. Or maybe the king's if this line on my arm doesn't move very far. I don't trust either of them, but I know for certain the king has a wizard. Didn't see anyone in robes at Duke Rehmir's."

The gnome grumbled constantly on the brief ride into town. His back was sore from sleeping on a thin mound of moldy straw. His head still hurt from being struck by an angry guard. The bottoms of his feet had gotten cold. The tops of his feet burned. The line on his arm was a little longer. And his hands and face itched terribly. Fenzig hated being uncomfortable.

He glanced at his small hands that clutched the reins and noticed there was a rash on his fingers. *Probably bugs in the duke's dungeon. Hungry ones. At least there aren't any rat bites. I hate rats. But I'm not too fond of bugs, either.*

Then he glanced at his feet, which rhythmically bounced with the pony's steps. The bottoms were pleasantly warm now, but the tops still burned. He stared at them. Amid the curls and all over his toes was a rash even worse than the one on his hands.

Those aren't bug bites. How did I. . . . "Of course," he moaned aloud. "That stupid ointment or hair cream or whatever it was Carmen, rather Carmella, had me spread all over. It didn't make my hair grow or any wrinkles go away. It's just making me itch. I'll bet I've even got a rash on my face."

Fenzig kicked the pony in the sides to speed its course over the town's cobblestone streets. He ignored the startled looks from townsfolk as he hurried past, almost knocking a few of them down. He steered the pony toward the center of K'Nosha, near the fountain where The Magnificent One had parked the wagon. But there was no evidence of the gaudily dressed male peddler, the black-attired female thief, or the wagon with its magical-paint sign. However, there were a few people milling about and grumbling as much as the gnome.

A few questions revealed that Carmen the Magnificent and

his gaudy wagon had left very late last night—shortly before some of his dissatisfied customers, who turned to grumble to Fenzig now, came calling to demand back their money—and more.

"You, gnome!" a bald man hollered. "You said that hair-growth tonic worked! It was because of you that I bought it. Because of you I've got this rash! This is all your fault."

Fenzig steered out of the bald man's way.

A woman who was pulling out clumps of hair by the fistfuls complained to Fenzig that the hair growth ointment did just the opposite of what the peddler had claimed. A second bald-headed man sported a rash similar to the one the gnome had. Trickles of blood ran down his forehead as he itched and scratched and glowered at Fenzig.

A younger woman grinned sheepishly and said she thought the hand cream was just fine, that it made her skin feel nice and smooth, but her mother's sore throat had not improved at all after drinking the entire bottle of sore-throat tonic.

"I've no idea where that crook went," snarled the woman pulling at her hair. "But if that peddler ever shows his face in K'Nosha again, I'll give him something much worse than a rash to worry about."

Questioning the sentries at the gate revealed nothing useful—other than the disturbing fact that several of the peddler's more disgruntled customers had left on horseback right after dawn—with swords and daggers strapped to their waists. A couple went north, one went south, and one struck out west across the open farmland.

North or south? Fenzig wondered. *South leads to Burlengren and King Erlgrane—which would be most convenient, and therefore most unlikely. North leads to all manner of places. East is out of the question because that would have taken Carmen right past the duke's estate. And west is over that rather uneven farmland, and I doubt*

Carmen would drive the wagon over that. I'll head north, he decided glumly, *and hopefully there'll be something left of him—or her, or them—when I get there.*

As the day grew older and the line on the gnome's arm grew longer, Fenzig had plenty of opportunity to reflect on his relatively short life. Most of his life had been pretty good, and most of the bad experiences fit nicely into these past several days. He tried to follow the wagon ruts that were worn into the road, while his mind wandered back to his childhood. He was too young to remember why his mother had left. Something about wanting more money and more things. A woodcarver, his dad said he never seemed able to provide enough for her. But he provided enough love for Fenzig and his brothers, and he gave them shelter and as much food as they wanted.

Maybe if I weren't so much like my mother, he pondered. *Maybe if I hadn't been so interested in getting wealthy, maybe things would have turned out differently. If I hadn't been so against trying to work honestly to earn a living. If. . . .*

A pair of riders coming south caught the gnome's attention. He waved cheerfully, and they stopped to greet him. A half-dozen questions later, the men revealed that they'd seen a bright wagon very early that morning. It was parked outside a small village farther north. They added that Fenzig wasn't the first person to ask them about the wagon. Two middle-aged men with severe rashes on their faces had stopped them about an hour ago, but they hadn't been nearly as pleasant about it as Fenzig.

The gnome urged the pony faster, and the miles fell away beneath the steady beat of the animal's hooves. Carmella had several hours' head start on him, and the wagon and horses were capable of moving faster than the gnome's pony. Still, Fenzig was counting on Carmella stopping to sell some wares—and collect more dissatisfied customers. He was hoping that perhaps the rash-covered men from K'Nosha had slowed the peddler down—without killing him.

The gnome arrived at the village late that afternoon. There was no sign of Carmella, though several people admitted to buying things from the peddler. No one evidenced a rash, though the gnome suspected that was simply because they hadn't yet had time to develop.

"He promised us a magic show tonight," a disappointed little girl said, "but two bad men came riding up, and Carmen the Magnificent rode away."

"Some things fell off his wagon. He was in a real hurry," a lanky farmhand added, holding up an all-too-familiar bottle. "It's hair tonic, see. My dad's going to love this!"

Fenzig closed his eyes, shook his head, and urged his pony farther north. "I know you're tired," he told the animal, "but you've got to keep going, or I'm going to be very dead."

By nightfall the gnome still hadn't caught up to the peddler, though by questioning a few more people along the road he knew he was still heading in the right direction. He tied the exhausted pony to a bush near a stream and watched it graze and drink its fill. The gnome was ravenous, but he wasn't about to eat grass, and he didn't know if the berries he saw were safe to eat. He drifted off into a troubled slumber and awoke before dawn—hungrier than he ever remembered being in his entire life.

Again the gnome and the pony set off to the north. Fenzig didn't bother looking at the line on his arm. He knew it was moving faster, that he had only a few days left, and that if he didn't catch Carmen or Carmella by tomorrow afternoon, he might as well give up.

Maybe I should have directed all my efforts into finding a wizard, the gnome mused. *Maybe another wizard could have negated the homing spell. King Erlgrane's wizard said only he could reverse the spell, but the duke said he'd take care of it. So King Erlgrane's wizard lied . . . I hope. That is if the duke wasn't lying.*

The pony snorted, rousing the hungry gnome from his thoughts. Ahead, near the road, two men were tied to a tree; their horses grazed contentedly several yards away. The men's faces were covered with a red rash, and Fenzig sped toward them.

Balancing himself precariously on the back of his pony, the gnome leaned over and yanked loose one of the men's gags.

"Cut us free!" the man demanded angrily. "Just look what that peddler did to us! Cut us loose right now!"

"My, my," Fenzig replied rather testily. "I don't see that you're in any position to be making demands of me, thank you."

"All right. *Please* cut us loose!" the man pleaded. The gnome suspected the man's irate tone was caused in part from having a rash that he couldn't scratch, what with his hands being bound at his sides by the rope that tied him and his friend to the tree.

"If I cut you loose will you go after the peddler again?"

"Yes! We'll help you. We'll help you tear that peddler limb from limb. We'll rip out his hair. We'll tear his clothes into little pieces. I can see you're a victim, too." The man had noticed Fenzig's red fingers and toes and was staring at his face. "Hair tonic, right? Or did he get you with the wrinkle-be-gone?"

Both. "I'm a victim most certainly," the gnome agreed, "but I don't want your help tracking Carmen. How long ago did he do this to you?"

"About an hour, two at the most. Now cut us loose."

"Sorry. Maybe on the way back."

Fenzig dug his heels into his pony's sides, urging it into a steady gallop and resolutely blocking out the curses of the men he'd left behind. *One or two hours—I'm getting close,* he thought. *I might still have a chance. I just hope Carmen or Carmella or the pair of them haven't fenced those emeralds someplace. I would have fenced them by now if I knew they were this hot.* The gnome continued talking to himself for well over an hour until he saw another village ahead and a throng of people gathered. He kicked the pony once more and sped toward the group that could only have a garishly attired peddler at the center.

"And here is my favorite—Carmen the Magnificent's Wart Remover. Guaranteed to eliminate all your warts in just one day."

The peddler looked truly flamboyant, Fenzig had to admit. Carmen, or Carmella, was dressed in a red satin shirt with billowy sleeves that sported white satin ruffles. The pants were lime green and voluminous, billowing like a ship's sail about his legs. He wasn't wearing a cape today. Instead, he wore a purple scarf that was covered with beads and sequins. It fluttered in the breeze, and the decorations sparkled in the noontime sun. A dark-green floppy hat festooned with a half-dozen orange feathers topped his head and shadowed most of his face, and his long blond hair hung loose about his shoulders.

Fenzig got off his pony, tied it to a post, and moved in closer, noting that Carmen the peddler had about the same build as Carmella the thief. The gnome was careful not to get too near. He didn't want to tip off Carmen or Carmella or anyone else who might be working for him or her.

"Give me some of that cold syrup you were talking about. I've got a bad case of the sniffles!"

"Right away, beautiful lady," Carmen said as he exchanged a bottle of pink liquid for a gold coin. "And how about you, ma'am? I'll bet you've been fretting over those few gray hairs that have been appearing. Try my exclusive Gray Away and you won't be fretting anymore."

"Ooh!" came a delighted squeal. "Gray Away sounds like just what I need. How did you know I was worried about my hair?"

Fenzig admired the way the peddler worked the crowd. Carmen knew what they wanted because he could read their minds with that necklace. He knew the things to say to get them to buy. He catered to them and complimented them and bilked them out of their hard-earned gold.

"And here's my newest remedy—Carmen the Magnificent's Cure-All. It will rid you of the gout, chase away the toughest flu bug, eradicate the mumps, and abolish bad breath."

The gnome was squeezed by the press of people trying to get closer to purchase Carmen's latest concoction. His small ears were filled with cries of "I've got to have some of that," "Oh, please sell me a bottle," and "I'll take two." After suffering a couple of unintentional jabs to his ribs, Fenzig dropped to his hands and knees and crawled between the humans' legs. He skittered to the front of the crowd, then made a dash for the back of the flashy wagon. He was stretching up to reach a hand-hold to help him inside, when he heard a wail that sent shivers down his spine.

"This cold syrup tastes terrible. And it's giving me a nosebleed! This isn't a cure. This is a curse."

"Ma'am," Carmen called quickly. "You're supposed to drink that before going to bed. That's why it's not working properly."

"If I drank it before I went to bed, you'd be long gone, and I couldn't get my money back. You're a swindler!"

"Yeah! This sore-throat tonic isn't working, either!"

"Good folks," Carmen pleaded, "you've got to give my medicine a little time to work. It needs a few hours to get into your systems and work its wonders."

"Wonders? It's a wonder you've got the nerve to sell this stuff."

Fenzig grinned widely—and leaned away from the wagon, looking around the side just in time to see a large, ripe tomato being launched by a tall farmhand. The tomato flew unerringly through the air and landed solidly with a squishy *splat* against the peddler's chest. Not that anyone would notice it, given how bright a red the shirt already was, the gnome mused. A few more tomatoes followed, as did potatoes, onions, rocks, and anything else the townsfolk had handy to throw. Some struck the peddler, the horses, and the side of the wagon. Others struck the customers up front.

Carmen tried his best to dodge and dip and jump about to avoid being pelted too severely. "This is uncalled for!" the peddler bellowed. "I came to offer you my best wares and you offer me taunts and vegetables! I'm leaving!"

"Good riddance, thief!"

"Get out of here, you stinking con artist!"

"Hey! Give us our money back!"

"Yeah, we want our coins!"

"After him!"

Fenzig gripped the handhold tight with his right hand as he felt the wagon lurch. With his left he reached for the knob on the back of the wagon, intending to open the door and climb in. But the wagon lurched again, and the gnome had to use both hands just to hang on. Carmen was obviously trying to move the horses through the crowd, though he wasn't having much success. The wagon pitched once more, then stopped, and the gnome heard the peddler yell at someone to let his horses go.

"You're not going anywhere!" someone called. Fenzig imagined the person was big, judging by the booming voice. "You're going to jail!"

"Yes! Take him to jail."

No! I can't let that happen, Fenzig thought. *If Carmen—or Carmella—cools his—or her—heels in jail, they'll keep the wagon and what's in it, too. Then I won't be able to get the gems or take Carmella to Duke Rehmir's. I've got to do something.* With that, Fenzig concentrated on his ring, felt himself instantly chilled, and became invisible. He leapt off the back of the wagon and started weaving his way through the throng of people pressing ever closer to the peddler. The horses were getting nervous and snorting loudly. But the people didn't seem to care.

"Ouch!" Fenzig yelled as a boot heel ground into the top of his foot. "Watch where you're going."

"Watch where you're walking!" Came an angry retort. "Get him!" the man with the hard boots added. "Jail's too good for the slimy peddler. Let's hang him!"

The people couldn't see Fenzig, but that didn't mean they couldn't bump into him, jostle him, and drop rotten vegetables on his invisible head. The gnome muttered a string of curses, which mingled with those being spewed by everyone else in the crowd, and he made his way toward the front of the wagon.

"Argh!" Fenzig spat as he was pressed between the wagon wheel and a burly man. The gnome pounded his fists into the man's belly, and at last the man backed up, looking for his assailant. The man's glare was directed at Carmen. *That's it,* thought the gnome. *Keep thinking the peddler's to blame for all your woes and hurts and you won't think to look for me.*

The gnome spied a dropped hoe on the ground in the midst of the crowd's feet. It gave him an idea. Risking more punishment, he crawled on his hands and knees between several pairs of legs and grasped the wooden haft.

Now we'll see if you give Carmen some room, Fenzig thought as he snuck toward the front of the crowd and jabbed the hoe handle into the back of the burly man's calf.

The big man whirled around and glanced at the person behind him. "Watch yourself!" he barked.

"No. *You* watch yourself!" came the vicious reply. "You're in my way!"

The gnome ducked and scampered forward just as the burly man landed a punch in the other man's stomach. At the same time, Fenzig stretched the hoe forward to trip a young woman who was reaching for a piece of Carmen. She fell forward against the wagon wheel, and the man behind her bent to help her up.

"You oaf!" she snarled as she slapped away the gallant gentleman's hand and kept up her attack by slapping his face. "You tripped me!"

"I did not! I was only trying to help!" The man put his hands on his hips in a pose of indignation, and Fenzig rapped him across the back of the ankles, causing him to pitch backward in surprise—right into the burly man.

The fistfight was growing larger, and Fenzig had to scamper this way and that to avoid being a target. *Good thing they can't see me or I'd....* "Ooof!" The gnome found himself being ground into the dirt as the fight moved over the top of him. He tried to stand, but found that someone was standing on him. His ribs ached, and he suspected a couple of them were at the very least bruised. "Get off me!" he hollered, then instantly realized how ridiculous he was being. No one could see him. Still, he had the use of his arms, and he started swinging the hoe with them, moving it back and forth, connecting with people's ankles and feet.

The cacophony of curses, yells, and connecting punches seemed deafening to the squashed gnome. He summoned all his strength in an attempt to do a pushup and dislodge whatever overweight villager was standing on his rump. He heaved and heaved and nothing happened, but then the person moved of his own accord when a shrill whistle cut through the air.

"What is going on here?" a new voice bellowed. It was deep and loud and had the sound of authority to it. "Break it up! Break it up!"

The yelling started dying down, and Fenzig took the op- portunity to scramble close to the wagon. *Maybe I'll just settle for the emeralds and not the lady thief and hope the duke understands,* the gnome thought as he clambered onto the back of the wagon. This time he had little trouble with the back latch. *Maybe I can find the gems inside—provided Carmen hasn't fenced them—and sneak out before the invisibility wears off. The crowd is welcome to the peddler for all I care. She deserves her fate. I just want the emeralds.*

"Who started this fight?" It was the same commanding break-it-up voice he'd heard before, and Fenzig craned his neck so he could see the speaker. The man wore a leather breastplate with some type of badge of office affixed to it. No doubt he was the town constable or some other type of lawman. "What is all this about?"

More cacophony resulted as the townsfolk proceeded to complain loudly and all at the same time about the peddler and his noxious mixtures. The criticisms, charges, grievances, and objections overlapped each other, and the gnome couldn't stomach listening to all the noise. He ducked inside the wagon and closed the back panel behind him.

"Now, hold it, folks. I'm going to talk to this peddler, and we'll get this mess sorted out." The sound of the constable's voice reached Fenzig even through all the shelves and boxes and vials and crates piled inside the wagon.

"No, you're not." This last bit came from Carmen, who hied the horses, which were now free from the press of the crowd.

The wagon lurched forward, and Fenzig fell on his rump, crushing a vial beneath him. The broken glass bit into his tender flesh, adding a new ache to his small body, and he wondered if whatever he was sitting in was going to give him another rash. The horses moved off at a run, and the wagon veered crazily from side to side. Pans, jars, bottles, and more were spilling off of the shelves and flying everywhere—even on Fenzig's invisible form. The gnome grumbled and pulled himself to his feet. He held onto a shelf, which was nailed to the wagon wall, to steady himself, and he opened the back door of the wagon just a pinch.

A bevy of townsfolk were chasing the wagon, though they had no real prayer of catching it because they were on foot. Then a figure on horseback caught Fenzig's eye. He was urging his mount around the crowd, shouting for the people to move. There were three more riders close behind him.

They do have a prayer of catching up, Fenzig thought. *In fact, it's almost certain they will.*

Thinking quickly, the still-invisible gnome groped around for unbroken bottles. He pulled the back panel of the wagon wide open and started flinging out the potions, aiming at the ground around the horses' hooves.

When the first landed and broke, pink smoke belched forth. The horse reared back, nearly tossing its rider to the ground. But he was a good horseman, and in a heartbeat he had the animal under control and had resumed the pursuit. The second bottle landed with a thud, the glass seemingly unbreakable, and the third and the fourth had little effect on the men or their mounts.

"Try the bottles with the blue liquid in them."

The gnome swore under his breath at the sound of Carmen's voice. The peddler must have used his necklace to discover he had company in the wagon.

"The blue liquid and the green liquid. They don't mix well. Throw them together, and you'd better hurry! They're gaining on us!"

Fenzig took Carmen's advice and gathered a handful of bottles that had blue or green liquid in them. He heaved them out the back of the wagon and watched in amazement as they broke on impact and discharged great puffs of colorful smoke and arcing streaks of sparks. The reaction looked like a miniature fireworks display and served to spook the horses. The men— including the town constable—were thrown to the ground. Their flailing limbs were barely visible amid the puffs of smoke.

"Did you get them?" Carmen called.

Yes, I got them.

"Good," the peddler replied. "Now why don't you come up front, and you and I can have a little chat?" The peddler hied the horses again and got them to go faster yet.

The gnome knew Carmen had to put more distance between himself and the angry villagers. The men would eventually get up, dust themselves off, retrieve their horses, and come after the peddler again. He halfway wished he hadn't thrown the blue and green liquid at them. If they'd caught Carmen, the gnome might have been able to explain about the emeralds, been allowed to take them, and go on his way.

"Now, now, now," Carmen lectured. "That's no way to think. Join me up here. The view's much better."

Fenzig grumbled and picked his way between the broken bits of glass and ceramic. *Is it always like this?* he thought, no longer bothering to talk. If Carmen could read his mind so easily, let him. *Do you always leave disgruntled customers behind—ones who would like to throw you in jail for eternity?*

"No," Carmen called back. "It's not always like that. I think my last batch of stuff had a few spoiled ingredients. Some people who used the lotions broke out in rashes. That usually doesn't happen. My elixirs simply do nothing. They're like sugar water. They generally taste good going down, but they neither hurt nor help you. Except for my hand cream, which is truly exceptional. I think I'm going to have to look at my recipes again."

You mean you have all of these nonsensical concoctions written down?

"Of course. I have to mix some things together to produce the colors and thicknesses. People don't want to buy clear liquid. It looks too much like water. But offer them something kelly green or dark purple, something that smells like ferns caught in a spring rain, and they'll shell out a few gold coins. People want something wildly exotic that offers the promise of a miracle cure. You know, something that. . . ."

The peddler's last sentence ended with a *clang*. He rocked forward in his seat, and the gnome grabbed the back of his shirt to keep him from plummeting from the wagon. Propping the peddler against the seat, Fenzig dropped the metal skillet he'd used to hit Carmen in the head and grabbed a length of twine. Climbing onto the driver's bench, he grabbed the reins and held them in his teeth. He made no move to slow the horses, as he was still worried about their pursuers. Balancing on the seat and keeping one eye trained on the horses' route, he deftly twisted the twine about Carmen's hands and feet. When he was certain the peddler wouldn't be able to worm his way loose, he yanked the medallion free from Carmen's neck. The gesture knocked off Carmen's hat—and his luxurious mane of blond hair went with it. The short-cropped black hair of the jewel thief was left behind.

"Carmella!" Fenzig exclaimed, dropping the necklace over his own head. The gnome wasn't surprised, though he hadn't been sure if Carmella was a female masquerading as the male peddler Carmen, or if Carmen was a male masquerading as the female thief Carmella. The former of those suspicions was correct.

I see how you do it, he thought as he stuffed the gaudy purple scarf in her mouth to make sure he could ride in silence. *I always believed it was best to blend in with the crowd so no one would notice me. On the other hand, you like to stand out in a crowd and get everyone's attention. But their attention is riveted on a flamboyant salesman who is easy to remember. No one ever sees the female in black who skulks into their homes and robs them. And I'll bet you use this,* he added to himself as he fingered the medallion around his neck. *I'll bet you read their minds to find out who is rich enough to get a visit after Carmen the Magnificent's magic show is over. I'll wager you used it on me to learn all about the emeralds and beat me to them.*

The gnome carefully turned the horses off the road and behind a copse of trees. He pulled Carmen's—rather Carmella's—unconscious body into the wagon, pushing aside a few boxes so he had enough space to stretch her out. Then he went about searching for the emeralds. It took him nearly an hour, but in the end he was successful. Carmella had hidden them at the bottom of a bag of rye flour.

I actually considered throwing this bag at those men, he realized with dismay. *I thought the flour might startle the horses. Talk about throwing away your life.* He cradled the gems in a fold of his shirt and carried them forward. As he sat on the wagon bench, he reverently ran his fingers over their sparkling facets. They were a handful, each about the size of his fist. In the sun they sparkled warmly and glistened like green fire. Fenzig admired their perfect beauty. *No wonder King Erlgrane wants them so badly,* he thought. *I've never seen any gems as exquisite as these. They've got to be priceless, or very close to it. I'll bet if I knew a wizard he'd get rid of this homing spell in exchange for one of these— maybe even for just a look at one of these.*

The green was dark and bright and flawless and almost mesmerizing, and the gnome had a hard time tearing his eyes away from the gems. However, the desire to save himself finally rose to the surface, and he thrust the jewels in his belt pouches and pulled up his sleeve. He scowled. The blue line had reached his shoulder.

"It's going much, much too fast. He said he'd never cast it on a gnome before." *I've got a few days left,* he judged. *Maybe a little more, but I doubt it. The line's moving so terribly, terribly fast, probably because my arm's so short. And I'm guessing it'll take me almost a day and a half to make it back to the duke's—and that's provided I stop only briefly to give the horses a rest. Sure hated to leave that little brown pony behind. Hope the duke won't be upset. No chance now of making it to King Erlgrane's on time. Bet the duke did something to speed up the spell so I wouldn't have a choice.* He returned to the inside of the wagon and found Carmen's stash of dried venison and a flask half full of water.

Satisfied he wouldn't starve before the homing spell killed him, the gnome picked up the reins and turned the horses around so they headed south. But he kept them off the road, guiding them over the farmland and behind a windbreak of trees as they passed near the village they'd just left so precipitously. The gnome had no desire to be spotted and chased. When he was a couple of miles past the village, he urged the horses back onto the road and made them pick up the pace.

He munched on the venison, drained the waterskin, and finally had hope that he might yet get out of this alive.

You can't have those emeralds. They're not yours to take. The voice was inside Fenzig's head.

"Huh? Who said that? Who said I can't have the emeralds?"

I did. You're reading my mind. You have my necklace around your scrawny neck, so you can read anyone's mind. It was Carmen—rather Carmella—who was thinking to him. *You don't understand. I didn't really steal the emeralds, and you certainly can't steal them.*

"You didn't steal them? Then who—looking just like you—snuck into the duke's place and lifted them off the mantel while I had to deal with the guards?"

Listen, you little idiot. You don't understand, but I'm going to explain it to you.

"No, you're not," Fenzig replied as he removed the medallion and thrust it in his pocket. "I gagged you so I wouldn't have to listen to you speak. And I'm not about to listen to you think. Now why don't you get some rest? You and I are going back to the duke's."

The gnome heard an angry "Mmmmph!" as Carmella tried to talk through the gag. It was about that time that the wagon passed the two men tied to a tree.

"I caught the peddler for you!" Fenzig called to them. "I'll send someone by to free you." He knew better than to release the two angry customers who were sure to slow him down—or worse. "I don't have time to help you right now. I've got a homing spell to beat."

RETURN TO THE DUKE

Fenzig drove the horses until well past midnight—until they were exhausted and he could barely keep his eyes open. The gnome's captive was more awake than he was, and she had made some progress on her bonds. He grimaced and tied them again, adding more twine and knots that she didn't have a prayer of undoing. Satisfied, he propped himself up on the wagon seat for a quick nap. He didn't even bother unhitching the horses. They could graze, and they could rest, and that was all that mattered for the moment.

Though there were a multitude of stars, it was too dark to see where the line was on his arm, so he fretted about it and guessed that it might be near his shoulder and well on the way to his neck. He thought about death, wondered if the end would be painful, and hoped fervently that something lay beyond this existence. Otherwise, what was the point to all of this?

I don't want it all to be over, he thought as he slipped off into a troubled slumber. *I don't want to die. There are so many things I want to do, so many places I want to see. There are so many things to discover.*

He awoke shortly before dawn, still tired. After a quick look at his trussed-up captive, he hurried the horses toward K'Nosha. He made relatively good time getting back, though he elected to go around the town rather than through it to get to Duke Rehmir's estate. He suspected there were still some angry townsfolk

126

who wanted a piece of the peddler, and there was nothing he could do to disguise the wagon from them.

Well, maybe the duke will let them have the peddler—after he's done with her, he thought happily. *I'd certainly like some retribution for this wonderful rash that's still giving me fits.*

Shortly after noon Fenzig found himself roughly ushered into the duke's study. His captive was unceremoniously carried there and deposited on the floor before the duke, who was sitting in his comfortable chair. The gnome noticed that the duke looked very tired and pale and probably hadn't slept much.

"I was successful," the gnome said proudly, pointing at Carmella and pulling the emeralds from his pouches.

The duke jumped to his feet, moving more quickly than Fenzig had suspected possible for one of his age and bulk. He grabbed the jewels from the gnome's small hands and held them to his eyes.

"No mars, no flaws. Still perfect, unharmed," Duke Rehmir whispered. He continued to stare at the emeralds for several minutes, letting their facets catch and hold the light streaming in from the window. Then he reluctantly tore his eyes away from them and carefully placed them on the mantel. "Thank you."

"You're welcome," Fenzig replied. "Now about this homing spell, the line creeping up my arm? You said you'd take care of it, make it go away. How about taking care of it now?" The gnome unbuttoned his tunic and craned his neck around to look at his shoulder. The line extended past where he could see. The gnome continued to twist and turn, and soon realized that if he couldn't see the end of the line, it had to be nearing his neck. He frantically felt about with his fingers, trying to find it that way. But his attempt was futile; the line was flush with his skin.

"The line is nearly to your neck," the duke said softly, notic-

ing the gnome's gyrations. Then he turned to his guards and
ordered them to release Carmella.

"Sir?" Fenzig pleaded. "The spell. You said. . . ."

The duke seemed to ignore him.

"But, sir? You promised. You said. . . ."

Duke Rehmir instead turned his attention on the girl thief.
"Why did you do this to me? How could you? I thought there
was a truce between us. I thought we were at peace."

The gnome was curious as to what was transpiring between
the two, who obviously knew each other, but he was more
concerned about his own well-being. If something wasn't done
to negate the spell quickly, his being wouldn't be well for long.
Fenzig took a step toward Duke Rehmir, but one of the guards
interceded. The human pointed a weapon at the gnome and
scowled.

"I didn't really steal them," Carmella said. "I picked up the
gnome along the road a few days ago and read his mind. I
learned that he was going to steal them. In a way, I thought I
was keeping them safe by getting them before he did, and in a
way I thought I'd get your attention. I guess I still felt like hurting you."

"You certainly got my attention, Carmella," the duke said
dejectedly. "But you've always had my attention; you just never
realized it. And you did manage to hurt me, so I suppose you
got what you wanted."

Fenzig listened to the banter with more than idle curiosity
now.

"Father—" Carmella started.

"Father?" the gnome blurted. "You mean she's your daughter?"

The duke nodded but still faced away from the gnome. "My
youngest daughter," he replied tenderly, "and a treasure in her
own right."

"Treasure!" Carmella huffed. "If you truly considered me a treasure, I wouldn't be standing here right now. I'd be sitting on your mantel with those . . . those . . . emeralds!"

"Carmella!"

"It's true, and you know it!"

Duke Rehmir sobbed openly, dropping his pudgy face into his thick-fingered hands. His great shoulders shook. Fenzig watched as Carmella's hard expression softened, just a little. She took a step forward and reached out to touch him, but stopped herself.

"Maybe I should be happy that I didn't hold as high a place in your heart," she said finally. "At least I'm still human."

"I don't understand," Fenzig stated. The gnome wanted to know what was going on, and he wanted the duke to keep his promise. "All this family stuff is puzzling and touching and has absolutely nothing to do with me. But Duke Rehmir and I had a bargain, and now he's got to . . . *arrggh!*"

Fenzig stiffened as a jolt of pain shot from his hand up his arm. His chest felt tight, as if the skin across it were much too small, and he struggled to catch his breath. The room was growing warmer, terribly so. It felt as if he were in an oven that was being stoked. He gasped for breath and felt his lungs burn.

His eyes bulged slightly, and he fell to his knees. *I'm dying,* he thought. *The homing spell is doing its job. It's killing me, and it hurts so very, very badly.* His chest grew tighter still, and a wave of hot darkness washed over him.

He heard voices, faintly, the duke's and Carmella's. They were distant, and they seemed to echo about the gnome, at first buzzing like bees. Concentrating, he picked out a little of what they were saying, hoping to find anything but the pain to fixate on.

"He has a homing spell on him, courtesy of King Erlgrane," the duke said.

"I know. I gained that from his mind within an hour of giving him a ride," Carmella answered. "It moved so quickly on him, I gather, because he was always so nervous, his heart beating so fast and speeding everything along."

"I told him if he retrieved you and the emeralds I would have the spell broken."

"You don't know how to break a homing spell." It was Carmella's voice, growing even more distant. "Only a wizard can do that."

"I know it takes a wizard. But I suspected that if he brought you back, you would be able to break it. Can you lift it?"

"You assume too much," she said icily. "Though I'll grant that you have learned something about what I've been up to, spellcasting and such. A homing spell is simple, but it is a very potent and vicious enchantment."

"Can you save him?"

"I hope so. I'm certainly going to try. He's a fine little fellow, and I enjoy his company. But the spell is already smothering him in its dark magic. I don't know if I can live with myself if he dies because I waited too long."

There were other words, but the gnome was beyond hearing them. His ears were filled with a roaring sound, similar to a massive wave breaking against a beach. Except the wave didn't recede. The noise persisted and grew and was drowning him.

Fenzig experienced a tingling sensation rushing up and down his arms and legs. He felt cold, then hot, then colder than he'd imagined possible. It was as if he were sitting in front of a fire and someone was putting ice all over him and, as soon as it melted, they started pouring the ice all over again. His head throbbed mercilessly, and he imagined that he could hear his own heartbeat. It grew louder and louder, competing with the roar, until it sounded like drums or thunder and overpowered everything.

The sensations seemed to continue forever, and Fenzig wondered if this was death and if all of death would be an eternity of booming heartbeats and heat and chills. Or was death only like this for people who lived dishonestly? Then the thundering of his heart softened, though his head still hurt, hinting that he still lived. The roar became muted, and through it he heard the indistinct words of Duke Rehmir and Carmella. The blackness turned to dark gray, then to a misty fog, then to the blurry image of Carmella hovering over him. He felt warm, unpleasantly so, but the feeling was not so bad as the hot and cold tendrils that had been racing over his limbs.

"He's going to be all right," he heard Carmella say. "See! The line on his arm is fading. I countered the spell just in time. But he will need to rest."

"I knew you could take care of it, dear."

She helped the gnome rise, easing him into the duke's comfortable chair. She ran her smooth hand across his fevered forehead and grinned at him. "Maybe if you'd been honest with me, admitted that was a homing spell when I first met you, I might have fixed it on the spot."

I doubt it, Fenzig thought. *There wouldn't have been any profit in it for you.* Aloud, he said, "You saved my life."

"She saved your life because you saved my other daughters." The duke's voice was stronger now, and the only evidence of his tears was slightly-red eyes. "I—or rather Carmella—kept my part of the bargain. Now, if you. . . ."

"Daughters?" Fenzig was curious. "You said I saved your *other* daughters?"

It was Carmella's turn. "The emeralds are my older sisters. Like you, they are the victims of King Erlgrane's wizard."

I don't understand, the gnome mouthed.

Carmella sighed and stepped back. "The wizard came to our manse one day with a message that King Erlgrane wanted the

131

hand of one of my sisters—any one of them. My father would never let Erlgrane inside these walls, so the message had to suffice. The note claimed the marriage would strengthen the friendship of the people of Burlengren and K'Nosha. I was too young to be included in the request, and I would have declined anyway. Of course, none of my sisters desired to wed him either. My father stood by their decision, and the wizard promptly ensorcelled them—turned them into emeralds right before our eyes. That was five years ago. I don't remember the exact words the wizard used, but it went something like—'the daughters you so treasure shall be treasures for all eternity.' I was spared. I guess I didn't mean as much to my father. But then, I guess there are benefits to not being so treasured."

The duke blustered, "Carmella, we have been over this again and again. I love you dearly. Because you were too young at the time to marry the king, you weren't taken in by the wizard's spell."

"You're a duke, a powerful man," Fenzig interrupted. "Couldn't you have paid off the wizard or. . . ."

"We couldn't force the wizard to undo his magic—he cast another spell and vanished in a puff of smoke. No wizard I've contacted since has been able to break the spell."

"Then let the people of K'Nosha and Burlengren know what the king's wizard did."

The duke chuckled. "Because King Erlgrane was safe in his castle, I couldn't successfully blame his wizard's evil deed on him. So few people have actually seen his wizard, anyway."

Duke Rehmir looked at Carmella. "It broke my heart to see your sisters like this every day. The only thing that saved me from complete despair was knowing you were spared."

"I was spared because I was never as cherished as they were," she continued. "You can't argue the point with me. I wore mother's necklace after the incident, knew what you were thinking. I was always a devious child, stealing things, playing pranks, never obeying you. I was never ladylike. I was not like my sisters."

The duke pursed his lips. "But I love you."

"In your way, and I suppose I should accept that as being enough." Carmella explained that her mother had died shortly after her sisters were transformed into gems. "Stress, I suppose, or perhaps she died of a heart filled with sadness. After she was gone, there was nothing to keep me here. Father grieved so much for my mother and my sisters that I just couldn't stay. I couldn't handle the pitiful atmosphere. So I took a few pieces of my mother's jewelry, a couple of her cherished vases and trinkets, and ran away from home. I sold most of it to live— except for her favorite necklace." She dangled her hand in front of the gnome, and Fenzig grudgingly gave her the medallion and watched her slip it over her neck.

"I stole everything else I needed, and I associated with all manner of people for a while—including a fledgling wizard who taught me a few enchantments. An actor I stayed with for a time taught me how to lower my voice, so I can sound like a man when I'm playing Carmen. Another taught me to sew. Evidently Father kept tabs on me, otherwise he wouldn't have known I could lift your homing spell."

"I tried my best to find out where you were and what you were up to," the duke said, "though I had no idea you were masquerading as a peddler. Why?"

Carmella shrugged. "I'm a thief. I admit it. And I'm very, very good at it. What better cover for a thief than to lead two lives—one that's so flashy and dashing that all eyes are trained on it, and another that clings to the shadows, unseen and undetected?"

"You could give up that life, come back here and stay with me," the duke implored. "I'll need help managing the estate. If

King Erlgrane is after the emeralds—your sisters—he is up to no good again. He will not rest until he has this land. He's tried so many tactics these past few years. The emeralds . . . if he possessed them, I'd have to give in."

Carmella paced back and forth. Fenzig watched the pair. Caught up in their politics and family tragedy, they were oblivious to him. "If you give him this estate, the people of K'Nosha and the Northern Reaches would suffer," she mused.

Perhaps I should sneak out now, the gnome thought. *I'm starting to feel stronger. I'll bet the guards won't give me a second thought. They're staring at the duke. Maybe I could even pick up a candlestick or two on the way out, a couple of pieces of crystal, trade them for a pony.*

"You know he always wanted this land. It's important strategically," Carmella said. "That's why he wanted to marry one of my sisters, why you were wise in not letting him inside these walls. He could have you quietly eliminated, and he would inherit the land through his wife. The land's position is perfect. From here he could expand, using his armies if necessary—and the armies he'd acquire from the marriage. And your palace is very defensible—more so than his own castle. He's been threatening war with his neighbors lately, and if he had this land, and his, he'd have a better position to strike at them. He would win."

"But my forces have grown stronger in the past few years, and he cannot take the land from me in a straight fight," the duke argued.

Carmella grinned slyly. "He wants the land so badly I suspect you are right—he planned to use the emeralds for leverage. And by having a thief steal them, it wouldn't look as if he were involved. The people would never know the foul act he'd committed."

"Of course!" the duke exclaimed. "Once he had your sisters—

the gems—he could force me to trade the land for them without the people being the wiser."

"Or," Carmella added, "he could have his wizard reverse the magic and make them whole again. He could forcibly marry one of them—what he wanted all along—and you would conveniently have a fatal accident. Then he would inherit the lands legitimately. Everything would look aboveboard. No one would realize there were dirty tricks involved."

"Either way he would win," the duke said dryly, "but I don't want him to win. I want your sisters to be flesh and blood again, and I have exhausted all possibilities within my grasp to do so."

"Except one," Carmella said, pointing at the retreating form of the gnome.

"Guards!" the duke barked.

One minute Fenzig's feet were clumsily hammering down the hallway, the next they were pounding across air. He felt himself being hoisted up by burly hands insinuating themselves beneath his armpits.

It's not fair, his mind wailed. *I want nothing to do with this family or with King Erlgrane. I want to go home to see my father, home where it's safe.* He struggled against them, still hopelessly weak from the malicious homing spell, and thought about calling on the last use from his invisibility ring. However, he suspected that would do no good. Carmella would use the necklace to find him through his thoughts. They'd just bundle him up in a tapestry again and thump him on the head.

The gnome was carried back into the den, dropped in front of the duke, and the door slammed shut behind him. Two guards remained in the room for good measure. They eyed Fenzig warily, and one fingered the pommel of his sword.

"All right," the gnome huffed. "What do you want? What am I supposed to do for you now? That's what this is about, right? Another task? The gods know rulers can't do things for themselves. Pull my strings, Duke Rehmir. I'm yours to command. Isn't that what you think? Well, I'm no one's to command anymore."

The duke furrowed his brow and regarded the gnome coolly. "Yes, I want you to do something for me. You're a thief. I've need of your thieving skills."

"What about my skills?" Carmella quipped.

"I don't want to risk you," the duke snapped. "It's too dangerous."

No, Fenzig mused, *might as well risk a stranger.*

Then the duke squatted down to be closer to the gnome.

Fenzig thought he looked like a bullfrog, all hunkered down with his belly sticking out to his knees. *And I'm the fly he's eyeing,* he thought.

"I want you to go back to King Erlgrane's," the duke began.

"No. Absolutely not!" Fenzig's tone was sharp, not caring that he addressed someone important. He crossed his arms in front of him in defiance. "Our deal's finished. You have your emeralds. You have Carmella. I met your terms; you had my spell negated; we're finished. Finished. Finished!"

"I want you to get to King Erlgrane's wizard," the duke continued.

"You're a maniac!" Fenzig yelled. "You know what he did to me the first time I met him! You know what he did to your daughters!"

"The wizard is capable of making my daughters whole again. You will help see that he does. He is their only hope."

"The wizard is capable of a great many things—things I want no part of. I think you'd better find someone else for the job," the gnome sputtered. "Find someone who'll volunteer for your fool's mission. I'm not volunteering. In fact, I'm refusing. No. Positively not. Under no circumstances will I go back to King Erlgrane's. Understand? There is no way you can force me."

"I can't go myself," the duke said. "I'm too recognizable, and I'm not a young man anymore. I don't have the stealthy skills you possess, and I'm afraid any attempts I might make would be met with quick failure."

"So I'll give you a few pointers. I'll teach you to be stealthy."

"You're small, and you can slip into places no one else could."

"Stop eating so much, and you'll fit into smaller places, too."

"Plus," the duke added, "the wizard and King Erlgrane will be expecting you. They would welcome you with open arms if they caught you on the grounds, thinking you had the emeralds with you."

"I don't want anything to do with their arms or anything else about them. I said no. Remember? In case you forgot I'll say it again. No. I am not going."

Carmella swept past her father and affectionately ruffled Fenzig's curls. "I don't blame you," she said. The gnome beamed, having found a kindred spirit who supported his decision. "I wouldn't want to go back there, either, but I think my father has a good idea."

"Bad idea."

Carmella took a step back and closed her eyes. She started swaying back and forth on the balls of her feet and weaving unseen patterns in the air with her slender fingers. She started humming, and Fenzig saw a glow form all around her hands. It was blue. And it looked very familiar.

"Worse idea," the gnome said.

The glow extended outward from her hands and engulfed Fenzig. It made him tingle all over, as if hundreds of mosquitoes were paying him a lunch visit. The air shimmered in front of his face, and it seemed as if he were looking out through a gauzy curtain of sky blue. The color intensified, as did the biting sensation over his exposed skin. The sensation was made worse, as he still ached from being trampled by the townspeople trying to get at Carmen the Magnificent. Then the color became a brilliant blue, then a dark blue the color of the sky after sunset, then it retreated down his arms and up his legs. The color centered itself around his hand.

"No!" he screamed. "Not again! You can't do this to me. Gods! What did I ever do to you to deserve this?"

"Think of it as insurance," Carmella said as she stopped swaying.

The gauzy curtain disappeared, and Fenzig was staring at another heart on the back of his hand, this one a little larger and not so perfectly shaped as the one cast on him before. "You're no better than King Erlgrane and his malicious wizard," the gnome snarled at the pair.

"On the contrary," the duke said as he rose from his bullfrog position. "The king does what he does for personal gain. I'm doing this for my daughters."

"This wouldn't have been necessary if you would have just agreed to help us," Carmella said. "But for once in my life I agree with my father. It's time to make my sisters flesh and blood again. My argument is with my father, not with them. They deserve better than to sit on a mantle. And whether you want to or not, you're going to help me save them."

The duke opened his mouth and started to speak, but Carmella cut him off. "I'm not going to let Fenzig risk his life alone. I'm going to Erlgrane's castle with him. We'll bring back Erlgrane's wizard—somehow. And once we have him here, we'll make him reverse the spell."

Fenzig was still staring at the heart on the back of his hand. "Let's take the emeralds to Erlgrane's instead," he heard himself saying. He swallowed hard, accepting his grim situation. "Let's get the wizard to reverse the spell there. It would be easier than bringing the wizard here, thank you. Besides, they expect me to bring them the emeralds."

Carmella and the duke shook their heads practically in unison. "That won't work," Carmella said. "If something goes wrong and we're captured, the king will have the gems and the leverage he wants—or he'll force one of my sisters to marry him."

"Or he'll force you," the duke said dryly. "You're older now, Carmella. You would fit into his evil plans just as well as one of your sisters. I really wish you wouldn't go."

She smirked. "Father, I've never been one to do as you asked, so don't expect me to start now. Just wish us luck. We'll get a good night's sleep, grab a hot bath and some clean clothes, and be on our way. If everything works out well. . . ."

Fenzig's growling stomach interrupted her.

"Maybe you should have the cooks fix us plenty of food to take along. Hungry, Fenzighan?" she asked.

The gnome nodded and numbly followed her out of the study, his eyes fixed on the heart that throbbed on the back of his hand.

Together Again

The pale yellow shirt was made of expensive silk and felt good against his skin, but it was much too big. Someone had taken tucks here and there, shortened the sleeves, and turned up the hem so Fenzig could wear it without tripping over it. But it still didn't fit the way a gnome shirt should. The black pants worked better, though the gnome was not pleased to learn they were a pair of Carmella's leggings that she'd hacked off well above the knees. They came down to the gnome's ankles and were a reasonably good fit, but he didn't like wearing something intended for a woman. He looked at Carmella and scowled.

"Oh, it's not so bad," she offered. "And if it's any consolation, they were my favorite pair. I ruined them just for you."

Fenzig continued scowling as he bunched up the shirttail and tucked it into the pants. He suspected he looked rather silly, like a frilly bumblebee with curly brown hair. Still, Carmella was attired in her Carmen outfit, a dazzling display of purple, chartreuse, scarlet, saffron, navy, and orange, so he figured he complemented her nicely. Stripes went in all directions around her lithe frame and caused the duke and the gnome to wince. Her hair was long and auburn this time, her blond wig having been lost somewhere along the road between the village and K'Nosha.

"What do you think?" she asked, grinning widely and spinning around in front of her father and the gnome. "I made this outfit myself, and I was saving it for a special occasion."

"I'll try not to think about it," Fenzig mumbled as he stared at the cooks, two of them gnomes, who were filling packs with hunks of cheese, loaves of bread, and an assortment of fruits and dried meats. He grinned as he saw them add a few dozen cookies.

"Let's go!" she urged.

"The long way around," Fenzig interjected. "We're not going through K'Nosha, not with all the rashes you caused." The gnome was pleased to note, however, that his rash was starting to fade.

They took the Carmen the Magnificent wagon, which had two fresh horses hitched to the front and a pony tied to a rope behind it. The gnome indicated their route around K'Nosha, and Carmella didn't argue. She seemed to sense exactly which way he wanted to go and followed it unerringly.

Of course she knows where I want to go, Fenzig thought as he looked around the corner of the wagon and watched the duke's estate fade from view. The palace was just a white speck on the horizon. Then it disappeared with the passing of a few hundred more yards. *She knows where I want to go because she's wearing that magical medallion. I can't even think to myself while she's got that on. I've no privacy. You're listening to me right now, aren't you Carmella?*

Carmella smiled weakly at him and took off the necklace, carefully placing it in a lavender pocket and patting it. "There," she said. "You can think all you want to without my listening in. And right about now you should start thinking about going home."

"Right," Fenzig said glumly, looking at the large blue heart on the back of his hand. "After we try to capture a wizard who could turn both of us into newts just by blinking his eyes. Then I can think about going home."

"Wrong," she said as she held the reins in one hand and

tickled the top of his head with the other. Then suddenly she turned serious, stopped the wagon, and jumped off the seat. She ran behind the wagon and returned a moment later, leading the pony. "You can go home now. Really. This isn't your struggle. This is my family's mess, and I'll get my family out of it. There's no need for you to risk your life for three women you've never met. I just needed to get far enough from my father's estate before I let you go."

"You're forgetting the homing spell," Fenzig said glumly. "That wonderful enchantment you cast on me. You didn't give me a choice in the matter, remember? I'm involved up to my hairy little armpits. Bring back the wizard or I'm dead."

"It's a tattoo," she retorted quickly. "I don't know how to enchant a homing spell. I'm not much of a wizard; I'm a much better thief. But I can make some pretty awesome tattoos just by thinking about it and mumbling the right words."

Fenzig's eyes grew wide, and he stared more closely at his hand. There was no blue line extending from the tip of the heart, and, if the previous homing spell cast on him was any indication, there should have been at least the start of a line by now. "A tattoo?"

She nodded and helped him from the wagon. "And you're stuck with it. The pony's name is Summer. I raised him myself and named him after my favorite season. Don't lose him or let any craven cats get him, okay?" She spun around and retreated to the back of the wagon again.

The gnome listened to thumping and rustling noises as she searched for something. *Maybe she'll give me some of those cookies,* he thought happily. *I would really like something sweet about now.*

But she didn't bring him food. Instead, she handed him the magical short sword her father had taken from him. "You earned this," she said. "Now, I've got to get going—and so do you."

"I don't understand," Fenzig said as he climbed aboard the dark-brown pony. "If this is only a tattoo, and you can't create a homing spell, then how did you get rid of the one I had—the one that almost killed me?"

"It is often easier to negate a spell or break an enchantment than it is to create one in the first place," she explained. "Think of a spell as being like a sand castle. It takes time and patience, a little bit of artistic ability, and a lot of sand to craft a nice one. But it only takes a few swift kicks or a bucket of water to ruin it. The same holds true with most spells. So I could erase your homing spell, even though I couldn't create one of my own. Of course, it takes a wizard to negate spells—not everyone can chase away magic. I've just never been enough of a wizard to negate the magic that makes my sisters emeralds."

"So I'm really free?" Fenzig asked with a hint of disbelief. "I can do whatever I want? I can go wherever I want?"

"Of course," she said as she climbed back on the wagon bench and grabbed the reins. "I'm kind of hoping you'll go visit your father. He was in your thoughts a lot."

"Yeah, I think that would be a good idea," the gnome said. "I haven't seen him for seven years." He looked toward the horizon, in the direction that would lead to the gnome's town.

"No. It would be a *great* idea," Carmella said as she made clicking sounds to get the horses moving.

Fenzig rode along beside the wagon. "Then why the tattoo? Why give me a mark to make me think I had another homing spell on me?"

"Silly," she snickered, "that was for my father's benefit, not yours. He wanted you to capture the wizard, and I let him think you were going to do just that. There's no way he would have let me go off to try this on my own."

"Do you really think you can capture him?"

Carmella pursed her lips. "I'm going to try, for my sisters' sake. I should have tried five years ago, but I didn't know anything about magic then, and I was pretty young. Besides, I was so filled with hostility toward my father that I wasn't thinking straight. At least I'm thinking a little straighter now." With that, she urged the horses faster and waved a farewell to the gnome.

I'm free, Fenzig thought as he watched the wagon clatter down the road. *I'm no one's puppet now. I can make my own decisions, and my first decision is not to get involved with any more wizards.* He nudged the pony toward his old home, opting to cut across the relatively open ground rather than take the road. His stomach grumbled, but he merely grimaced and thumped it once with the heel of his hand.

I can fill you up in a few nights when we get to my father's, he thought. *You're not going to starve, and I'm not going to raid any more windowsills to fill you up.* He strapped the magical short sword to his waist as he went. *I can sell this for lots of money and try my hand at an honest trade, maybe woodcarving with my father. Maybe peddling some real merchandise. I'll bet either profession would be more challenging than thieving, and I'll wager they'd be a lot less dangerous.*

He didn't catch up with Carmella until late that night.

"I thought you might need some help," he said as he joined her for venison stew, "and I thought you might need my expertise. After all, I've snuck into King Erlgrane's castle before."

"And got caught," she added, passing him a plate of cookies.

"So I'll know what not to touch this time, thank you."

"Or what *to* touch," she said. "But it could be dangerous."

"It *will* be dangerous," he said, adding to himself that at least it wouldn't be boring. After all, he was doing this of his own free will. *Risking your neck isn't so bad if you're doing it because you want to,* he thought. *And I guess I'm not quite ready for a steady, safe, stable job . . . yet.*

"I'm glad you came back," she said, passing him a second plate of cookies. "I could use the company and the help. Listen, I have a plan."

Morning found the gnome full, rested, and seated next to Carmen the Magnificent, who was wearing an even more outrageous outfit than she had the day before.

I hope I don't regret this, he thought, blinking to avoid the bright light sparkling off the maroon sequins on Carmella's vest. *This will be dangerous, and we could end up dead if we're not careful. But I couldn't let her try this stunt alone. I just couldn't. Wouldn't be honorable. Besides,* he added, looking out over the sun-tinged landscape, *I have to see how this all turns out. I hate not learning how a story ends.*

They entered the gnome town early that evening. Fenzig had talked her into stopping there. It was within walking distance to King Erlgrane's, and the gnome really didn't like the idea of going into Burlengren in the garish peddler's wagon. "We don't want to attract attention this time," he told her. "Erlgrane and his wizard are smart. They might be able to see through our disguises." In addition, Fenzig desperately wanted to get into some clothes especially made for gnomes.

Carmella squealed with delight when she saw Fenzig's birthplace. The town, called Graespeck on a small wooden sign, consisted of dozens upon dozens of mounds of earth—all with polished walnut doors set into them and woven grass welcome mats out front. Every window had a curtain, a few of them made of colorful fabric, and a handful of the homes had boxes of flowers growing on the window ledges. Some of the homes had grass on top, instead of straw or shingles. The grass was carefully and lovingly trimmed like a well-manicured lawn. Others had wildflowers or carefully tended rose gardens nearby. There were vegetable gardens behind about half of the mound-homes; others had animal pens or things relating to their occupants' businesses. One had a smelter and a lean-to behind it. Another had an anvil and forge, along with the trappings for making horseshoes.

"This is just delightful," Carmella gushed. "Everything is just so adorable and so small. So awfully cute."

Cute. Ugh. Fenzig rolled his eyes. *I've never considered Graespeck adorable, he thought. I've considered it practical, cozy, friendly, and boring. It's functional—not cute.*

A throng of gnomes came out to meet the wagon, attracted by its bright paint and the promise of what might lie inside. They were a sea of small folk, all barefoot and all wearing curious and cheerful expressions.

"They're so charming," Carmella said, "and small. I can't imagine why anyone wouldn't like gnomes. Look at their little noses."

Yeah. They have noses that look a lot like mine. Fenzig rolled his eyes again and waved to his father, who was at the edge of the growing crowd. The older gnome beamed and elbowed his way up front. Fenzig climbed down and was a little embarrassed that his father hugged him as if he were a child.

"What do you have for sale?" a young gnome woman asked.

"Yes, what kind of tonics and elixirs? Anything to eat?"

"Yes! What do you have to eat?"

Carmen the Magnificent stood and doffed her green and grape cap. "I have wondrous pills to cure your ills," she began in her deeper voice. "I have syrups and creams and lotions and potions, ready and waiting for your consumption. My prices are the best in the land."

"No!" Fenzig yelled. "You don't have anything for sale!"

Carmen blanched; then thin lips tugged upward in an

awkward grin. "Sorry. It's an old habit. Fenzig's right, folks. I forgot that I sold out of just about everything while we were in K'Nosha."

"Everything?" The young female gnome was persistent and looked terribly disappointed.

"Well, I do have a couple of bottles of lilac cologne left."

The young gnome practically glowed with anticipation. Fenzig grimaced, but Carmen the Magnificent quietly assured him the bottles really did contain cologne.

The sale concluded—at a discount at Fenzig's insistence—Fenzig, his father, and Carmella retired to the woodworking shop. Carmella had to crawl into the place on her hands and knees, and once inside she had to sit cross-legged on the floor. All the furnishings were gnome-sized, and the ceiling, at its highest point, was not quite four feet tall.

Carmella proceeded to take off her hat and wig, share the rest of the cookies, and tell Fenzig's father about their planned excursion to Erlgrane's castle.

Fenzig explained about the horrible curse Carmella's sisters had endured for the past three years and how terrible the duke felt over the entire situation. The gnome carefully omitted the part about his failed attempt to steal from the king and the subsequent homing spell that was cast on him for punishment.

"So we need to stay here until late tomorrow afternoon," he said at last. "We want to reach Erlgrane's castle after dark. It's safer that way."

The gnome's father was both worried and impressed, but agreed they could stay.

"And to repay your hospitality," Carmella volunteered, grinning, "I shall entertain all of Graespeck tonight. I'm quite a showman, you know."

Indeed the show was splendid. The entire population turned out as Carmen the Magnificent created bouquets of flowers out of thin air, caused scarves to fly high above everyone's heads, and made it snow—briefly. Carmella strutted about and basked in the gnomes' admiration.

"Think of a color," Carmella said, leaning close to a gnome child. "Any color. Concentrate. That's it. I've got it—your favorite color is purple!" She produced a bright purple marble from behind the child's ear and handed it to her.

The child giggled with delight, and the crowd clapped wildly.

"And your favorite color is blue!" Carmella exclaimed to the child's mother.

"That's right!" the mother squealed. "How did you know that?"

"Ah, my dear, it's magic," Carmella said, returning to the makeshift stage and cavorting some more.

Yes, it's magic, Fenzig thought, happily surrounded by his old friends. *It's a magical necklace, one that won't let anyone keep secrets.*

Carmella let her bright red cape flutter to the ground and drew an elegant hand to her forehead. "Someone in the audience is admiring Fenzig's new tattoo. They want a tattoo also. Am I right?"

"You're right!" shouted the young man to Fenzig's left. "Wow, how did you know that?"

"Then step right up, and I'll give you a magical one! Carmen the Magnificent aims to please. And nothing pleases me more than performing for you!"

Fenzig watched as his friend was engulfed in a blue light. He imagined that the young fellow was feeling nonexistent insects racing all over his skin. In the end, the young gnome opened his shirt and displayed a blue tattoo in the shape of a lion in the middle of his chest. "It's terrific! Marvelous!" he cried.

"And best of all, it will never come off!" Carmen announced.

"Never?" the gnome asked.

"Never!"

"That's wonderful!" the gnome replied, admiring the lion and showing it off to all his friends.

Fenzig glanced at the heart on the back of his hand. *Never?* he thought.

"I want one, too. A dragon!"

"Me too," someone else squealed.

"Oh, please don't forget me!" a young woman cried. "I'd like a bouquet of flowers on my arm. Flowers that will never come off."

Never come off. Fenzig kept staring at his hand. *Wonderful.*

INTO THE LION'S DEN

Their faces blackened with a greasy soot mixture Carmella provided, the pair of adventurers stuck to the growing shadows and cautiously approached King Erlgrane's castle. They had left their more colorful clothes behind in favor of tight-fitting black outfits that didn't rustle when they walked. And they'd made sure they had plenty of sleep. They needed to be alert and at their best.

Erlgrane's castle, though not as large as the duke's manor, was nonetheless impressive. A thick stone wall ringed it, with four evenly spaced attached towers that served as guard posts. There was no place along the walls the guards could not see— except for a place close to one of the towers, where the shadows were thick and where the light from the windows was dim. Fenzig and Carmella scaled the wall there, the gnome climbing up it as if he were a monkey, and Carmella using a thin silk rope with a small grappling hook on one end. The only sound they made was the soft *clink* of the hook as it cleared the top of the wall and found purchase.

The pair crouched on the top of the wall and watched the tower window. When they were satisfied the guards inside, and the sentries patrolling the grounds, were oblivious to their presence, they landed softly on the thick grass on the other side. From this vantage point, King Erlgrane's fortification was revealed in all its glory. The moon poked out from behind a cloud just enough to illuminate the pale gray stones. The main

150

building was in the center of the yard, standing four stories high with a crenellated, dark-red roof. Connected to it was a tower six or seven stories tall. Another tower of about the same height was set farther back and was of more recent construction; the gray stones were of a different color and the mortar that held them together was stark white. Carmella whispered she suspected that the farther tower housed the troops and the king's servants and was used as another lookout.

Fenzig said he didn't care what it was used for. He wanted to get in and out as quickly as possible. The gnome directed Carmella's attention back to the northern tower that was attached to the building, indicating that was the one he had entered, and they scampered toward it. Soft light spilled out the casement window slits—the galleries along the base of the castle where archers stood, ready to fire on trespassers. So quiet and careful were Carmella and Fenzig that not one bowman was alerted.

At the base of the tower Carmella looked up and shivered. She glanced at her silk rope and judged its length, then she looked at the gnome and shook her head. There was no purchase for the grapple except the window, which was all the way at the top, and her rope wouldn't reach quite that far. She ran her fingers over the stones, which she whispered were too smooth to make good handholds.

Fenzig motioned for her to stay put, and he slung her rope over his shoulder. He winked at her and started up like a monkey, his fingers and toes fitting perfectly in the grooves between each stone. The gnome loved to climb, and he made this scaling attempt look effortless. He wanted to show Carmella that he was the better thief, and he suspected he was duly impressing her. He chose the same high window as before, and he peered in before climbing onto the ledge and disappearing inside.

After a few moments the rope snaked out. The end dangled about five feet above Carmella's head. She stretched up with her fingers but couldn't close the distance, nor could she gain enough purchase along the bottom stones to climb even a little.

Then, as the gnome watched, she backed away from the tower—five feet, ten, fifteen, twenty. Fenzig feared someone would see her, as she was not crouching. Then she took off running at the wall, and just below the base of the tower she sprang up like a graceful cat. Her fingers closed about the end of the rope, and the momentum carried her against the stones.

The air rushed out of her lungs from the impact, but it didn't slow her. She took a deep breath and started up as if she were ascending the side of a low mountain. Hand over hand she climbed higher, bracing herself against the stone with her feet. The gnome wondered if this was how she'd scaled the wall at her father's manor, or if she'd climbed the ivy and was immune to its sleepy effects.

It was not an easy squeeze through the window for Carmella. Only because she was thin and small did she make it, and her garments were torn here and there from the effort. Inside, she briefly hugged Fenzig, ignoring his concerned glances at the deep scratches he saw through the tears in her clothes. Then she glanced down the stone steps that descended steeply from the landing. The lantern that flickered partway down the steps cast dancing shadows down the stairwell and illuminated the impressive wooden door.

Is this it? she mouthed. *The one you broke into?*

Fenzig nodded yes as he moved to the door. For a moment it seemed as if the gnome was living the night of the failed robbery all over again. The locks were difficult to open, one a particular challenge he remembered all too well. But eventually they yielded, and the pair slid inside. Carmella clung to the shadows along the wall by the room's entrance, and Fenzig quickly went to the largest pile of gold coins. Kneeling, he stuffed only the coins from the top of the mound into his small bag. He had no desire for the copper or iron coins beneath. They spent well enough, but they wouldn't buy as much, and they took up just as much space. He spied a pair of silver belt buckles and stuffed them in the bag for good measure. He might as well make away with something during this trip.

Just as he was standing to head for another pile of coins, he was interrupted by Erlgrane's wizard.

"You should be dead," the old man said as he stifled a yawn. "I should be in bed, and you should be food for the worms. I judged that the homing spell would have finished you nearly an entire day ago. But it didn't, and here you are again. I don't care what you did to break my spell, but I intend to break you, *thief.*" He spit out the last word as if it were a spoiled piece of fruit. "You were a fool to return here."

The wizard was flanked by two guards, who moved into the room, their boots chinking over the coins spilled across the floor. "My magic is complex and powerful," the old mage muttered as he raised his hands and started gesturing, tracing wild patterns in the air with his spider-leg fingers, "and I don't like it when someone stops my enchantments. Furthermore, I don't like you. The king didn't ask much of you, scoundrel. The theft of three gems wasn't such a high price to pay for your miserable life, was it? You should have done as he wished. You certainly had the talent for the task. Talent, though not the wits."

Crackling energy formed in the air where the wizard had waved his hands. Vibrant green and sparkling blue, the lines whirled like snakes as they moved toward the gnome. Fenzig gulped and pivoted, placing the magical light serpents between himself and the guards.

Then he drew his sword, which glowed a faint blue. "You'll not take me without a fight, wizard," Fenzig spat. "I don't like you, either, and when I'm done with these guards, I'll cut you to pieces." He puffed out his chest for good measure and watched the two guards wave their blades. Their swords were longer, and they thought they had the edge on the gnome with the short sword.

They boldly advanced on him, impish grins on their puglike faces, and at the same time Carmella stepped out of the shadows behind the chamber door. She raised a brass urn high above her head and brought it down with a resounding *bong* on the wizard's head. The wizard crumpled to the floor just as Fenzig brought his weapon up to parry the first swing of his attacker.

The blades connected, a flash filled the room, and one guard cursed as his sword turned to rust and then disintegrated. The second guard was already in midswing, though he was looking over his shoulder to see what had happened to the wizard. His aim was off as a result, and the gnome pivoted and thrust out with the short sword. The magical weapon missed the guard's sword, but it struck his armor. Another flash of light was emitted, and suddenly the guard was standing there in padded clothes staring at his unconscious taskmaster.

Fenzig pressed his attack before the dumbstruck guard could react. He brought the short sword up to touch the longer blade, and the flash that rusted the weapon blinded the other guard, who had just stepped to the side, hoping to gain a better position from which to attack the gnome. When the light faded, the weaponless and armorless guard started backing toward the door—providing an easy target for Carmella and her urn.

But one guard refused to take his eyes off the gnome. Muttering a string of curses, he crouched and grabbed an iron candelabra. He swung the makeshift weapon wide—above the reach of the gnome's sword—and brought it down in a vicious arc. The move caught a surprised Fenzig in his shoulder, and he winced as the metal bit deep into his flesh. The gnome cried out and dropped to his knees as he dropped the magical sword. The guard stepped in closer and lifted the candelabra above his head, intending to bring it down on the gnome in a killing blow, but Carmella rushed forward, barreling into him. The guard fell across the gnome, and Fenzig managed to crawl out from beneath him and retrieve the magical sword.

Carmella stood on the guard's back, and Fenzig touched the tip of his short sword to the guard's makeshift weapon. The gnome didn't want any errant heavy objects lying around that might be used against him.

We've got to tie them up quickly, Fenzig thought. Carmella was wearing her magic medallion, so the thief didn't bother with words that might carry down the stairwell. Bad enough that the brief swordplay had made noise.

Carmella nodded and stepped out onto the landing to retrieve her rope. The pair quickly used it to tie the guards together. "Now how am I going to get out of here?" she whispered. "I needed that rope to climb back out the window."

We couldn't go out that way even if we wanted to, the gnome mentally scolded her. *There's no way the wizard would fit through that small opening. And we've got to take him with us.*

"I'd make him fit." She snatched up a couple of beautiful scarves she'd found amid the treasure and used them to gag and tie the wizard. She checked him over very carefully, as for an instant she feared she'd killed him with her blow. If he were dead, her sisters would forever be emeralds on her father's mantel. Carmella breathed a sigh of relief. The wizard still lived—he was breathing shallowly, but regularly. He would wake up soon, and he'd likely have a headache to go with the growing bump on his head.

This was indeed an excellent plan, Fenzig thought as he surveyed their trussed-up captives. *We didn't have to search for the wizard; setting off his magical alarm brought him right to us.*

Now, let's get out of here. We'll go down the stairs and out one of the doors along the casements, with the wizard in tow. We can easily carry him between the two of us. A proverbial piece of cake.

"Fenzig!" she whispered harshly. "Change in plans! Give me your ring! Now!"

Why? What could you possibly want with an invisibility ring? It has only one use left, and it's mine. You have a magic medallion.

"Give it to me, please," she implored. "There's no time to explain. Things have just gone very wrong."

No, he thought. *You can't have all the magical jewelry you see.*

"Then forgive me," she said. Carmella launched herself at him just as the sound of many footsteps reached the gnome's ears. "More guards are coming, and we don't have a chance against them."

So you're going to escape and leave me here! Fenzig's mind screamed. *What about the wizard and your sisters? Are you giving up on your sisters?* Her strong arms pinned him to the floor, and she pulled the ring off his finger and placed it on one of her own.

"No, I'm not going to leave you here," she whispered, "but the wizard and the guards saw you. They didn't see me, and I intend to keep it that way." That said, she disappeared just as the clamor of footsteps coming up the stairs reached the gnome's ears.

"Some partner you turned out to be," the gnome sputtered. "I told your father I work alone, and I should have kept it that way." *She must have known the guards were coming,* the gnome angrily mused, *because of her medallion. She read their thoughts. But she could have warned me. She could have. . . .*

A dozen men in chain mail burst into the room. These guards were armed with broadswords and looked much more formidable than the ones lying at Fenzig's feet. But he wasn't going down without a fight. He had no desire to return to King

Erlgrane's dungeon and whatever fate might await him there. Fenzig cursed, flourished his magical blade, and advanced. *Bad odds,* he thought, impossible odds. *But I've got magic on my side, and I'm mad. I think I'm much better with this thing when I'm mad.* He swung the sword up to strike the oncoming blade of the lead fighter. There was a flash, and the man's weapon rusted.

Fenzig barreled into another, the tip of his sword sliding across the armor of three men in the process. A trio of flashes filled the air, and before any of the men could react, the gnome swung his weapon up to strike at their blades, rendering them rusted and useless. In the space of a few heartbeats, the little thief had reduced the effectiveness of his foes by a third.

Two others went down, tripping over a long brass candleholder that someone had thrust at their feet. *Well, at least Carmella is doing something,* Fenzig fumed, *but I could have been much more effective with that ring. You'd better hope I get out of this, or my ghost is going to haunt you forever.*

Nimbly dodging a wide swing by one of the burliest fighters, the gnome narrowly avoided being decapitated and brought his short sword up. The blade cut through the guard's chain mail, instantly rusting it, but then kept on going, digging into the man's abdomen. Fenzig stepped back and tugged the sword free. A pained look grew on the man's face, and Fenzig frowned. The gnome watched the man clutch at his wound and pitch over. His angry fellows rushed the gnome, and it was all Fenzig could do to parry their attacks.

"Look out for his sword!" one of the more astute fighters bellowed. "It's magic!"

Despite the warning, the room was filled with flashes of light as the guards' blades struck the gnome's and instantly rusted and fell apart. Fenzig dashed between the legs of two men who had given up on weapons and were simply trying to grab the little thief.

I think I killed someone, Fenzig thought as he swung his blade around to strike the side of one of his assailants. A flash resulted, and another fighter was left in padded clothes. Two more men went down behind him, struck from behind by a chest tossed by an invisible Carmella. *I've never killed anyone before,* the gnome thought with dismay. *And I don't want to have to do it again. Ever.*

Fenzig's heart pounded from fear and exertion. His face was red, and he took in great gulps of air as he danced over the tops of coins and eluded the swords and fists of the fighters. Seven men, all who were left standing of the dozen who'd attacked, were after him. After a few more thrusts with his short sword, Fenzig had rendered them all weaponless, but they were still dangerous. They circled the gnome warily, keeping their distance and looking for an opening. Carmella managed to pick off two of them before the rest rushed the gnome and tackled him. Fenzig thrust upward with the magical short sword, and it neatly slid between the ribs of one of the men. The gnome tried to pull it free, but his hand was slippery with blood, and the press of men did not give him enough room to maneuver.

Gods, I killed another one! he cursed himself.

Their weight on him was unbearable and forced the air from his lungs. He gasped for breath and inhaled hot air tinged with sweat and blood. He heard groans as some of his attackers struggled to rise, and he also heard more footsteps pounding up the stairs.

I've lost, he thought sadly. *The king will surely kill me this time. Carmella, get out of here now!*

Some of the fighters rose off him. Their weight was easing, and he could breathe more easily. But just as he began to entertain the slightest notion that he might escape, a meaty fist swung forward and connected soundly with his small chin. The room spun, the smell of the sweaty fighters intensified until it became overpowering, and Fenzig lost his grasp on consciousness.

He awoke in King Erlgrane's audience chamber, the one where he had enjoyed the delicious meal. His face hurt from being pummeled, he had the coppery taste of blood in his mouth, and he noticed that a few of the guards who held him captive must be hurting, too. Some had bandages on their arms, and more than one was sporting a bruised or broken nose. At least he wasn't the only one in pain.

Even the king's wizard was suffering. Fenzig noted that the old man gingerly held the back of his head where Carmella had struck him. Through narrowed eyes, the wizard glared at the gnome. He raised a bony finger and waggled it at the thief.

"The little scoundrel did not bring your emeralds, sire, and he managed to break my homing spell. To add to the insult, he tried again to rob you."

The king raised his lips in a snarl, looking all too much like a rabid dog the gnome had seen once when he was a child. "Insolent wee-one," the king snapped, his face growing red in anger. "I will kill you for this. Slowly. I promise you. I want those emeralds. And you shall pay for not bringing them to me. I have thought of nothing but them for the past few weeks. They will be mine, do you understand? They will sit in *my* study, not the duke's. Those stones are the key to everything I want: power, position, property, and wealth. You were to be the means to an end, but now I see I'll have to resort to more drastic measures. A new plan, one born of your failure. If I have to, I'll go after them myself. Those emeralds will be mine—at any cost."

"I could try again," Fenzig offered, hoping to buy himself a little time.

Jean Rabe

"I should have known not to trust a thief—even one ensor-celled to do my bidding." The king paced in front of the gnome. His hands were balled into tight fists, the knuckles white. "Did you even try, thief? Or did you just run in search of a wizard who would break the magic?"

"I tried," Fenzig said meekly, "but the duke caught me. I managed to escape, and on my way out of town I ran into a wizard who was kind enough to lift the spell."

"You are an idiot!" It was the old wizard's turn now. "If you were free of my spell, and you didn't have the emeralds, why did you come back here? Why didn't you simply run back to your absurd gnome town filled with mounds of dirt and ridiculous little people with foolish little brains?"

Fenzig inwardly fumed at the insults leveled against his race. He knew gnomes to be a kind, good-natured folk. They kept apart from humanity simply because things of human design were too large. They enjoyed the comfort of burrows, and only a few had chosen the thieving profession. Most were hardwork-ing, honest folk.

"I came back because I had no coins. I didn't have so much as a copper piece to my name, and you have all this wealth. Sure, I knew the treasure in the tower wasn't your main hoard, but there was enough there to make me happy."

"And didn't you think you'd be caught again?" the wizard posed. "Did you think the alarms no longer worked?"

Fenzig fidgeted nervously. "Well, I thought I could bypass your alarms, and I didn't think you'd expect to be robbed twice in so short a time. Who'd expect to be robbed twice?"

"And your accomplice?" the king asked. "Who broke into the room with you? Who else shall share your death sentence?"

"I was alone," Fenzig said, taking a defiant pose. "I always work alone."

"I was struck from behind!" the wizard bellowed.

160

"By one of your own clumsy guards," the gnome retorted.

"Sir?" One of the guards addressed the king. Erlgrane nodded, granting him permission to speak. "I saw no one else in the false treasure room. I saw only the gnome. He was waving a sword about that rusted any metal object it touched."

"A sword I gave him," the king said evenly. "A sword that killed two of my men and is now again in my possession."

I wonder if Carmella got out? Fenzig mused. *As angry as I was that she took my ring, I can't help but hope that she made it. A woman couldn't possibly last more than a day in Erlgrane's dungeon. Better that I take the punishment than a frail woman who is barely more than a girl.*

The guards shook Fenzig, rousing him from his thoughts. "Move!" a pair barked in unison.

The gnome looked up at the king.

"You signed your own death warrant, scoundrel—both by coming back here, and by being empty-handed. Those emeralds were the only things that might have saved you." King Erlgrane glared at the thief and motioned for the guards to hurry the gnome along. "I will have those gems, no matter what."

Fenzig looked over his shoulder at the still-fuming monarch. He wondered if the king was mad. He was certainly obsessed. "Would they have saved me, sire? Would you really have let me live if I had brought the emeralds to you? Or would you have killed me so I couldn't have told anyone about what I did for you?"

King Erlgrane didn't answer; he twirled on his expensive leather boot heels and strode from the room.

"Same cell?" Fenzig asked the guards. "I kind of missed the place. The rats and I were getting along rather well. And the food. Mmm. I can't say enough about your food."

"You're not bound for the dungeon," the one on the right snapped.

"Then where?" *Am I to die already?* the gnome wondered. *Don't I even get to fret about it for a while in a dark, damp cell? You know, torture my mind before you have at my body.*

The guard only chuckled as he prodded the gnome in the back with the tip of his very sharp sword.

A CAGEY SITUATION

The guards nudged Fenzig down a long and twisting flight of stairs—the steps of which were steep even by human standards. The gnome suspected he was three or four levels below the ground by the time they finally stopped—deeper than he'd been when he was in the dungeon. The walls were slick with moisture, and the place smelled fusty and very old, perhaps older than the castle that sat atop it.

The gnome's short legs ached, and he was exhausted, but the guards wouldn't allow him so much as a pause to catch his breath. They pushed him toward an ironbound oak door, the only door he'd seen since starting his downward journey. The guard to his right tentatively touched the handle before unlatching it, as if the metal might be hot. When he opened the door, he did so very carefully, nudging it just a crack. The guard pressed his eye close to the opening, then breathed a sigh of relief. Apparently satisfied that whatever awaited beyond was harmless, he swung the door open wide and shoved the gnome in.

Fenzig's mouth dropped open, and shivers danced up and down his spine as he took in his new surroundings. Before him stretched counter after counter filled with vials, bowls, cups, and various other metal and glass containers. There were small mounds of colored sand, feathers, shriveled eyeballs, finger bones, and animal claws. Tall, clear vases were filled with bubbling green liquid. Braziers burned something that produced a noxious-smelling red smoke. All sorts of painful-looking metal implements—small and large—were arranged on a low bench. There were crates stacked high all about, and against every wall there were shelves crowded with scrolls, books, and stacks of parchment. The gnome uneasily noted a few dark reddish-brown patches on the floor, which he suspected were dried blood, and there was an unsettling feeling permeating the very air.

This is worse than the dungeon, Fenzig thought. *I don't care if it's not dirty, and I don't care that there aren't any rats . . . but there are other animals,* he noticed as he glanced up.

The ceiling was tall, close to thirty feet, the gnome guessed. Suspended from it were about a dozen iron cages affixed to ropes and pulleys. Inside the various-sized cages were animals: monkeys, dogs, cats, weasels, and exotic creatures the gnome couldn't identify.

"Move!" one of the guards barked.

Fenzig gulped and took another step into the room.

"Move over there!"

The gnome looked to where the guards were pointing and felt his chest tighten in fear. He was shoved roughly from behind, propelled a few feet closer to an empty cage that rested on the floor near the center of the room. One end of a chain was attached to the top of the cage, the other end was hooked to a pulley contraption that connected to the ceiling.

"C-c-couldn't we discuss this?" Fenzig stammered. "If you put me in that cage, you'll be treating me like an animal—like those animals. Wouldn't you rather put me in the dungeon where you can taunt me? You'd have much more fun."

"Move!" both of the guards barked in unison.

I'm not going into that cage, the gnome thought. *If I go in that cage, they'll winch me up where all those animals are. I'll starve, or I'll be experimented on. I won't go. I simply will not go. If I have to die, let them kill me quickly and cleanly.* Defiantly, he plopped himself down on the damp stone floor and crossed his arms.

The angry guards picked him up and carried him to the cage. Fenzig struggled against them, but he was tired from the fight in the tower and the long trek down the stairs, and they had the advantage of size and numbers. Within the space of a few heartbeats, he'd been tossed in the iron cage, the door had been slammed and locked behind him, and he felt himself being hoisted up until he was better than a dozen feet in the air, about even with a small cage holding a sorrowful-looking baboon.

"What's going to happen to me?" he asked the retreating guards. "This is that old wizard's lab, isn't it?"

One turned and craned his neck up at the gnome and nodded. He didn't say anything, though he offered Fenzig a sympathetic look. But the guard who was in the lead laughed long and hard. Together, they left the chamber and slammed the door behind them.

The gnome closed his eyes as he listened to their retreating footsteps. When he could hear only the sound of his own labored breathing, he opened his eyes. The baboon, which barely fit in its cage, was regarding him intently. *Odd,* the gnome thought, *the animals don't make any noise.* He returned the baboon's stare and cringed.

On closer inspection, he saw that its fur was matted, and festering sores were evident along its ankles and wrists. Its face was scarred and pockmarked, and it showed no energy. Most of the other animals were in similar shape, and some were worse. They had no hope or spirit left, so they cowered in silence. One in particular caught the gnome's eye, now that he had a better vantage point. The weasel that he'd first spotted from below had six legs, as if an additional pair had been grafted to its sides. He wondered if the other animals higher up, the ones he couldn't quite see, had extra appendages.

He strained and peered into the darkness, his curiosity pushing him. At the edge of his vision he spotted two cages, side by side, their black-furred occupants practically blending in with the shadows.

"Craven cats," he whispered. "Why would the wizard catch craven cats?" The gnome swallowed hard, returned the almost-human gaze of one of the beasts. It flicked its tails at him—this one had three—and the leafy appendages at the end dribbled acid that seemed too weak to threaten the iron bars of the cage. "The wizard didn't catch craven cats," Fenzig hushed. "He creates them."

The gnome remembered back to the Haunted Woods when he encountered the beasts, remembered wondering what malicious god birthed the craven cats. He shook his head. "The eyes are human," he said. He stared at the twin beasts hanging high above him. "Were you human? Is the wizard populating the woods with monsters to keep people out of them? And if so why? Is he hiding an army of craven cats in there? An army that would be used for . . . what?"

The cats snarled in unison and Fenzig's thoughts turned quiet. *Will I be turned into a craven cat, too? No. The king wants me dead. Though I suppose being a craven cat could be considered dead. Gods! I don't even want to think what the wizard is going to do to me. Give me four ears and shave my head? Dye me purple? Kill me by turning me into something else?* Fenzig wondered. *Well, they're definitely going to kill me. Eventually. I just hope they won't hurt me too much before they get the job done. What is this place, and what on earth possessed me to come back here with Carmella?*

"I think it was your sense of chivalry that brought you here," the air answered.

"Carmella?"

"I told you I wouldn't abandon you, even if you do think I'm a *frail* woman. But it looks as if we're going to have to abandon our plan to get Erlgrane's wizard. There are just too many guards, and who knows where the old mage is now. Maybe we can try later if we get a few reinforcements. Our priority right now is to get out of here."

"Then get me down! Please!" Fenzig's tone was harsh, but his face showed he was happy to see her. Well, not exactly see her, as she was still invisible. But he could tell where she was, as she had started to lower his cage. "Why didn't you help me earlier—when all those guards were piling on top of me?"

"The odds were too bad. The guards and the wizard had seen you, but they hadn't seen me," she said as she continued to bring his cage toward the floor. "I let them think you were working alone; that way I could stay hidden and help you out when there were fewer people about."

The cage landed on the stone floor with a dull *clank,* and Carmella set about trying to open it. "Where's the key?" she asked.

It's not here, Fenzig thought. He noticed she was still wearing the medallion, so he decided he might as well think to her rather than talk. *The guards took it with them when they left.*

"Terrific," she replied.

You claim to be a thief—pick the lock, he mused.

"I'm not that kind of a thief."

He heard some grumbling and a few soft footsteps; then he watched as the metal implements on the bench were shifted around. A thin silver rod with a sharp point floated in the air toward him and started working at the lock.

Move it this way. That's it. Then this way, Fenzig mentally instructed as he motioned with his hands. *You're not too bad; you just lack a little finesse.*

"Thanks," she muttered.

The cage creaked opened, and the gnome scrambled out. The backs of his legs were sore from being cramped inside the cage, but he blocked out the sensation in favor of concentrating on his freedom.

"Uh-oh." Carmella sharply inhaled. "We've got. . . ."

The gnome ignored her and pointed toward the door. "Up those steps and. . . ."

But before the pair could take a step, the door slowly opened and the wizard padded inside. His eyes immediately locked onto the gnome, and he sputtered. "Thief! You might escape that cage, but you cannot escape me!"

"Company," the gnome said, finishing Carmella's interrupted sentence.

"King Erlgrane said you were mine to do with as I will, just so long as I killed you in the end. I have plans for you, scoundrel. You shall be part of my next grand experiment." The wizard slammed the door behind him and started mumbling.

Fenzig suspected the old mage was calling down another magical spell, and he didn't want to be the object of it. He sprinted across the stone floor and ducked, just in time, behind a crate. He didn't see the effect of the wizard's enchantment, but he heard it—a loud crack that sounded like a bolt of lightning—and he smelled it—a hint of sulfur in the air.

"Fool! We can play this cat-and-mouse game for a time if you wish, but I will win! You haven't the resources to best me!"

Fenzig risked a peek over the top of the crate and saw the wizard painting symbols in the air with his spider-leg fingertips. These didn't look like the blue and green snakes he had made earlier in the tower. These looked like the outline of overlarge hands. As the gnome watched, the wizard spoke a string of what seemed to be nonsense words and pointed toward the crates. The glowing hands flew through the air and started grabbing crates, moving them about and revealing Fenzig's location.

"I have you now, thief!" the wizard spat. He gestured, and the magical hands shot toward the gnome.

Fenzig ran, his bare feet slapping over the cold stone floor. Although the gnome was fast, he wasn't as fast as the wizard's enchantment. The hands scooped him up and dangled him a few feet off the floor.

The old wizard smirked and slowly glided toward him.

Carmella! Where are you? Do something! Fenzig's mind called out. *He's coming closer and he looks decidedly unhappy. He's. . . .*

Before the gnome could finish the thought, he saw a pair of metal spikes float through the air behind the wizard. It was Carmella carrying them, of course, Fenzig knew, but he wasn't sure what she intended to do with them.

Be careful, Carmella. Those could kill him. Try to take him alive. If you can, we might still save your sisters.

"Gnome," the wizard sneered, "I've always wondered what it is about your race that makes you so short and squat, and gives you hairy feet and nimble fingers."

"We're born that way," Fenzig retorted as he squirmed helplessly in the grip of the magical hands.

"You're quite a bit different than a human—on the outside," the wizard continued. "All of your kind are." He was rubbing his hands together in a gesture Fenzig had seen greedy merchants display. "Maybe if I cut into you a little, I can see how different you are on the inside." With that, the wizard reached into the folds of his robe and produced a sharply honed, thin-bladed knife.

Fenzig gasped.

"Oh, don't worry," the old mage sneered. "This will hurt, but it won't kill you. I have too many experiments to conduct to let you die so soon. I'll make sure you stay alive for a good, long while." He brought the knife in closer to the gnome.

"No, you don't!" an invisible Carmella spouted. She was just behind the wizard now, with the metal spikes in her hands held out to the old man's sides. She brought the flat sides of the spikes inward with a considerable amount of force, and Fenzig heard the wizard's ribs make an ugly crunching sound.

The wizard pitched forward to his knees and gasped in pain and surprise. At the same instant the magical hands holding the gnome vanished, and Fenzig fell several feet to the floor. He landed solidly on his rump and cried out.

"So you did have an accomplice, little thief," the wizard jeered. He held his right side with a shaky hand and started gesturing again with the left. "No matter, really. Now I will have two people to experiment upon."

Carmella was bringing the metal spikes in for another attack, but as she closed to within a few inches of the wizard's body she stopped, motionless. The wizard swiveled and rose, eyeing the spikes that seemed to hover in midair. Then he gestured again. The air shimmered and sparkled, and a moment later Carmella was revealed. She looked frozen, as if she were a life-like statue.

While the wizard's attention was trained on her, Fenzig slid behind a counter and stretched his fingers up, seeing what he might find. *Hmm, now here's something that might be useful,* he thought as he filled his hands and pockets.

"You look familiar," the wizard hissed.

Fenzig knew the old mage was talking to the frozen Carmella.

"I can't place you, but I will. I never forget a face, and I have seen your lovely visage before."

Fenzig slid around the far end of the counter, hoping to come up behind the wizard. *I don't like this,* he thought. *I don't like being in a wizard's laboratory, especially when the wizard is powerful and can grow extra legs on animals, create craven cats and freeze people.*

"Where'd your little friend go?" the wizard asked. "He was here just a moment ago. Ah, there you are, thief."

The old man's voice was coming from above the gnome, and when Fenzig glanced up he saw that the wizard had leaned over the counter and was looking directly down on him. The gnome snarled and threw his hands into the air, releasing the sand he had so carefully carried. The colorful grains flew upward and into the wizard's face.

The old man coughed and wheezed and rapidly backed out of Fenzig's view, but the gnome pressed his attack. He sped around the corner of the counter and barreled right into the mage. The wizard teetered on his slippered feet for only a moment before he fell to the floor.

Fenzig followed him, scrambling up the man's bony form until he stood on the wizard's chest. "Don't move," the gnome growled. "Not one move. Not one inch. Not one gesture. Not one word."

"Otherwise we might be the ones cutting into you." Carmella had somehow broken free of the spell that held her. "Nice work, Fenzig." She dropped the spikes and shook her head as if to clear her senses. "I don't know what that spell was, but I didn't enjoy being the target of it. I could see everything, yet I couldn't do anything."

She took a step toward the wizard and looked down at him. His face bore a pained expression, and he continued to wheeze. Fenzig looked down, too, and realized he was standing on ribs that likely were cracked or broken from Carmella's blows. He jumped to the floor to stand next to the wizard and grabbed the wrinkled face between his small hands. The wizard stared unblinking at Fenzig, his rheumy blue eyes meeting the gnome's intense gaze. Even though the mage seemed powerless, his eyes unnerved Fenzig.

"I've found some cord," Carmella volunteered. She sat on the floor and started wrapping it around the wizard's hands. "You can't gesture if you can't move your fingers. That means you won't be able to cast any more spells."

The wizard shifted his gaze from the gnome to her. "Who are you?" he said in practically a whisper.

"I look familiar because I'm Duke Rehmir's youngest daughter," she said as she finished tying his hands together. That task finished, she tore off a piece of his robe and stuffed it in his mouth. "I'm the one you didn't turn into an emerald."

"Great, he can't go anywhere now or do anything! We got him!" Fenzig said aloud. "But now we have to get him—and us—out of here. You're not invisible anymore, and I know the old man isn't about to do anything that might help us leave. He'll probably try to foul up our escape attempt. Who knows when the guards will be back. Maybe this place is part of their regular patrol."

"I doubt it," she replied. "If I were a guard I wouldn't want to come down here. The place reeks of evil."

"Fine, but do you have any brilliant ideas for getting us out of the castle? We need to hurry. There probably isn't much darkness left."

Carmella smiled weakly at Fenzig. "I told you I studied with a wizard for a while. He didn't teach me much because he didn't know too much himself. Outside of teaching me how to make tattoos and how to break down not-so-powerful spells, he taught me how to sense life and the pasts those lives experienced."

"That'll be real useful here. You can find out what the wizard had for breakfast yesterday."

She frowned. "And he taught me the only other spell I know, a spell that makes things smaller. I always thought it would come in useful if I broke into some treasure room. I could cast it on the treasure. That way I could put a lot of tiny valuable stuff into a little space."

"Can you use it to shrink him?"

"I don't know if it works on people, but I'll give it a try. I was actually intending on casting it on him in the treasure room. Stick him in my pocket, and then we'd climb back out the window. But things didn't turn out that way." Carmella sighed and rocked back and forth, closed her eyes. Her face grew flushed, and her breathing became irregular. "Nothing to lose," she whispered.

For a moment Fenzig feared she would collapse, and he'd be faced with taking both her and the wizard out—which would be impossible. But then the color drained from her face and her eyes fluttered. Her hands glowed softly, and she placed them on the wizard's chest.

The gnome saw the wizard jerk and twist spasmodically, as if he were having a seizure. This continued for several long moments, and just as Fenzig felt sure the wizard would perish, the old man started to shrink. Fenzig jumped back for fear he would grow smaller, too. The wizard seemed to fold in upon himself, becoming shorter and thinner. Even his clothes and the cord wrapped about his wrist shrunk.

Carmella pulled her hands free and watched the transformation continue. Within moments the wizard was Fenzig's size, though of a much slighter build. A few moments more and he was but a foot tall, like a child's doll. The process continued until he was half again that size, a little shorter than Carmella's hand from the heel of her palm to her fingertips.

She grinned broadly. "I guess I'm not such a bad wizard after all."

"You're a great wizard," Fenzig said. The gnome's mouth hung open as he stared at the diminutive wizard. "Will you be able to make him big again when we get to the duke's?"

She pursed her lips. "I should be able to. If the shrinking spell works, the regrowth version should, too. You're next. Stand back."

"What?" Fenzig screamed. "No way. I like being small, but

I'm small enough."

"Listen, our chances of escape will be much better if only one of us has to get out. I can carry you and the wizard in my pockets."

"No," Fenzig protested, "I can carry *you* and the wizard in *my* pockets. I'm a far better climber than you are, and if I get caught, I can drop you in some nook or corner so you can use your magic and try to escape later. They didn't see you, remember?"

"Chivalrous to a fault," Carmella said. "Either that or you're afraid of my magic. Too bad I don't know any humans like you." She swayed again and mumbled, directing the enchantment on herself this time. Within moments she was even smaller than the wizard, and she looked up at Fenzig and put her hands on her hips.

"Well," she asked in a voice as faint as a whisper, "aren't you going to get us out of here?"

The gnome grinned and carefully scooped her up and placed her in his breast pocket. He wasn't quite so careful with the wizard—despite the old man's ribs. He put the mage in his pants pocket and padded toward the door. He paused under the animal cages and glanced up.

I'd like to free you, too, he thought. *I'd like to take you all out of here, but it just isn't practical, and you're all in very bad shape. You're going to die here, and there's nothing I can really do about it except feel sorry for you.*

"Not everyone or everything can have a happy ending," Carmella called in a voice that sounded like a distant whisper.

Can you please take that necklace off? Fenzig pleaded to her. *I'd like to think to myself for a while.*

The gnome didn't take the stairs, but instead climbed the stairwell wall. His fingers and toes fit perfectly in the niches between the stones, and it was far easier and quicker than trying to maneuver over human-sized steps. At the top, he heard guards talking. They were pondering what experiment the wizard would conduct on the gnome, possibly turning him into a miniature craven cat.

Fenzig shivered and slipped past them, clinging to the shadows and making his way out of King Erlgrane's castle. The sky was a pale gray tinged with pink, indicating dawn was fast approaching. The shadows were not as plentiful as they'd been when he and Carmella had broken in, so the gnome relied on speed, running across the open courtyard and hoping the sentries were too tired to be paying attention. Scaling the outer wall was easy after everything he had already endured, and making his way back to Graespeck was not difficult either.

Carmella remained tiny the whole trip. In fact, when Fenzig glanced in his pocket, he saw that she was sleeping. He didn't bother to wake her—not even when he climbed on the Carmen the Magnificent wagon and bid farewell to his father.

"I'll be back," Fenzig said. "I'll not stay away so long this time. I promise. And when you see me again I might be looking for a job as an apprentice woodcarver."

The older gnome beamed, and Fenzig smiled back.

Carmella woke up after the wagon had been on the road to K'Nosha for a few hours. She climbed out of Fenzig's pocket, and he set her tiny form on the seat next to him. The gnome watched her wiggle her fingers and cast another spell. This one, too, was successful, causing her to grow back to her normal height.

"I can take the wagon the rest of the way if you want," she offered. "I'll bet you're tired."

"I'm hungry," Fenzig replied, and he watched her retreat into the wagon. "I think there are still a few tiny cakes left," he called, "and how about some cheese?"

The miles melted away, and by the time a couple of days had

passed, all the food in the wagon had disappeared. Carmella and a still-hungry Fenzig found themselves at the duke's estate by midmorning—with no sign of pursuit from Erlgrane's men. The gnome suspected the king had no idea his wizard was gone, as the monarch likely didn't venture down to the old mage's catacombs.

Carmella waved to the guards at the gate. Word of their arrival traveled quickly, and the duke was waiting for them at the manor's front door.

"Carmella!" the duke beamed, rushing toward her and helping her down. He hugged her fiercely, then grinned at the gnome. "Come in, please," he urged. An arm about his daughter's waist, the duke ushered them inside.

"I was so worried about you," the portly man said as he led them up the stairs and to his study. "I was afraid I might lose you, too, Carmella. I was. . . ."

"We were successful," she said happily, interrupting him. "We have the wizard."

"Where?"

Fenzig could tell Carmella wasn't used to all the attention, and she seemed a little uncomfortable. She extracted herself from her father's affectionate grip and went to stand before the mantel, where the three emeralds glimmered.

"Where is he?" the duke persisted.

"Here," Fenzig said as shuffled forward to join them. He gently pulled the tiny wizard out of his pocket. "It wasn't easy catching him, sir," the gnome began. "There was this laboratory, and all these creatures, craven cats, and magical spells were going off, and then we had to escape without anyone seeing us, and—"

"And we caught him," Carmella finished, bending over and gingerly taking the wizard from the gnome. She grimaced when she noticed the old man was pale and that his robes were spotted with blood. With her index finger, she felt about his ribs. "I think I hit him a little too hard," she said as she tugged the tiny gag from his mouth and felt his forehead with her fingertip. It was hot from a fever. "And he refused to eat or drink anything during the trip."

"I've attendants who can see to him," the duke said. He gazed at the diminutive wizard sitting in Carmella's palm. "But I want your sisters tended to first. Do you understand, wizard? I want my daughters whole again."

Though obviously in pain, the miniature wizard looked defiant.

Carmella knelt and set the tiny figure in front of the fireplace. Taking a step back, she concentrated and closed her eyes. Her fingers traced a colorful pattern of pale green light in the air. The pattern expanded to take in the wizard; then the pattern grew—as did the old man. Within moments, the wizard was full-sized again. He looked much worse, now that everyone could see him more clearly. He sat down, breathing harshly, and his lips were tinged faintly blue.

"I'll get my attendants, a healer," the duke offered.

"I don't want your healing, Rehmir," the wizard cursed. "I want to see you crushed by my master, King Erlgrane. He'll have these lands—even if it means your wretched life. If he can't have them through marriage to one of your daughters, he'll gain them by force. They'll be his. Just wait and see. I will not restore your daughters to you."

"Then let him come try to take my lands," the duke said hotly.

"He will," the wizard hissed, "but he'll try to take the gems first. He's consumed with the idea of possessing them. It's all he's talked about recently."

"Erlgrane's mad," Fenzig whispered.

"Madness and genius are often confused," the wizard

returned. "I prefer to consider my king in the latter category, and he's wise enough to know that if he has the emeralds—your daughters—he will have your land and your loyalty, willingly given or not. And from your precious land, he can more easily strike out with his armies, envelope the Northern Reaches and beyond. He intends to control everything to the north seacoast and perhaps even to the west."

"The gnome's right," the duke said. "The king is mad."

"Maybe he'll have me turn your last daughter into a gem, too, another bauble for his collection," the wizard sneered. "Or maybe I'll cast the spell without his bidding. Is your land more valuable to you than your own flesh and blood? Or do you so badly want another emerald to decorate your mantel—one more jewel for my king to take?"

Fenzig saw the duke shudder, the wizard's venomous words hitting a soft spot. The portly man's shoulders sagged, and his lips trembled. "If I just give him my lands maybe he'll give my daughters back their lives and leave them alone," Duke Rehmir said sadly. "I'm tired of looking at them, sitting above the fireplace. I don't want anything to happen to Carmella. I. . . ."

"Father, no!" Carmella barked. "You can't mean it! What about the people of K'Nosha? What about. . . ."

Her words trailed off as the wizard let out a groan. Carmella and the duke turned to look at the old man. The gnome was standing behind him, his small fingers pressed into the wizard's throat.

"You're dying," the gnome spat at the wizard. "You're dying, and you know it. The king's attendants might be able to save you. Maybe. He's got a few skilled healers, so all the townsfolk say. If you want the chance to live—the chance to serve your mad king for a few more years—then you'd better save the duke's daughters. Your giving them back their lives will not affect any struggle between the king and Duke Rehmir. In fact, you're not doing anything could guarantee a war. If you die, Duke Rehmir's daughters will always be gems. I'd say that gives the duke ample reason to war against Erlgrane."

The wizard glowered at the duke and Carmella, then he gasped as Fenzig increased his grip.

"So, wizard," the gnome continued. "If you care for your king, you'll do something about the duke's daughters."

The mage twisted his head and tried to dislodge the gnome's fingers, but Fenzig was strong and healthy, and the wizard was weak.

"Your answer," Fenzig growled. "You can't serve your king if you're dead, and without your releasing the spell, your king could be attacked. Your decision."

"I will *try* to return Rehmir's daughters," the wizard said finally. His voice was strained because of Fenzig's viselike grip. "But I can make no guarantees. Know you that the spell I cast on them is years old."

"Five years," the duke replied.

"Enchantments that old are sometimes hard to break."

"I have every confidence in you," the duke added.

"I will need to stand."

Fenzig shook his head fervently. The gnome wouldn't release his grip until the duke nodded.

"If you try anything," Duke Rehmir began, "you'll find *my* fingers about your throat. And I can guarantee I will lead my men against Erlgrane." He helped the wizard to his feet and untied the old man's hands.

The wizard's eyes narrowed to thin slits, and he glanced at Fenzig and Carmella. The pair of thieves were standing together, near the emeralds spaced evenly on the floor in front of the fireplace.

"I do this because you give me no real option," the wizard said, "and because your daughters are not to blame for your idiocy." Then he doubled over, coughing and wheezing, and the duke grabbed him and supported him about the waist. "If this works, Duke Rehmir, you will have all your daughters again, but you will still lose. King Erlgrane will triumph in the end. He will find a way to come take your daughters as easily as he could find thieves to steal the emeralds. He is more powerful than you realize."

The duke started to reply but thought better of it. He stood quietly and watched the old mage weave a pattern of golden light in the air. The wizard mumbled a singsong chant filled with ancient melodic words. His voice rose and cracked as the light pattern brightened, then the glow seemed to move of its own volition to encompass the emeralds.

Fenzig held his breath, praying that the old wizard wasn't performing one last evil deed by further harming the duke's daughters. But as the gnome watched, he saw a bit of brightness come to the wizard's eyes.

The emeralds shimmered, and the light that surrounded the gems was quickly absorbed by them. Their facets sparkled with an unearthly beauty and held Carmella, Fenzig, the guards, and the duke spellbound. It looked like green fire captured inside hunks of crystal. Then the light started to fade, and the emeralds grew dark, almost black.

"No!" the duke cried. "This can't be. Please. . . ." Before he could finish, the darkened gems shattered. In their place on the floor in front of the fireplace, three beautiful women stood, all with dark hair and eyes that flashed like Carmella's.

The duke rushed forward to embrace them. The wizard, no longer supported, fell to the floor in a heap. Carmella stepped toward her sisters, tears streaming down her face, happy to join in the family reunion.

Fenzig felt like an intruder on the cheerful scene and turned his attention on the wizard. He padded toward the old man and sat on the floor next to him. The wizard's eyes were fixed, and a thin trickle of blood spilled from his mouth.

"He's dead," Fenzig whispered.

"You're alive and well!" the duke cried to his daughters.

FAMILY REUNION

"My name is Elayne."

Smiling sweetly, the tallest of the girls bent over to shake the gnome's small hand. She had flowing blond hair, the color of corn silk, with soft blue eyes that lent her face a kind appearance. "I can't thank you enough, Fenzighan," she said. "I owe you my life, truly. I never thought I'd be human again. I never thought I'd be able to talk again, or to touch my sisters."

"Neither did I. I'm Ruthe," another girl interjected. She didn't at all resemble Elayne. Her hair was much darker, the shade of walnut tree bark, and her eyes were bright and intense. Her voice was a bit stronger and lower pitched, almost sultry. The gnome immediately decided he liked listening to it. "You answered my prayers, wee-one. I was the emerald in the middle, and I was so tired of sitting on that mantel, watching father stare at us. His eyes haunted me."

Ruthe's voice mesmerized Fenzig, and he listened to every word. Questions tumbled, one after another, from her lips: near musical queries of what had happened in K'Nosha and Burlengren during the past several years, where Carmella had been, and how Carmella and their father had found such a fine, small hero to rescue them. The duke did his best to answer her, but even he seemed a bit overwhelmed.

Fenzig decided this daughter looked so much like Carmella they could pass for twins—provided they wore their hair the same. Ruthe's eyes sparkled in the light streaming in through the window—just as Carmella's sparkled when she sold her wares, and he found himself wishing Ruthe would go on talking forever just so he could listen to her enchanting voice.

Grinning at the gnome and finally stopping her stream of sentences, Ruthe knelt on the floor in front of him and kissed the top of his head. "And this is Berthrice," she added, indicating the third girl. "Our oldest sister."

Berthrice glanced at the gnome and scowled. "It was horrible," Berthrice began in a voice as grating as Ruthe's was pleasant. Her blue eyes narrowed as she crossed her arms in front of her chest, as if she were trying to draw herself all into one spot, giving her a pinched appearance. She looked uncomfortable. "Maybe I should have accepted King Erlgrane's proposal five years ago. I'll grant you he is an evil man, but I don't think living with him could possibly have been worse than living on that mantel. Never moving. Never. . . ."

"Berth!" Elayne snapped. "How can you say that? Erlgrane never wanted you. He never really wanted any of us. He wants only the land and Father's manor."

"I'll tell you how I can say that!" Berthrice snapped back. She drew herself even closer together, drew her lips into a thin, unbecoming line. "It felt as if an eternity passed while we sat on that mantel. I could see everything. All of us could see everything."

"See?" the duke asked.

"See!" Berthrice hissed. "See! He should have blinded us while he was at it. All we could see was this damnable study and Father's sorrowful face!"

Fenzig looked at her quizzically, wondered how she could be so different from her sisters and how her voice could sound . . . sound . . . so much like a hungry crow.

"While emeralds, we could see, we could smell the smoke from Father's pipe." Wiping a tear from her flushed cheek, Berthrice turned to Duke Rehmir. "Day after day, I saw you come into the study, Father. You'd sit in the chair and watch us. Sometimes you'd cry. Sometimes you'd just smoke your pipe and stare at us. I was angry that you couldn't do anything to break the wizard's spell—that it looked like you were doing nothing. I was angry that Carmella was still human, that *she* was spared. That spell was a terrible curse, worse than death. When you weren't here we saw only the furniture and the walls. The view never changed. It was madness."

The duke swallowed hard. "I wasn't aware you could see, or smell, or. . . ."

"And hear," Elayne added. "We heard everything."

"We heard you talking to us," Ruthe broke in. "When you'd come in here late at night and talk to us, pretending that we were still flesh and blood and were listening, that made things bearable."

The duke grabbed Ruthe's hand and squeezed it gently. "My life is bearable now that all of you are back, no matter what Erlgrane threatens me with next."

"That wagon ride wasn't bearable," Berthrice said. Still venting her rage, she continued to complain, tapping her narrow foot. "When Carmella put us in the sack of flour in the wagon, I thought we were finished. All that white! It was like being stuck inside a warm snowbank. And then *you* plucked us out and kept handling us," she added to the gnome. "You ogled us and ran your dirty little fingers over us. Worse, I thought you were going to drop us when the wagon bounced down the road. What if you had dropped us? What if we'd cracked? We could have died!"

"But we didn't," Elayne said. She put her arm around Berthrice and gently hugged her. "Yes, it was horrible. But it's over now thanks to Fenzig and Carmella. We're not on the mantel anymore—or in a sack of flour. We've a grand life ahead of us.

We have a lot of catching up to do. And we've no reason to dwell on the lost years. Let it be behind us—forever."

Berthrice nodded, her facial expression softening a little. Then she looked down on the gnome again. "Thank you for saving me," she said finally and with what appeared to Fenzig to be some effort. "Thank you for saving my sisters, too."

Fenzig stared at the three beautiful human girls. He tried to imagine what it must have been like to sit for five years as gems on a mantel, always watching and hearing what was going on around them, but not able to interact with each other or anyone else. The gnome shuddered. Indeed, it would have been horrible. He was pleased and proud that he had been instrumental in saving them.

Carmella moved so silently up behind Fenzig that the gnome didn't hear her. He jumped when she tickled the top of his head. "We all owe you a big thank-you," Carmella said. Her voice had a happy lilt to it, and Fenzig's grin became even broader. "You've given us a family reunion. I have to admit that I never thought I'd see my sisters again."

"I never thought I'd have a family again," the duke added.

"And I was surprised to see Erlgrane's wizard," Elayne said. "I can't say I'm sorry he's dead."

"No," Fenzig added, thinking about all the poor animals in the wizard's laboratory. "But what are you going to do with his body?"

Duke Rehmir and his four daughters glanced at the wizard's form.

The duke sighed and padded over to it. "I'll have the wizard's body sent back to King Erlgrane," Duke Rehmir said. "That will make Erlgrane even more angry, but the wizard should be buried where he lived. I can't send the body to his relatives— the wizard kept his name hidden, so no one knows who his relatives might be."

"Why not just bury him here and let King Erlgrane wonder what happened to him?" Fenzig considered that the best option. "Dead is dead. The wizard isn't going to care where you bury his body."

The duke drew his lips together, tapped a finger against them in thought. "That wouldn't be proper. Besides, I suspect Erlgrane has ways of finding out what occurred. Perhaps he has lesser wizards in his employ who can divine what happened. In any event, I sense a long-overdue confrontation coming between myself and the king."

"A war?" the gnome queried.

"Perhaps, but it's not very likely. I know if Erlgrane tries to bring his troops here, he will lose. Mine is the greater force—and even if he is mad, he has to realize that."

"Besides," Carmella interjected, "the people of Burlengren might rise up against King Erlgrane if he makes war on us. They don't want a fight that will threaten the lives of their men—whom the king would likely call into service. K'Nosha and Burlengren have been peaceful for decades. I don't think anyone except the king wants that to change."

Fenzig was surprised the woman knew so much about politics and the affairs of cities, having been on the road as a peddler for so long. The gnome wondered if she would stay with the duke, who seemed like a reasonable man—for a wealthy potentate anyway.

The duke's four daughters stood behind him. Three of them looked almost identical in elegant, fancy dresses and artfully styled hair—and chattering like twittering birds nonstop. They looked young, as if they hadn't aged a day while they were gems.

Carmella had cleaned up and was wearing new clothes, but they consisted of dark-blue leggings and a light-blue tunic—somber daytime attire for someone who frequently wore a clashing rainbow. The duke just stood there and beamed at his daughters.

"I need to be on my way," Fenzig said at last. He looked out the window of the study and saw that the sun was nearing its lunchtime position.

"Won't you stay and have a meal with us first?" the duke asked. His tone was gracious. He was treating Fenzig as an equal now, not like the contemptible thief he'd viewed the gnome as a few days ago.

"Well, I am rather hungry," the gnome quipped.

"And my father's cooks are awfully good," Carmella added.

That said, Fenzig stayed for three more days, enjoying the meals Duke Rehmir's excellent staff prepared. He ate more than he had in the last two weeks put together, which satisfied his gnome stomach. *This one final dinner,* he told himself. *Then I need to be gone.*

"I'm amazed you can eat so much and not gain any weight," Carmella giggled.

"It's part of being a gnome," Fenzig said as he reached for his third piece of cinnamon-peach pie.

It was nearing sunset now, and the gnome made it clear he wanted to start back to Graespeck. Despite pleas from Carmella and her sisters that he stay overnight, he declined. He knew that if he stayed much longer, he'd be tempted not to leave at all. The duke's estate was fancy, and the food was very, very good. There were a few other gnomes here, in Duke Rehmir's employ. He'd have like company. But the estate was just too grand to suit his tastes.

"I really must be going," he repeated.

"Then before you go, I'd like to repay you for saving my daughters—*all* of my daughters," Duke Rehmir said. "Come with me."

Fenzig was led into a back corner of the manse, where guards were plentiful. On a nod from the duke, one of them produced a leather bag, one that was nearly two feet long and about half that wide.

"You're a hero, Fenzig, and, as such, you deserve a reward." The duke threw open a massive walnut door, behind which were piles of coins, bowls filled with gems, and open chests brimming with jewelry and objects of art. "My treasury, Fenzig. You may take as much as you can fit into that bag."

The gnome looked at the bag, at the room filled with riches, and then he glanced up, dumbfounded, at the duke. "I can't take anything from you," Fenzig said. "I helped because . . . well, I guess because I wanted to. I don't need a reward." He quickly added that the homing spell Carmella cast on him was actually just a tattoo—he hadn't been forced to do anything.

The duke laughed. "And a lovely tattoo it is." He nudged the gnome into the room. Practically everything inside sparkled and glittered and brought tears to the little thief's eyes. "Go on. You won't be stealing anything. I'm giving it to you. Whatever you want, take it."

Fenzig moved forward, mesmerized. The gems and gold and everything was like a dream come true—and he'd been *let* in here. He didn't have to sneak and break in. He didn't have to steal. It was a gift. He took another look over his shoulder at the duke, who made a motion with his hand for Fenzig to continue.

All right, Fenzig thought. *I'll take just a little. The man has more gold than he can spend in his lifetime, and he won't miss what little bit I take. Look at those rubies! And that pearl necklace! And look at those gold belt buckles! And that beautiful short sword! And all those coins! And that—*

Fenzig stopped thinking and started filling his bag. He took whatever was within easy reach and looked expensive, but he was very careful not to take the most valuable pieces—those should remain for the generous duke and his lovely daughters. He stood transfixed by a crystal case on a pedestal. Inside were pins in the shape of butterflies. A dozen, they looked like they were on display like an insect collection. But these insects were trimmed in rubies, sapphires, jacinths, and diamonds. He blinked and looked away.

The short sword that caught his eye had a carved ivory pommel, and the duke indicated he should take it and its tooled leather scabbard. Fenzig didn't wait for a second invitation to strap it around his waist.

The bag was bulging and almost too heavy to carry by the time Fenzig was ready to exit the room. "I'll have enough wealth to live on for years," he said, grinning. "I won't have to work. I won't have to carve wood with my father." The smile started to disappear from his face. "I won't have to travel. I won't have to do anything." He set the bag down amid all the other baubles.

"This isn't going to make me happy," he said at last. "Wanting riches is what got me into trouble in the first place. Having riches might get me into a worse mess. I learned my lesson. I don't need this much stuff. Nobody needs this much stuff. And I don't need to be rich." *Wealth never made King Erlgrane happy,* he thought. *And wealth hadn't made the duke happy—having his daughters back did.*

With that, Fenzig opened the sack, selected four walnut-sized gems and a handful of coins, and put them in his pocket. They'd buy him food, a small wagon, and plenty of supplies—things he could use to give himself a fresh start.

He looked up at the guards, who were smiling at him. He offered them a wide grin in return; then he glanced at the duke one last time. "I've got what I want," he told Duke Rehmir. The gnome patted the sword, deciding he'd keep it for self-defense. He might pass through the Haunted Woods again, and he wanted something to keep the craven cats at bay.

"I wish you'd take more," the duke said.

Fenzig shook his head. "It would only weigh me down."

"Your pony, Summer, is waiting out front," Carmella told him, smiling.

"Summer? I don't know what to say." Fenzig was at an uncommon loss for words over the gift of Carmella's prized pony.

"Say you'll come back and visit," the duke replied as he escorted the gnome to the front door where Summer was waiting.

As Duke Rehmir and his four daughters waved farewell from the steps, Fenzig mounted the pony. Surreptitiously wiping a tear from his eye, he turned his back on the happy little group and rode away. *I'll miss you Carmella,* he thought, for once hoping she *was* wearing the necklace.

As the gnome headed away from the manor house, he wondered if the shop in K'Nosha—the one with the lovely green-and-yellow quilt—would still be open. *My aunt would love that,* he thought; *I could buy it for her.*

He urged Summer into a fast trot around the garden, over the sculpted lawn, and through the gate. He was nearing the border of the duke's property when he spotted a rider coming at a fast pace toward him. The setting sun painted the black-cloaked man with a hint of orange, and Fenzig wondered if he was a messenger bringing important news to Duke Rehmir.

As the man approached more closely, however, Fenzig gasped in surprise and pulled hard on the reins to turn Summer about. The little pony responded quickly, but the man steered his mount to cut across the gnome's path, blocking off his escape. He threw back the cloak and dismounted in one fluid motion.

King Erlgrane! The king was wearing the same type of chain mail as his guards wore, and he had very few pieces of jewelry about him. He was not wearing anything that would readily identify him as a monarch, and the realization that the king was traveling incognito filled Fenzig with dread.

"You will die, wee-one," the king hissed. "It took all the resources of my lesser wizards to learn what you have done, where you were. And now, you will die. By my hand!"

As Erlgrane drew his sword and advanced on Fenzig, the gnome swallowed hard and slid from Summer, tugging his new short sword from its scabbard.

"You have thwarted me, scoundrel, for the last time," the king spat. "You kept me from the emeralds."

"They're not emeralds anymore," Fenzig said as he took a defensive stance. The thief was nervous. He knew he lacked any real skill with the sword, and this one wasn't magical and wouldn't rust the king's blade and armor. "They're Duke Rehmir's daughters again."

"And you've done something to my wizard."

"Guilty," the gnome replied. "He's dead. And his body should be arriving at your castle about now."

"Fool! Above everything else, you have kept me from claiming this land," the king continued.

"The land is Duke Rehmir's, and you've no right claim to it."

"It will be mine!" Erlgrane snapped. "I told you days ago, thief, that I would take it myself if I had to. It should be mine simply because I want it!"

"Your army isn't strong enough to take it," the gnome quipped. Fenzig nearly dropped his sword, his hands were sweating so.

"But if I kill Duke Rehmir, I *will* claim it. I will force a marriage with one of his daughters, and then the land will legally be mine. Or I'll have it by killing them all. No one will be the wiser. No one will know, because no one knows I'm here."

"No one?"

"I slipped out of my castle and donned a guard's uniform.

The people of Burlengren and K'Nosha will never know I had a
hand in the Rehmirs' upcoming tragedy."

"But *I'll* know," the gnome said as he stepped back to get
away from the advancing king. "Even if the duke dies, even if
you're successful in killing him, his daughters will know, too."

"You'll be dead," Erlgrane said icily, "and after I've ensconced
myself within the duke's palace, he will die, his daughters will
die, too, one by one, in horrible, unfortunate accidents. I'll
grieve for them, truly. But no one will suspect anything."

"You're mad!" Fenzig cried. He hoped his voice might be
loud enough to carry and alert some of Duke Rehmir's guards.
"You're truly mad—a dangerous lunatic!"

King Erlgrane lunged forward, slicing with his longer blade
and cutting through Fenzig's tunic. The blade sliced skin, too,
and a thin red line formed on the gnome's chest. The wound
was not serious, but it stung, and it distracted the gnome, who
did not bring his own sword up fast enough to parry the king's
next thrust.

This time Erlgrane struck at Fenzig's hand, meaning to
disarm the gnome. Instead, the blade crashed into the pommel
of the sword just above the gnome's fingers, and pieces of ivory
flew this way and that. Stunned, Fenzig dropped the blade, then
cringed as Erlgrane stepped on it.

"You're no fighter." The king's voice was even and tinged
with sarcasm. "You're a common scoundrel who had no business getting involved in any of this. Stand still, and I'll make it
quick. Just like I made. . . ."

Erlgrane didn't finish his tirade, instead raised his blade high
above his head. The last rays of the sun caught the metal and
made it glow as if it were newly forged.

"No!" the gnome bellowed. He pushed off with his feet and
threw himself at Erlgrane. The impact startled the monarch,
and he stepped backward but did not fall. Fenzig, however, fell.

He dropped to the grass and snatched up his now-free short sword. He rolled to the right as the king's blade flashed and came down—the tip landing into the earth inches from where the gnome had been, a heartbeat before.

Fenzig continued rolling, then sprang to his feet when he'd gotten some breathing room between himself and the king. In the distance he heard shouts, and he prayed the duke's guards realized something was wrong.

Will they get here before Erlgrane finishes me though? the gnome wondered. He sprang to his left, avoiding another thrust, then he pivoted and danced around behind the enraged monarch.

That forced Erlgrane to turn, and Fenzig took advantage of the few seconds he'd won by darting in and slashing at the king's legs. The gnome's first blow was ineffectual, but the second sliced into the king's thigh and brought a howl of rage and pain from the monarch's lips.

"Insolent dog," Erlgrane cried. "I'll have your head." The king heaved back and swung his sword in a quick and deadly arc.

Fenzig dropped to his rump and watched as the blade cut through the air several inches above him, then he thrust his own weapon upward, meeting resistance as it sank deeply into the king's undamaged thigh.

The gnome suspected he'd cut the monarch to the bone and cringed as the king fell backward, the short sword still lodged in his leg. Fenzig grabbed the king's sword and tossed it out of Erlgrane's reach. The gnome couldn't decide if he should pull the short sword free, or if that might hurt the king even worse.

Instead, Fenzig hovered over the monarch, yanking off the gold necklace he wore, tugging off his ruby signet ring, unlatching the bracers—anything that might identify Erlgrane as royalty—and stuffing all of them into his pockets. King Erlgrane only rocked back and forth on the ground and continued to howl. The gnome tossed dirt on him to soil his garments.

"I have another wizard, wee-one," he cursed. "He will retrieve me—I guarantee it. I will not be so easily undone. I will have what I want. And I will have you and Rehmir and all his daughters dead. Already I have made you pay for your insolence. All I need do now is finish my work! Everything is in motion! I will not be undone!"

The monarch was still howling when the guards arrived—led by Carmella atop her Carmen the Magnificent wagon. She was the first to the gnome's side, and she fussed over the bleeding cut across his chest.

"I'll live," Fenzig said, but he groaned and swooned a little for the added attention.

"So will this fellow," one of the guards observed. He pulled the short sword from Erlgrane's leg, and the king screamed even louder. "But he'll need a poultice and some rest—and right away. Was this scoundrel trying to rob you, Sir Fenzig?"

Sir Fenzig? I like that, the gnome thought.

The king moaned something barely intelligible, and the gnome and Carmella exchanged quick glances. She nodded almost imperceptibly to the gnome.

"Why, indeed he was trying to rob me!" Fenzig said sternly. "And aside from being a thief, the poor fellow is quite mad. Claims these lands are his, and that he's a king somewhere. But he doesn't look very kingly. He looks like a common ruffian who stole someone's chainmail." The gnome tossed the king's jewels in the back of Carmella's wagons.

The guards laughed as they none too carefully picked up Erlgrane and placed him over the back of the largest horse.

"Then we'll throw the thief in the duke's dungeon and have the attendants minister to him there!" the guard announced.

"Good," Carmella replied. "Make sure he stays in the dungeon a very, very long time. And be sure to have my father look in on him later today, would you?"

"Yes, ma'am," the guard said, nodding to her.

The guards headed back to Duke Rehmir's manor, and Fenzig and Carmella grinned broadly.

"Are you sure you don't want someone to look at that? Put a poultice on it?" Carmella asked, once again examining the oozing wound on Fenzig's chest.

Fenzig shook his head. "I don't want to be near another king or duke or castle or palace for quite some time. I'm looking forward to a nice, cozy burrow where I can mend on my own."

"No more traveling?" Carmella's eyes sparkled in the fast-waning light. "I told my father just a short time ago that I had a couple more places to visit before I could come back here and make any attempt at putting down roots."

The gnome's curiosity was piqued. "Where are you going?"

"West," she stated as she squared her shoulders. "There are a few towns over in that direction that have never heard of Carmen the Magnificent, and they don't know what they're missing. Want to come with me?"

Fenzig groaned. "I vowed to go straight. I promised myself: no more stealing, no more conniving. I'm going to be an honest gnome."

"Pity," she said as she helped him up, dusted him off, and handed him the short sword. "The pommel's cracked."

"King Erlgrane did it," the gnome said, "but better a split pommel than a broken wrist."

Carmella tousled his hair. "Yeah, I'd rather see you intact than in pieces, too. Well, I'd better be off. I've a lot of miles to cover, and I want to be well past K'Nosha before the stars come out." She climbed up on the wagon and winked at Fenzig.

"Think there's a weaponsmith in one of those towns you're going to?" he asked. "Someone who could fix this sword?"

"I'm sure of it," Carmella said. "Maybe he'd even trade the

labor for a bottle of Carmen's Cure-All." She hied the horses into an easy gait.

As Fenzig urged his pony alongside the wagon, he looked up at Carmella and sighed. Who was he to argue with fate? "I have a better idea," he said. "Back in Graespeck there are all sorts of recipes for stomachache cures, headache remedies, and the like. We could stop there, get the recipes, then head west. I'll bet the potions would work on humans just as well as they work on gnomes. And they do work. . . . Well, most of them do, anyway."

"They just might do the trick at that," she said, laughing. "Think somebody in Graespeck would show me how to brew them?"

"Definitely," Fenzig answered.

"Of course, I'd have to add a few touches of my own to give them color."

Without saying another word, Carmella angled the wagon toward burrow town. The gnome broke into a broad grin and hurried Summer to catch up.

GRAESPECK REVISITED

"You've been awfully quiet for the past forty or so miles."

"Just thinking," the gnome said.

"Aren't you happy? You should be happy. At least a little happy," Carmella prompted. "The king's in my father's dungeon, we're free of the concerns of any nobility, and you just finished the rest of our sugared dates, which definitely should have made you happy. Besides, we'll be visiting your people right before suppertime—with an empty wagon. That's what you wanted, isn't it?"

"It's not entirely empty," Fenzig returned. "My stomach or the wagon."

"Well, we don't have any of my concoctions left to sell."

The gnome made a face and shook his head.

"All right, all right," she huffed. "My concoctions are *almost* gone. So I've really got nothing to sell your gnome friends."

Fenzig poked out his bottom lip and met her stare.

"Nothing much anyway. Look, Fenzighan, all we have left are just a few jars of hand cream—which never hurt anybody as far as I know. And I made a special point to save a couple of vials of my wild roses cologne—which I bought, I didn't make. I couldn't have *completely nothing* to sell to your people now, could I? Remember that cute little gnome lady who bought my lilac cologne? She was so happy. I couldn't disappoint her."

"Sure you could. Right this very minute you're disappointing those folks who bought your . . . your. . . ."

"Toothache eraser?"

He nodded.

"Hair-growth tonic?"

He nodded again and frowned.

"Don't be so glum, Fenzighan. After all, we unloaded practically everything on those two villages. Made a healthy profit, too. You weren't so glum when you were looking at all the gold pieces. Didn't take us far out of the way, either, only a two-day side trip. Pleasant countryside. Pleasant weather."

"It was at that," the gnome admitted, brightening a little. *And pleasant company,* he added to himself.

"Besides, I thought you said you were happy that I'm going to try a fresh start—selling those gnomish formulas you mentioned instead of my mixtures. And if I'm really making a fresh start, I might as well do it by getting rid of. . . ."

"Your tummy-soother, worry-reliever, and the rest of it?"

"Exactly," she said smugly.

Fenzig offered her a slight grin and took a turn at the reins. "Yeah, I thought making an honest living for a change might be a good idea for the both of us. Making a dishonest one certainly got me in a fix. But I didn't mean for you to start over by selling those . . . those. . . ." Fenzig again found himself at an uncustomary loss for words.

"Carmen's Cure-All? Headache-be-gone? Gray-away?"

"Yeah, what you call cure-alls and what-not, all the stuff in the wagon. I didn't mean for you to sell that stuff to some poor, unsuspecting souls who'll be itching for days, who won't grow the hair you promised, and who will still have sore throats long after the syrup you sold them is gone."

"They'll get over their sore throats sooner or later anyway," Carmella giggled. "And if you're so upset about it, then why'd you help me?"

"Weak moment."

She jingled her coin purse. "Once a thief, always a thief, dear Fenzighan. But we'll try these gnomish formulas, provided the good folk of Graespeck will reveal their secret recipes."

"They'll reveal their secrets. Most gnomes don't keep anything secret for long. Just don't sell them anything. No hand cream. No cologne. No nothing."

"All right." She reached over and ruffled his hair. "But I've got all these wonderful, garish costumes in the back of the wagon. So don't hate me if after a while I go back to my old ways."

I don't think I could ever hate you, Fenzig thought. *You saved my life, and I'll never forget that. I owe you.*

"Thanks," she answered. "But you don't owe me anything."

The gnome glowered at her, realized she was wearing her necklace that let her read others' thoughts, hadn't taken it off after her last sales pitch, but had been on her guard enough not to. . . .

"Answer your thoughts until now," she finished for him. "I slipped up. Sorry. Force of habit. I'm used to listening in. Happy now?" She put the necklace in her pocket and set her hand on his shoulder.

Carmella listened to Fenzig's tales of growing up in Graespeck as the miles disappeared. It was far different than her life, though she and Fenzig both were raised by their fathers. She was pampered, taught all the important social graces—how to walk, sit, which eating utensils to use for which course, how to read, how to dance, how to hold a tea cup in a ladylike manner. But she was always in her older sisters' shadows—because she was young, because she wasn't quite as attentive or practiced as they, and because she was a bit of a scoundrel. And she always felt smothered, yearning for the more colorful life she knew could be had beyond the boundaries of her father's estate. Life was indeed more colorful outside his high, stone walls, she'd learned. And she was looking forward to seeing the colorful gnomish people in Graespeck again.

"No." Fenzig tugged on the reins, signaling the horses to stop.

"Now what are you worried about?" she huffed. "What could. . . ." Her words trailed off as she spotted what the gnome was staring at—a broken sign.

It was the small wooden sign proclaiming that Graespeck was just around the turn in the road. It was split in two and spattered with red paint. Fenzig slipped down from the wagon and hurried to pick up the pieces.

"It's just a sign, don't be so upset. A red wagon probably hit it."

"It's not paint. It's blood," Fenzig said, glancing down the road. Then he took off running, his stumpy legs pounding toward the village.

Carmella urged the horses along, careful not to let them trample the gnome.

"Gods!" Fenzig cried when he stopped in his tracks.

It was all Carmella could do to stop the horses in time so they wouldn't run over him. She jumped from the wagon and in a heartbeat was at his side, was looking out over what was left of the gnome village.

What had been dozens upon dozens of mounds of earth—all with polished walnut doors set into them and woven grass welcome mats out front—was now flattened ground. The dirt was practically level, as if men with plows and oxen had worked the homes into farmland. Colorful, lacy curtains were caught in low-hanging tree branches. Vegetable and flower gardens had been shredded. Animal pens were open, the livestock long gone. The only intact burrow-homes were a pair of businesses at the far end of what was once Graespeck. One had been a smelter with a lean-to behind it, though there wasn't a lot of the lean-to remaining. The other had an anvil and forge, along with the trappings for making horseshoes.

"Gods," Fenzig whispered. "What happened?" The gnome stood unmoving for several minutes. "What could have leveled a town?"

"Magic, maybe," Carmella said numbly as she padded by him, went to the nearest home. At her feet was a polished walnut door with deep scratches in it. She knelt and sifted through the ruins, heard him call for his father behind her, silently prayed he would get a response. But his voice was the only one she heard.

She continued to dig, looking for sigils and glyphs, magical markings that might indicate what spells were used to destroy the gnome town. The type of spells might point a finger at the wizard.

Nothing. No clue. No response to Fenzig's shouts.

"Nothing!" she hissed, furiously digging now, searching the furniture fragments she came across. Everything was broken, nothing carried a sigil or any other kind of magical mark.

Fenzig continued to call for his father, was running from flattened mound to flattened mound, searching for a trace of him. The gnome's calls were more frantic now, coming raggedly as he was losing his breath.

Carmella stopped to watch him as he moved to the next flattened mound. There was practically nothing left to distinguish one family's home from its neighbor's. The little things that had made each burrow different, and which had thoroughly delighted Carmella, were scattered everywhere—flower boxes, lantern posts, wooden trim, life-size animal carvings—and were all broken. She surmised Fenzig only knew which home had been his father's because of the flattened mound's position in the village and because there were a few more pieces of broken wood around it.

"Father!"

"Fenzig, stop," she said, pushing herself up and joining him. He was tearing savagely at the earth, sobbing and cursing. And for once she was glad she didn't have her necklace on to eavesdrop on his thoughts. "He's not here, Fenzighan. No one's here."

"You can't know that!" he spat, as he continued to dig. "He might be trapped under the dirt. Everyone might be trapped!"

"No one could be alive under that," she said sadly.

"You can't know that, either!"

"Yes, I can." She stepped back, toward what she guessed was the center of the village, and planted her feet wide apart. Then she closed her eyes and started swaying, started mumbling words that didn't come from the human tongue and that sounded vaguely musical.

Fenzig paused and turned to watch her, fell on his rump and wiped at his tears with a dirty hand. "What are you doing?"

"Searching for life," she whispered. "Remember? It's one of the few spells I told you I had mastered. Shhh. Let me finish."

The gnome thought he saw the air sparkle around her face, thought he spotted those sparkles, like pale fireflies, dart away and flit across the flattened mounds of earth. He tried to follow the miniature lights, but the sun was still up, making it difficult for him to see them. There! He finally caught one in his gaze, followed it, watched it return to her, then melt into her face.

She gasped and opened her eyes. "No one alive in these homes," she said, gesturing at the flattened mounds. "But there's someone—or something—in there." She pointed toward the far end of what had been Graespeck, indicating the blacksmith's place.

Fenzig leapt to his feet and ran toward the building.

"Fenzig, wait! You don't know what's in there. Maybe a wizard. Maybe. . . ."

The gnome disappeared inside, and a scream cut through the air.

Carmella ran headlong toward the small building, gulping in air as she went. Working the life-searching spell, which she sometimes used on the road to determine in which direction the larger village might be, had exhausted her. "Fenzig!"

She dropped to her knees and scampered inside, blinked to make her eyes adjust to the darkness. Fenzig was standing in front of an old gnome, one covered with dried blood and dirt. The old one was gibbering, rocking back and forth and looking furtively between Fenzig and Carmella, babbling gnomish words.

"He's terrified," Fenzig said. "He doesn't recognize me, screamed when he first saw me. I asked him what happened, but he just spouts gibberish."

"Translate the gibberish for me," she urged. "Maybe I can make some sense of it."

Fenzig shook his head. "There's no sense to it. He just says the darkness swallowed this place."

"My necklace!" Carmella reached inside her pocket, and was about to put it over her head when Fenzig's small fingers stopped her. "But I could read his mind. Learn more."

Fenzig tugged at the necklace. "He's one of my people. If anyone's going to look inside his head, it should be me."

Carmella didn't argue, relinquished her mother's necklace, sat back against an earthen wall, and waited. She watched Fenzig cautiously approach the old gnome, sit across from him and try futilely to calm him.

Fenzig was speaking in the gnome language, fingering the necklace and asking the old one what happened to the village and to the people. He translated most of his questions to Carmella, and then translated what he found in the other gnome's mind.

"All he thinks about are people running. *My* people running into the woods. He couldn't run, wasn't fast enough to escape what he calls the 'smothering blackness.' So he hid in here, waiting for the blackness to swallow this burrow and him with it. But it didn't come." Fenzig backed away and groaned. "He's mad, Carmella. His thoughts are like a whirlwind. There's no way to find out what happened here—at least not from him."

Fenzig brushed by her and went outside. After a few moments she followed.

"I've got to look for my father, Carmella, and the rest of the people." He pointed a stubby arm toward the woods in the distance. "That's where they went—if anything of what he was thinking is correct. I need to see if they're all right. If my father's okay. But I just wish. . . ."

"That you knew what did this," she finished—without benefit of the necklace.

He nodded.

"Listen, I'm not much of a wizard, Fenzighan. I'm better at breaking down other people's spells than I am at making my own. But I do know a few."

"Like your firefly spell that finds people?"

"Yeah. That's a rather simple one. This one, the one that would let me know what people had for breakfast yesterday, is a lot more complicated, but works on the same principle. Maybe I can remember how it goes. Wait here with me, please." She sat with her back against the blacksmith burrow, splayed her fingers on the ground to either side of her, then dug her fingertips into the earth.

Fenzig watched her, torn between chasing after his people and seeing if she might be able to learn what happened here.

The foreign words starting tumbling from her mouth again, and, in the shadow cast from the mound, the gnome saw the pale firefly lights form about her head again. The glow intensified, and the lights began to dance down her neck, across her chest, then down her arms and into her fingertips.

With the magical necklace, Fenzig was picking up her thoughts, though he didn't understand them. They were filled with words that meant nothing, concepts that seemed far beyond his comprehension. "The earth," was all he could pick up, but he concentrated harder, hoping something that was going through her mind might make sense to him. He concentrated harder, and in that instant he was overwhelmed with images.

Graespeck was alive. The burrows were intact, the residents were milling about tending gardens, cooking, gossiping over clotheslines, going about their daily business. The sun was sinking in the sky, signaling dinnertime.

Fenzig smelled the aroma of fresh-baked raisin bread, picked up the scent of a roast pig that must be turning on a spit just out of sight. And there was a trace of honey-glazed peaches in the air. He was at the blacksmith shop, his back to it, and he was facing out onto the village, just as Carmella was. He couldn't move or talk, was like a fly on the wall observing what was transpiring.

Must be what Carmella is seeing and thinking with her spell, he thought. *But I don't understand. Everything looks normal. Wait, there's my father!*

Fenzig's father dragged a newly made bench down the center of town, toward Apple-Pie Annie's, who must have commissioned it from him—and whom no doubt intended to pay for it with apple pies. The woodworker was whistling a tune, paused outside a window to sniff the bread. Then he resumed his course for a few yards before he suddenly released the bench and spun to look at the western edge of the village. There, highlighted by the orange sky, were dark shapes, six-legged creatures that were slowly, but methodically, approaching.

The other gnomes outside spotted the beasts, too. Some

stood, curious, while the older and more practical ones ran for weapons and things that would function as weapons. Fenzig's father tugged a wicked-looking woodworking tool free from his belt and started toward the west.

"What are they?" Fenzig heard Apple-Pie Annie holler. The grizzled woman was peaking around the edge of a burrow and squinting into the setting sun. "Panthers?" She had keen eyes—at least she did while Fenzig lived here. "They look like panthers!"

Not panthers. Craven cats. Fenzig felt his mouth drop open in horror, heard himself holler for his father and the others, instantly realized his words weren't part of this scene. For the briefest moment, he considered taking off Carmella's necklace, blotting out what was happening. *No,* he told himself. *I have to see.*

The cats slunk forward, unafraid of the gathering throng of villagers. Eight, Fenzig counted. Eight craven cats. *What would they be doing here? The beasts were only known to be in the Haunted Woods, weren't they?* "And in a laboratory deep in King Erlgrane's castle," he whispered.

The lead beast snarled, and its six legs started churning over the ground as it neared Graespeck. The others followed, all snarling, acidic saliva spattering the ground. One of the gnomes rushed forward to meet the cats' charge. Fenzig didn't recognize the young man, who must have joined the village in the past seven years since he'd been gone.

The young gnome swung a club, bashed it into the lead cat's side. The cat snarled, and its twin tails snapped at him as it went by. The cats following were more vicious. Two threw themselves upon the gnome and tore into his flesh. Fenzig tried to blot out the sounds of the cats snarling and the young man screaming. Then the air was filled with a myriad of screams.

Only a handful of gnomes, including Fenzig's father, stood

their ground. The rest were running to the southeast, toward the forest.

Fight them! Fenzig screamed in his mind. *There are only eight. There are dozens of you! Fight them!*

The gnomes rushed past him, not seeing him, as he truly wasn't there. Running headlong out of the village, they continued to cry in terror. And through the press of their bodies, which Fenzig could only imagine feeling, he spied more cats. *Nine, ten,* he counted. *Gods! There are well more than a dozen.*

The beasts' snarls rose to a horrible cacophony of sound, and even the few gnomes who tried to fight the initial charge fled. Ferret saw his father, stout legs churning across the road that ran down the center of the village, and spotted the old man who was in the building behind him. The old gnome was laboring, clutching his side and falling farther and farther behind the rest of the villagers, and no one was stopping to help him. He fell to his knees and started crawling frantically, seeking shelter in the blacksmith's home while the craven cats chased all the gnomes away.

The largest of the beasts pulled some of the lagging gnomes down, quickly silencing their screams by ripping into their small bodies. Fenzig shut his eyes, but still the scene persisted in his mind because of the necklace and because he was still locked into Carmella's thoughts. Eight, nine people dead that he could see, maybe more beyond the edge of the village. His father?

Then the craven cats turned their attention to the burrow-homes. There were eighteen of the beasts now, Fenzig counted, and they were methodically tearing at the dirt with their three pairs of claws. Acid wore away the doors and shutters, acid-dripping tails ruined carefully tended gardens, destroyed lifetimes of work and memories.

In the span of several moments, the entire gruesome scene

played itself out. The sky darkened and still the cats tore at the homes. The stars illuminated their fiendish work, then the stars faded and the sky started to lighten. Hours upon hours it had taken the creatures to level the village. Hours, and . . . one of the cats' ears pricked up. The beast snarled and started toward the far end of Graespeck—where only two buildings remained. The rest of the pack started following, and Fenzig knew they were intent on these buildings, were going to flatten these, also, were going to find the mad old man inside.

But why were the buildings still here now? he wondered. *Why is the old man alive? What happened?*

He watched the cats approach him, though he knew they weren't really slinking toward him, but the building that existed behind him two days ago. In morbid fascination he noted their rippling muscles, admired their graceful forms. *Why are they here? And why didn't they ruin these buildings? Why?*

Within a heartbeat it was clear to him. The first rays of the morning sun stretched out from the east. The cats stopped, almost as one, glanced at the horizon, then bolted to the north, toward the Haunted Woods.

"Just like they left me when I was in the woods. They don't like the light of day," Fenzig mused.

"Monsters." It was Carmella's voice.

The scene melted away, leaving an orange glow from this day's sunset painting the carnage.

"Our two-day side trip," Fenzig said. He dropped to her side and shook his head. "If we hadn't sold those concoctions in the villages. . . ."

"We'd have been here," Carmella finished. "We would have died, like some of your people, or have been driven off."

"But you're a wizard. You could have. . . ."

"Done nothing. My spells are not powerful. I can't create balls of flame or strokes of lightning. I can't bring down magical hailstones or turn an acre of earth to air. I couldn't have done anything to stop even one of those monsters, my friend. I can undo other spells, find out where people are, where they've been. That's it. I'm sorry."

The gnome looked at her. She was telling him the truth, the necklace he wore revealed that. And he knew that she was right. If they'd been here, they would have fled, or more likely died.

The peddler's face was sweat-streaked, her short, black hair was plastered against her head, and her breath came raggedly. The spell had taken a lot out of her. Fenzig helped her stand.

"Let's find my father," he said.

She nodded and followed along. Normally, the gnome would have had trouble keeping up with her long legs. Now, fatigued from her magic, it was the other way around.

"Wonder why the monsters would attack your village?" she huffed.

"They're called craven cats, but I'll agree with you that they are monsters. I used to think they were only in the Haunted Woods."

"So I wonder what provoked them to come here?"

"Erlgrane's wizard."

She reached forward to stop him.

"Impossible," she huffed.

"No, not at all impossible. When I was in that cage in his laboratory, I saw two craven cats dangling from the ceiling. Erlgrane's wizard made the craven cats, from people, I think. And if he could make them, he could control them, send them here."

"That's not what I mean. Fenzighan, this attack happened two days ago. The wizard died many days before that—in my father's study. And he couldn't have summoned these cats before he died. He was with us—in your pocket, barely alive."

Fenzig shrugged and resumed his trek toward the woods. "All

right. So it wasn't the old wizard. But it was some wizard, one of Erlgrane's lesser wizards. I recall what Erlgrane said to me when we were fighting at the edge of your father's estate.

"I have another wizard, wee-one," Fenzig remembered the king saying. *"He will retrieve me—I guarantee it. I will not be so easily undone. I will have what I want. And I will have you and Rehmir and all his daughters dead. Already I have made you pay for your insolence. All I need do now is finish my work!"*

"The king arranged this," the gnome said sadly. "He told me as much."

Carmella pursed her lips. "If that's true, then how?"

"He said he had another wizard. A powerful king can have all manner of wizards, I suppose. Doesn't matter who he has in Burlengren. I intend to go back to his castle and find a way to deal with them." The gnome continued marching toward the forest, shutting out Carmella's argumentative thoughts, and ignoring the dried pools of blood on the ground, where he knew the craven cats had brought down and devoured some of the gnomes. Tired, he forced himself to walk as fast as he could manage and thrust, to the back of his mind, the sensations from his aching chest and feet. He didn't want to be caught in the woods—any woods—after dark again. He wanted to find the rest of his people and. . . .

"And then what?" he muttered aloud. "Then what'll I do with them? There's no more Graespeck." He heard Carmella struggling to keep up behind him, considered slowing down to accommodate her, and then thought better of it. The sun was halfway swallowed by the horizon. He didn't have much light left.

"Father!" Fenzig cried as he neared the treeline. "Father!" He called other names, too, the names of gnomes he recognized from his recent trip to town with Carmella. He hollered until he was hoarse, until he wore himself out enough that the peddler finally caught up.

"Fenzighan," she huffed, as she tugged on his sleeve and sagged against a tree. "I can find life, remember?" She slid down the trunk, grimacing when she heard her shirt snag against the bark. "Just give me a moment."

The gnome did, grateful for the brief rest. He sat next to her, watching her hands, spotting the firefly lights around her face now that it was darker. They danced about her head for the briefest of moments, then flitted off into the embrace of the trees. He lost sight of them. It seemed like an eternity, this waiting, though the gnome suspected only minutes passed. The shadows hadn't gotten a chance to get thicker before the lights returned and melted into the smooth skin of Carmella's face.

"There's a spring, about a half-mile or a mile deeper into the woods," she said, weakly gesturing with her hand. "That way." Her breath was even more ragged than before, the continued use of her limited magic taking a toll on her. "There's plenty of life there, not animals, too strong I think. Lots of life. Gotta be your people. Not much of a wizard. Sorry, Fenzighan."

"Thanks, Carmella. I. . . ." The gnome studied her face. Her eyes were closed, and her head sagged on her shoulder. She'd fallen asleep from the exertion. Fenzig quietly got up and relied on his thiefly skills to move silently so she could rest. He briefly worried about craven cats. If they came, Carmella would be a quick meal, alone and unprepared. But if they came, Fenzig knew it would be only minutes later before he became dessert.

"Father!" It was twilight by the time Fenzig found the spring and the gathering of gnomes around it. The small cookfires the gnomes had burning led him here—either Carmella's gesture was a bit in the wrong direction, or his feet had led him a little off course.

The elder gnome hugged his son, began talking about the

craven cats, about being not able to stand up to the beasts. Fenzig didn't stop his father, though he knew exactly what had happened because of Carmella's spell and had even witnessed some of the atrocities that happened as his father was fleeing. Other gnome voices buzzed around him: Apple-Pie Annie, Alicia, Leonard Smithsward, Nura, and more. To complicate matters, he was picking up so many of their thoughts with the necklace he'd forgotten to return to Carmella, that he was getting a terrible headache. Extricating himself from his father's embrace, Fenzig plucked the necklace off and stuck it in his beltpouch. *She must know how to use this so she only hears one person at a time,* he thought.

"Father, it's dark. We've got to get out of here," Fenzig said. "I've a friend at the edge of the woods."

"That peddler?"

"Yes! She helped me find you. I don't want to leave her alone. I can't. It's possible the craven cats could. . . ."

"Come back. Yes, we all know that. We won't run this time."

"Not that it would do any good," Apple-Pie Annie grumbled. "We're no match for the beasts."

Fenzig tugged on his father's sleeve. "All of you, c'mon!"

"Where are we going?" his father asked softly. "We've nothing to go home to."

In the end, a rested Carmella was able to convince the Graespeck gnomes that K'Nosha was the place to go. But she hadn't yet convinced Fenzig.

"Fenzighan, don't be a fool!" she lectured. "You can't go to Erlgrane's castle."

"I intend to do something about those other wizards, make them pay," the young gnome fumed. "Settle things."

"Oh, do you? And how will you do that? By ending up in the dungeon again? The last two times you broke into the castle you were caught."

"We were trying to get caught, remember?"

"We would've been caught even if we hadn't tried. You're a thief, not a hero!" She paced in front of him, balled her fists, then spun to face him. For emphasis, she bent over until she was nose-to-nose with him. "I'm not about to lose my best friend because he hasn't the sense of a common ground squirrel. Even though Erlgrane's rotting in my father's dungeon, there are guards in his castle, wizards probably, people who don't know their king's a prisoner. What are you going to tell them, Fenzighan? The king won't be coming back? Don't hurt the gnomes or anyone else anymore? That'd be smart. You'd start all sorts of power struggles. Maybe there'll be fights to see who the next king is. Maybe the guards and wizards will scheme and try to get Erlgrane back. And you'd start it all."

"Best friend, really?"

"You'd be an idiot to go to that castle. We'd be far better off to go back to my father's estate. We need to warn him about the band of craven cats, Erlgrane's lesser wizard. I might not always agree with my father," she continued to fume. "But he's wise, and he'll know what to do. Maybe we can use Erlgrane for leverage. Did you think of that? Get his people to cooperate if they know he's our prisoner. Then we might have a nice, peaceful, safe way at our fingertips to deal with whoever and whatever's left in the king's castle."

"Best friend?"

Carmella nodded.

"That's nice. I'm not sure I've been a best friend before." Fenzig seemed insatiably pleased with himself, temporarily forgetting that they stood in a demolished gnome village with the stars winking into view overhead. "All right. K'Nosha for all of us. But it's gonna take a lot longer to get there," he said, indicating the throng of displaced gnomes.

Early morning found Apple-Pie Annie and Leonard Smithsward perched on top of the Carmen the Magnificent wagon, with Carmella and Fenzig taking turns at the reins. A half-dozen other gnomes, including the mad old man from the blacksmith's, were squeezed inside, and a couple hung from the back. Fenzig's father proudly rode Summer. The rest of the Graespeck residents walked in front, to the sides, and behind the garish wagon, all of them chattering—about the wagon, Carmella, Fenzig, and the craven cats.

It took the entourage of one human, two horses, and one hundred and sixteen gnomes seven days to reach K'Nosha—the garish wagon was prudently hidden outside of town. And it took a little less than one day for Carmella to call upon the kindness of the citizens and encourage them to take the gnomes into their homes for a while.

Apple-Pie Annie, the appointed gnome spokesman, retold the craven cat attack in great detail and made it clear the Graespeck gnomes intended to return to their village and rebuild it, and that the K'Noshans' charity would be repaid as soon as possible.

Fenzig was quick to interject his speculation that King Erlgrane was behind the attack.

And Carmella added she wanted to make sure the gnomes would be safe—that everyone in K'Nosha would be safe from the influence of King Erlgrane's magical and human forces. When she could guarantee that safety, she said she'd have someone personally lead the gnomes home.

"Duke Rehmir will deal with Erlgrane's forces," she finished, noting with satisfaction that the crowd of humans and gnomes were hanging on her every word. "My father will not let that foul man's tyranny spread to K'Nosha and the Northern

Reaches. My father will enforce the peace we've come to love!"

Amid the cheering, Carmella and Fenzig slipped away from the crowd. "Now to tell my father about all this in person," she whispered. "He's not one for surprises."

"When's dinner?" Apple-Pie Annie's voice cut through the air behind them.

An Affair of State

"The day after tomorrow, Carmella."

"But, Father . . . why not tomorrow morning? Why not now? Armies can travel at night. *Do* travel at night. The men could. . . ."

Duke Rehmir gently held his youngest daughter's hands. "I intend to do something, Carmella. I intend to do the very thing you suggest. In fact, I've already taken the necessary steps—and that was without knowing about the gnomes and Graespeck and those horrible craving cats. . . ."

"Craven cats," Fenzig quietly corrected.

"In the days since you've been gone, Carmella, I've increased the number of my troops by a third. The general has recruited young men from K'Nosha and from the Northern Kingdoms. They flocked to my banner when there was even the slightest suggestion they'd see some action. I fully plan to march them . . . peacefully I hope . . . into Burlengren, right to Erlgrane's castle. My general hopes to *peacefully* come to terms with the men at Erlgrane's estate, give them evidence that we hold their king and give them an opportunity to walk away or join us. Erlgrane has no heirs, only distant relatives, and if I do not try to absorb the land into my own holdings, take over the entire area, there could be a civil war in Burlengren. And any war there could adversely affect us and all of the people of K'Nosha and farther north."

"Set yourself up as the king? Of the entire area?" Fenzig

asked. "Is that really such a good idea? I mean, I know somebody has to do something about the wizards and the craven cats. But wouldn't you be happier just tackling the whole affair while just staying a duke? Less worry, less responsibility. Let someone else take over Burlengren."

Duke Rehmir seemed not to hear him, continued to talk above Fenzig's softer gnomish voice. "Carmella, I will hope with all of my heart that my soldiers' presence won't start a war. But just in case, I'll make sure the general has enough men with him to quash any resistance."

"But the wizards, Father. . . ."

"The general will have plenty of men, Carmella, plenty. And the general is more than capable of resolving matters—peacefully or otherwise."

She relaxed a little, squeezed his hands, and glanced down to offer Fenzig a smile. "Then why wait, Father? Why not head them out tonight? You'd be a far better king for Burlengren and the southern lands, the entire area, than whoever could possibly arise out of Erlgrane's castle. King Rehmir. I like the sound of that, I think. Why not start everything moving now?"

"You think he should be a king, too?" Fenzig asked Carmella. But she was caught up in her father and the moment and didn't hear the gnome.

The duke sighed and shook his head, released her hands, and gestured for her and Fenzig to join him and his three other daughters, who were already seated in the dining room. "Not now, Carmella. The day after tomorrow. You see, also in the days since you've been gone, I've been planning a gala event. I need to celebrate the return of Elayne, Berthrice, and Ruthe. I want the town to know they are here and well, end all the speculation of where they've been these past five years. I *need* to do this, to tell them all the truth."

"The horrid rumor circulating in K'Nosha was that we'd all

eloped with common men in the Northern Reaches," Berthrice said. She looked down her long nose at the gnome as he settled down to the dinner table. "A simply horrid rumor. Barbaric. Can you imagine, eloping with unlanded men?"

"That was only *one* of the rumors," Elayne added. "Some people thought we'd locked ourselves away in here, thinking those outside the estate were too good for us. Father hadn't told anyone about . . . about. . . ." The words were hard for her, and she drew her rose-tinted lips together and met Fenzig's stare. "Father never told anyone beyond the estate that we had been turned into gems."

"I couldn't. If I had revealed that news to anyone," Duke Rehmir interjected, "they would have thought me mad. I needed to keep peace in my lands, and I had no proof what Erlgrane's wizard did. The wizard and king were too crafty. I always feared that wizard. Now I can tell everyone what he did. And what Erlgrane was up to."

Ruthe nodded. "You did the right thing, Father, keeping things quiet until now."

"So now you're throwing a party," Carmella said, a touch of sarcasm in her voice. "That's surely the right thing to do. Wonderful."

"Ah, indeed it will be wonderful. There'll be an orchestra. Nobles from the north, businessmen and landholders from town, a few of the richest and most influential men from Burlengren. The cooks have dreamed up a magnificent feast. It has been so very long since I've had a reason to celebrate."

"The gnomes of Graespeck have nothing to celebrate," Fenzig muttered half under his breath.

Duke Rehmir finally acknowledged the gnome and scowled. "To cancel the gala event now would be to invite more rumor, and word might reach Burlengren that something is truly up, alerting the men at Erlgrane's castle. We can't have that."

"You don't think marching a bunch of soldiers to Burlengren the day after tomorrow isn't going to alert someone?" Fenzig quipped. "Don't you think Erlgrane's men are already on their guard? You've had their king locked up for two weeks. Even if they don't know you have him, which I suspect they do, they have to know he's somewhere, that something's up. His old wizard is gone, too. Dead. Don't you think they'll be ready for something regardless of what day your men go? So why wait? Maybe there're already power struggles going on with all Erlgrane's shirttail relatives."

"He has to wait." Berthrice glared at the gnome, drew herself up, and squared her narrow shoulders. "To cancel the party, little Fenzig, dear Carmella, would be foolish. Everything has been planned. We have new gowns."

"The general will march the very next morning," the duke said, ending the discussion. "And Carmella and Fenzig, you will be the gala's honored guests." He clapped his hands, and the servants brought out steaming bowls of sweet potatoes, noodles, and smoked turkey.

The conversation meandered to the topic of the Graespeck gnomes, as Carmella regaled her sisters and father with the details of what her magical spell revealed in the leveled village. Berthrice seemed to lose her appetite when Carmella described the craven cats and the several gnomes who were killed, and quickly switched the subject to fabrics and dyed lace. However, by the time desert came, the duke's youngest daughter again commanded the conversation and explained about placing the homeless gnomes with the good folk of K'Nosha.

Mmmm, apple pie! Fenzig thought. He didn't need to listen to Carmella's account—he'd been there and knew exactly what had happened, and he could care less about lace and fabrics, colors and textures. Fenzig was quick to dig in and grab two pieces of pie, noting with pleasure that the cooks hadn't skimped on the brown sugar and cinnamon. But with every bite, he hoped the Graespeck gnomes were being fed well, too. And with every swallow he hoped Duke Rehmir was doing the right thing by planning the "peaceful or otherwise" takeover of Erlgrane's lands. King Rehmir. The gnome wasn't sure he liked the sound of that.

The orchestra started practicing midmorning. After Fenzig's second breakfast, he strolled into the smaller of Duke Rehmir's ballrooms to listen to them. It sounded pleasant enough, especially the flutes. But it was human music, and it therefore lacked all the intricacies, harmonies, and the exacting syncopation of gnome compositions. It just wasn't very interesting. He'd been told that the orchestra would be performing in the largest ballroom tonight, where the acoustics were better. But they couldn't practice there now since the room was being decorated. This smaller ballroom would soon be set up with tables, where tonight's feast would be served. Fenzig idly wondered what was on the menu.

Between breakfasts—Fenzig knew to eat two breakfasts, as lunch would be scant because the cooks would be working on the gala's feast the rest of the day—the gnome wandered into the largest ballroom. He had to concentrate to keep his mouth from dropping open in awe. The floor was white marble, polished to make it gleam like a jewel, and the pale gray veins in the tiles had been matched to form patterns. The ceiling, two stories above, was covered with magnificent frescos of human women in elaborate gowns. They were dancing, though the gnome did not spot any depicted musicians. The walls were stark white, but thick garlands of scented cloth flowers were being hung between the ornate lanterns that were evenly spaced throughout.

Fenzig thought the walls needed a few paintings here and

there, so people didn't have to crane their necks toward the ceiling to look at art. The gods knew Duke Rehmir had enough paintings everywhere else in his palace, he could have put some here. But, on second thought, maybe the duke didn't want attention focused on the walls—he probably wanted all eyes on the room's occupants, especially his daughters.

The raised marble platform at the far end of the room was where the orchestra would sit, the gnome noted. Already, padded chairs were being placed there for the musicians' comfort. More padded chairs were being added along the walls so the guests who were not dancing would have a place to sit.

Wines and finger desserts would be served in here after the meal, a female gnome chef explained. Fenzig made a note to ask her, Grechen, what the different types of dessert would entail. Maybe he could put in a request.

Shortly after noon, and shortly before that same gnome chef had promised him a light lunch, Fenzig made his way to the fourth floor, searching for Carmella. He hadn't seen her since his first breakfast, needed to know what she was up to. The gnome had done a lot of thinking, mostly about himself and his people from Graespeck, and some about Burlengren. He was going to leave the duke's estate tonight, after the gala, or leave the very first thing in the morning. It wouldn't be polite to leave before, he decided. He'd rent a room in K'Nosha—one of the gems the duke gave him earlier would pay for plenty of days of room and board.

He just didn't fit in here, though the food was just about the best he'd ever eaten. He didn't care for Duke Rehmir's new-found interest in expanding his territory by taking over Burlengren. He didn't care for Carmella's eldest sister Berthrice. And the few gnome cooks were pleasant enough, but he had nothing in common with them—except food. He simply didn't fit in—not the first time he was here, and not now.

I'll stick around K'Nosha just long enough to see how everything works out with Burlengren, long enough to get some gnomish formulas for Carmella, long enough to make sure my people are going to be all right, he thought. *Wonder if Carmella's gonna come with me again? Wonder if. . . .*

"Are you looking for Carm?" It was Elayne, the sister Fenzig particularly liked.

He grinned at her and nodded, stared at her hair, which cascaded in tight curls all around her shoulders. There were strands of pearls woven here and there, and the gnome considered the entire creation rather nice to look at. She touched a slender hand to her hair.

"I'm getting ready for the party," she explained. "Carm is, too. They're trying to fit her with one of my dresses. She'll be beautiful."

"So can I see her? We've got things to talk about. Important stuff."

"Can't it wait a little while?" She smiled sweetly and tilted her head.

"I guess. But just a little while."

"And can't we find something a little more . . . dressy . . . for you to wear?"

"Dressy? Gnomes don't like to be dressy. At least I don't like to."

"Appropriate." She settled on that word instead. "Something more appropriate for you to wear?"

Fenzig fervently shook his head. He wasn't about to have another of Carmella's outfits cut and tucked so he could fit into it. Maybe he'd just find a place to wash what he had on, tidy up a bit and. . . .

"I'm certain Carmella would really like it if you dressed up for the party. I could send for something in town. Something in just your size. Green, perhaps. Blue. That's my favorite color."

"Maybe something new, I guess."

"Blue, then?"

"Gray."

"Perfect."

"And black. I like those colors."

"Don't like to stand out, do you?"

Fenzig shook his head.

"Nothing too ostentatious, then, my little friend. I promise. Come along, let me get some measurements, and we'll have you fixed up in an hour or two."

The gnome grudgingly complied. Getting fussed over by Elayne was better than wandering around the estate. And it would have to do since he couldn't talk to Carmella for a little while. . . .

A little while turned out to be at Duke Rehmir's grand gala. Fenzig was dressed in billowy gray pants that were gathered at his ankles, just above black leather shoes that were a tad tight. It was the first pair of shoes he'd had on in years. His shirt was black silk, and he was forced to admit it felt good against his skin. Beneath its folds he wore his beltpouch, which he refused to leave even in Elayne's good care. A gnome couldn't be without his riches close at hand, he argued.

Fenzig was among the first to the dinner table, and was the first to be impressed. There were more pieces of silverware than he could imagine what to do with; three glasses, each of a different size and tinted blue to match the plates in front of him; linen napkins embroidered with the duke's crest; and scented candles sculpted in the shape of castles.

Carmella arrived just before the wine was poured. At first Fenzig didn't recognize her. She was dressed in a sweeping gown the color of ripe watermelon flesh. Tiny beads edged the sleeves and high neckline and sparkled in the light of the chandeliers, reminding the gnome of the magical fireflies she created with her spells. Her hair was tightly curled, and her head topped with a glistening tiara. It made her look like a princess, which the gnome suspected she would be considered when her father took over Burlengren and Erlgrane's estate.

She waltzed gracefully into the room, took a seat next to the gnome, and with an elegant gesture opened the napkin onto her lap.

"You look beautiful," he whispered.

"I feel silly," she returned. She edged her index finger under her collar. "And I itch. I'm not used to wearing so many clothes."

You better get used to it, princess, he thought. *A king probably has lots of gala affairs.*

"I can't wait until this is over. My sisters, well, just look at them. They probably want this to last forever. They spent all day getting ready and. . . ."

Fenzig pushed her words aside as introductions were made—he futilely tried to attach names to outfits in the event he'd have to talk to these folks later. And he nodded politely to Berthrice, Elayne, and Ruthe, dressed in elaborate dresses of scarlet, dark blue, and ivory respectively. He let the dinner conversation drift about him like buzzing insects as course after delicious course was served, and as his stomach was suitably filled to bursting.

The dance that followed, and that Fenzig observed from his perch on a padded chair at the back of the room, was as impressive as dinner. The gnome had never seen so many expensive dresses and in so many colors. And he'd never seen so many humans move so precisely.

Duke Rehmir was dancing with a broad-shouldered woman with a hawk nose. She wasn't near so pretty as the other ladies swirling about the room, and when she laughed, it reminded the gnome of glass breaking. It made him cringe. She wasn't young—or old—she was somewhere in between. And she was clumsy. The gnome noted that she frequently stepped on the duke's feet and that her skirt seemed to get tangled in her legs— which made her titter with that glass-breaking laugh. *The duke is being especially kind to this particular guest to dance with her,* Fenzig thought. He suspected no one else would be so willing.

Carmella had been dancing—for the third time—with a young man named Gregory, who, Fenzig was told, was a landowner from the Northern Reaches. The gnome wasn't paying close attention to who was doting upon Carmella's sisters. Though he had noted that several different men had been dancing with the charming Elayne.

Duke Rehmir again breezed by with the hawk-nosed woman. He was holding her close, and they were dancing slow—probably so her skirts wouldn't tangle the legs of other dancers. *Gods, it looks like he likes her,* Fenzig thought. He cringed again as her laughter cut above the strains of the orchestra. *Maybe the old man was looking for the companionship of a woman closer to his own age. But couldn't he do better than that?* Now that he had all of his daughters back and was facing the almost-assured possibility of becoming a king, maybe he was looking for a queen. He certainly was dancing with that one woman long enough. And close enough. *Gods!*

"No maybe about it," one of the gnome cooks whispered when Fenzig left the ballroom for the cozier confines of the kitchen.

"He's got his eye on a very special one," explained the cook who had earlier introduced herself as Grechen. "Been courting her since the day after he got his daughters back and Carmella left. She's rich, just inherited land to the west. She's nice enough, has a crooked nose, but the duke hasn't minded. Good of him to overlook her faults."

Fenzig wrinkled his face. That was the woman. The hawk-nosed one. Yuck.

"On top of everything," Grechen continued, "it would be a good political match. Very good. Her lands and the duke's. It would make both of them more powerful."

He hated talk of politics. Gave him indigestion. Already his stomach was sending up a reminder of what he'd had for an after-dinner treat. Strawberry something.

"I think it was getting his daughters back that changed Duke Rehmir," she confided as she bustled back and forth preparing trays of tiny deserts. "He's not depressed anymore, hasn't moped about for a minute. Having them around has given him more energy, a zest for life and for power. A reason to court that woman. I can't recall her name, Lady Elsbell, Elpeth, something with *El* in it. Anyway, it has given us a lot more work to do. He keeps all of us so busy preparing dinners for important people, fixing lots of late night meals for he and the general—they're planning to take over Burlengren and Erlgrane's lands to the south, you know." This last she whispered. "Then there's been the elaborate picnics by the pond for he and the lady friend. He's getting terribly serious about her, and terribly quickly. Probably misses romantic female companionship. And probably thinks he should have himself a wife again—since he's going to be a king. Cupcake, Fenzig?"

The gnome uncharacteristically declined. "I lost my appetite," he said sadly. "I think I'll go for a walk."

ALWAYS A THIEF

"Lost your appetite? Really?" The gnome cook looked offended, as if something she'd laboriously created hadn't agreed with Fenzig. She wrinkled her brow and poked out her bottom lip. It was definitely one of the better perturbed faces Fenzig had seen one of his people put on.

He shrugged and smiled.

"You can't be serious," she continued. "Please say you're not serious. I made a special trip into the market for colored sugar for the icing." She thrust the cupcake at Fenzig, and he grudgingly took it. "See, it's blue! Elayne's favorite color."

It looked like the morning sky, smelled like blueberries, and made his head spin.

"It's not your cooking, Grechen. Your cooking is wonderful," he said as way of an excuse. "Best I've ever tasted, in fact, a masterpiece for the palate. I just can't eat anymore." In truth, he didn't want any more not because he *couldn't* eat any more—he could always eat more—but because all the thoughts of politics and armies whirling around in his head had depressed him and agitated his stomach. It was merrily churning away and making him a little bit dizzy.

"Upset stomach?"

Maybe in a manner of speaking, he thought, although he shook his head "no" so she wouldn't run off trying to find some remedy that would make Carmen the Magnificent blush. *Upset stomach? Well, on second thought, definitely in a manner of speaking.*

He didn't think he could stomach any more of the rich life at the duke's palace.

"I've been eating at least three of everything it seems, and if I eat one more bite, Grechen, I'll probably explode. You'll be spending days cleaning bits of me off the kitchen walls and the ceiling."

The image took Grechen aback. She swallowed hard and offered him a polite smile. "Then maybe you better save that cupcake for later."

"Why, that's just what I intend to do!" Fenzig beamed, passing the cupcake back to her. "And, if you don't mind, could you save me one or two extra for a midnight snack?"

She grinned broadly and gestured to a low cupboard. "I'll put a dozen in there," she whispered. "Just for you."

He nodded and slipped from the kitchen, taking the back stairs down into the catacombs that ran beneath Duke Rehmir's imposing palace. Fenzig had planned on going outside, enjoying a leisurely walk under the stars, visiting Summer, whom he'd come to consider a great listener, and thinking up an "I'll see you later" speech to give to Carmella. Then he had planned on walking into town and finding a room at a boarding house, settling in for a while, and discovering something other than politics and kingships and armies to occupy his mind.

"Being a thief isn't so bad," he told himself as he continued down the damp stone steps. "I certainly can't join my father's woodcarving business—it doesn't exist anymore." So it was back to being a thief, a prospect that didn't bother him as much as he thought it should have. "I'll just have to be a little more careful who I steal from."

The light was scant here, as the lanterns were spaced far apart, and the wicks were turned low. No use wasting oil on a part of the palace where few people bothered to visit, he suspected was the rationale. Fenzig didn't care for the darkness, as he associated it with things he didn't like—rats, craven cats, and bad dreams mostly. And it also reminded him of his stint in King Erlgrane's dungeon.

But he could fare well in the darkness when he put his mind to it. His gnomish vision was excellent, and he could easily pick through the shadows. "Not so bad at all, being a thief. Thieves don't concern themselves with warring on people or taking their lands or making the proper alliances or having such elaborate parties for their daughters. Though the food was very good, thank you. Thieves just take a couple of baubles now and then, things people can live without. And I never, ever took everything anyone had. I've got morals, after all."

He wondered if kings and other politicians had as many morals as most thieves he knew. Then he silently cursed himself for such thoughts. Duke Rehmir had been kind to him—much more than kind to him, all things considered. Fenzig knew the duke would make a much better king than Erlgrane had, and the duke didn't have any wizards, that he knew of—outside of Carmella, who he suspected wouldn't stick around for long. Politics didn't seem to interest her, either.

Fenzig's silent footsteps took him into the thickest shadows, where the light from the lanterns didn't quite reach. He hadn't realized he was heading to Duke Rehmir's treasure chamber until he was just outside the door. At least he hadn't consciously realized it, he told himself. "I really was gonna take a walk outside," he whispered. "But since I'm here, I might as well look inside. Just to see if he's added anything new. Just for something to do."

Poking around amid jewels and coins and valuable sculptures sounded like a much better idea than listening to the orchestra and watching all the people dance. There was no one his size to dance with, and it bothered him—just a little—seeing people dance with Carmella. Fenzig wasn't jealous, not in the romantic way, as he only thought of Carmella as a friend. But he was jealous in a "best friend" way. Carmella hadn't spent more than a few moments with him this evening, she'd just been too preoccupied with everyone else.

I'm not going to steal anything, he told himself. *I'd never steal from Duke Rehmir. He gave me gems, after all, and he's been very generous. So I couldn't outright take something from him. I just wanna have a look. Just for a minute. Just for . . . what have we here? This is new.*

The gnome finished picking through the shadows surrounding the massive door. It was bound in iron, and three great locks held it shut. When the gnome was here before, at Duke Rehmir's insistence, he hadn't noticed the locks. He searched his memory. No. There weren't any locks. But the duke didn't care much about his wealth then, before his daughters returned, hadn't seemed to care much about anything. The thief supposed when you were adding to an army that you had to pay and feed and when you were planning on becoming a king, you had to care about your treasure horde and make some effort to protect it. Besides, with all those people upstairs, you'd had to take the precaution of locking the vault—just in case some of those folks were less than honest and chanced to find their way down here.

The first lock was achingly easy, and Fenzig made a mental note to discuss Duke Rehmir's slack security. *I can tell him how to construct much better locks. Why, I could probably fashion them for him. Any thief could get by these.* The second was a little more difficult, but only a little and only because it was almost out of reach.

The third lock was above Fenzig's head, and he had to climb up the iron bands on the door to get to it. This was a more complex lock, it felt newly forged to his sensitive fingers, and it brought a smile to the gnome's lips. It was going to present him a little bit of a challenge. Finally, a chance to have some sport tonight!

This is much better than listening to that boorish orchestra, he thought. *Much, much better. Much better than not dancing, than watching Carmella, than watching the duke and his new lady friend. What great fun!*

He chose a different pick, a thinner one that let him get farther inside the lock. Pressing his ear to the mechanism, he felt about with the pick until he met resistance, wriggled it back and forth, and finally heard a soft *click.* It took him several moments more, and twice he had to change picks, before he finally got it open. "So maybe I don't have to help him with security," he said. "Well, not much help, anyway." Fenzig climbed down the door, gleefully rubbed his hands together, and went inside.

He remembered there being a lantern to the right of the door, and so he quickly found and lit it, setting his thieves' tools next to it. His vision was keen enough in the darkness, but he wanted light so the jewels would sparkle and so he could appreciate them better.

Within a heartbeat he had the wick high enough so that the gold coins glimmered, and the gems caught the light and practically glowed. "Yes," he said approvingly. "Everything in its place, just like before, just like I remember. Coffers, statues, gilded frames, music boxes, butterfly jewels, chests. . . . Hmm. Better be sure everything's still here. Just as a precaution. Just to help the duke."

Indeed, the gnome convinced himself he was only helping out Duke Rehmir by being here, as he was certain the servants and soldiers didn't have time to bother about sifting through pearl necklaces and platinum vases to make sure nothing was amiss. And he convinced himself once more that nothing would find its way into his possession. After all, his beltpouch was beneath his silk shirt—so it wasn't immediately accessible, and his pants were just a smidgen tight after all he'd eaten tonight, so he couldn't risk the seams by putting something in his pockets.

"What's this?" The gnome stopped in midstride on his way toward the butterfly pin collection. "Magic?" On the floor, mere inches from his toes, was a pattern, barely discernable because coins had spilled over part of it, and barely glowing. The gnome batted his eyes and stooped to look at it more closely. "Magic, definitely." It was a glyph, a magical maguffin that when walked upon or across would signal a warning someplace.

"So Duke Rehmir has fine security after all," Fenzig pronounced. He didn't remember there being a glyph here before when he was let into the treasure room. Though he supposed the duke could somehow deactivate it when he wanted.

"Who put it there? Carmella?" *No, she couldn't have. She was with me. Except for today when she was getting ready for the party, which means she wouldn't have had time to come down here and do this for her father. I understand it takes a while to craft one of these. So the duke has access to a wizard somehow.*

There was something familiar about the pattern, but the gnome couldn't quite put a finger to it. "I'll just have to walk around you," he told the glyph. "Wonder how many wizards the duke has in his employ. Never asked him if he had any, didn't strike me as a man who favored spells and such. So it doesn't mean he isn't the type. Probably relied on wizards to help him build this palace. Well, never mind. About those butterflies. . . ."

His short arms stretched out to touch the crystal case. Inside, golden butterflies, bedecked with emeralds, sapphires, jacinths, and garnets, glittered in the light like their wings were gently flapping. "The duke's daughters should be wearing these. They're so pretty. Shouldn't be locked up where no one can see them."

"They're locked up so no one will steal them."

The words were crisp and came from behind the gnome. He whirled, losing his balance and falling on a mound of unyielding gold coins. The air rushed from his lungs. "Ketterhagen!"

The general didn't know the gnome, though Fenzig had spotted him the first night he broke into Duke Rehmir's palace. "General Ketterhagen, I'm not stealing anything," Fenzig sputtered. "I was just looking. The duke let me down here before, so I figured it was all right. And the party was boring. Well, it probably wasn't boring for humans. But I didn't have anyone to dance with, you see, and the music just wasn't. . . . And I was upset with all the talk of politics and Burlengren and kingships and armies. I was going into town to a boarding house. But I thought I'd take a last look around. Doing a favor for the duke, actually, though he doesn't know it yet. I was checking his security—which is quite good by the way, but it could be better and. . . ."

The gnome's words were tumbling together, blurring so fast in a nervous frenzy that the aging general had to struggle to make them out. The older man finally gave up, obviously not in the mood for the gnome's explanation anyway. He gestured, and two guards materialized from the hallway behind him, and strode forward, their hard leather heels clinking harshly over the coins. They grabbed Fenzig up by the armpits, shook him to see if anything valuable would fall out, then held him up to Ketterhagen.

"It was a good thing for Duke Rehmir I wasn't with my troops this night," the old general said. "I wouldn't have heard the alarm."

"Alarm?" Fenzig managed to get the word out, then the guards squeezed him harshly to keep him quiet.

"The magical alarm on the door. A chime rings in my chambers if the door is opened. If I'd been with my troops, I wouldn't have heard it." Ketterhagen gestured again, and the guards nodded in unison, then carried Fenzig from the chamber. The older man followed, closed the door behind them and didn't bother to refasten the locks.

"Duke Rehmir," Fenzig risked. This time the guards didn't squeeze him. "If you get the duke, he'll explain that I've been here before, that I'm a guest. That it's okay."

"You're a guest, all right, wee-one," Ketterhagen returned. "A guest of the dungeon."

"The duke. . . ." the gnome persisted.

"Is having a party tonight and is too busy to be disturbed by the likes of a little thief. He will deal with you in the morning." With that, Ketterhagen left, his slippered feet making practically no sound in the long, stone hallway.

The guards carried the struggling gnome deeper into the catacombs, through a maze of corridors and down a series of steps he hadn't traveled before. The air was chill here, and fusty, as if little fresh air ever reached here. The light came from guttering, fat-soaked torches that were placed far apart. Cobwebs covered the ceiling like the ornate fresco covered the ballroom ceiling, and Fenzig's keen vision picked out all manner of crawling things in the webs—and the husks of little things that had died there. Mold grew on the walls here and there, adding to the unpleasant atmosphere of the place.

Fenzig chattered to the guards, about the duke, about him being a hero because he helped rescue his daughters, about him being Carmella's best friend, and about how someone should go get Carmella or the duke and tell them how sorry he was for revisiting the treasure chamber. But the guards ignored him, didn't say a word until they reached a particularly dank corridor. Then one chuckled. Stagnant water lay in puddles along the stone floor, dripping down here from who knew where. Fenzig's eyes noted rat droppings in profusion where the walls met the floor. He thanked the gods that Elayne had talked him into wearing these shoes.

"Carmella wouldn't like it that you're taking me here," he said softly. "She wouldn't like it at all."

"Lady Carmella doesn't like thieves," one of the guards returned.

"Neither does the duke," added the other, as they rounded a corner. The light barely reached here, and Fenzig imagined that the guards were having a difficult time seeing. However, his own vision was good enough to make out all the dismal details.

The gnome gulped. Cells lined both sides, old iron-barred cells that obviously hadn't been used in a very, very long time. The bars were rusted, and the hay inside the cells was so old and moldy it was hardly recognizable as hay.

The gnome was entrusted to the taller of the two guards, while the other fumbled about his waist for a key ring. "This one'll do," he said to his companion. The guard had selected the closest cell and fitted one key after another in the lock until at last he was rewarded. The door opened with some difficulty, and filled the air with a keening protest of the bottom iron rung being rubbed across the stone floor. The sound jarred Fenzig, and he clamped his teeth shut.

The gnome was tossed inside, discarded like too-old potatoes, and was again greeted with the bone-hurting keening as the door was closed, and then locked.

"We'll check on you tomorrow, thief, after the duke has arisen and decides what to do with you."

"Do with me? Why, he'll order that you let me out immediately. He'll be angry you put me here!" Fenzig retorted. "You'll be looking for new work! I'm an honored guest. Why, I'm a hero. And Carmella will. . . ."

But the gnome's words were lost amid the guard's retreating footsteps, their muttered words about being replaced soon for the change in shift.

"Gods! I hate it in here," he moaned, as he selected a wall farthest away from the mound of hay that at one time might have been a prisoner's bed. He slid down the wall, suspecting that he wiped away part of the dirt with his silk shirt in the process.

There was just so much dust and dirt here. It had been unused for a long time. Fenzig wondered just how long. A thick layer of grime covered everything. Reminiscent of Erlgrane's dungeon, the film of filth coated the stone floor, the walls, and the mound of moldy old straw. It covered everything.

Fenzig wrinkled his nose in disgust and picked up several new odors—rats, which he had learned to identify in Erlgrane's dungeon, stagnant water, human waste. The latter piqued his curiosity, as it indicated he had company down here.

"I bet you don't like this place any better than I," he said loud enough for the other guests to hear. He was answered with a high-pitched squeak from one of the rats in his cell.

"I hate rats," he grumbled. Squinting, he spotted a bony trio in the far corner. They looked practically emaciated, and were not near so bold as the rats in the king's dungeon. "Nothing to eat down here, huh, fellows? Guess I should have brought Grechen's cupcake with me. See, they won't be feeding me down here, so you won't be getting fat off any of my scraps. I'm going to be out of here very soon. Very, very soon, in fact. Soon as Carmella hears what happened. Why don't you go bother the other prisoners?"

The rats continued to squeak and stare at him, kept their distance and continued to make the gnome fret. "I really hate rats. Wonder if the rats are any healthier in the cells of the duke's other guests." *Other guests? Guest,* Fenzig corrected himself. *A very important one. King Erlgrane. Carmella said the king was in her father's dungeon.*

"Hey, your majesty!" Fenzig bellowed. "How's it feel to be

down here? Your dungeon's no better than this! So how do you like a taste of your own hospitality? Huh?"

The gnome's answer was a muffled "Mrphrgm!"

"What's the matter? Craven cat got your tongue?" He chuckled at his little joke, pushed himself to his feet, and padded toward the barred door. "Hey, your majesty! Talk to me!"

The reply was again muffled, making Fenzig squint across the hallway, into a cell on the other side. Poking through the darkness, he spotted the bedraggled form of King Erlgrane. No longer imperious, the monarch was chained to the wall by his legs and arms, and a thick gag was stuffed into his mouth. He looked thin, the clothes sagging on him, reminding the gnome of a rag doll and indicating that he hadn't been fed well, though the wound on his leg had been tended to. The gnome knew he was at least receiving some sustenance, else he would have been dead by now. But he thought the duke would have taken better care of his important prisoner.

"You're not going anywhere for quite some time, I'm sure." The gnome noted that there was a faintly glowing symbol on the floor of the king's cell. Apparently the duke was taking as many precautions as possible so his royal prisoner would not escape.

"Can't go anywhere, eh, your majesty? Can't talk either 'cause of that gag. Too bad. Bet you can listen, though. And I'm going to give you the proverbial earful. See, I'm gonna be getting out of here, soon. Very soon. And you'll still be here. Maybe forever. You certainly don't deserve any better." The gnome continued to berate the king, taunting him mercilessly and practically endlessly, expounding on Duke Rehmir's plans to march into Burlengren and seize Erlgrane's holdings. When Fenzig was finally out of breath, he stepped back from the bars and sighed. His little tirade had made him feel better—a little. But it was not so satisfying as having someone nearby who could talk back—give him evidence that his verbal jabs were hurting.

The gnome started to pace, his leather-soled shoes sticking here and there where something—he didn't want to guess what—had adhered to the stone. He batted his hands in the air when he inadvertently walked into a curtain of spider webs.

"Gods! I hate this place!" he howled. The gnome wanted out, wanted to be away from this place, away from kings and dukes, and far from human orchestras that played simple tunes that clumsy, hawk-nosed women danced to. He wanted to be on his own, anywhere. And he wanted the king to acknowledge his insults.

"Wait a minute." He stopped, whirled, and returned to the bars, tugged up his now-filthy silk shirt. His short fingers fumbled about in his beltpouch. Fumbled, quested. "There!" he exclaimed, tugging free Carmella's magical necklace. He was sad he'd forgotten to return it to her after she loaned it to him in Graespeck. But his sadness instantly vanished when he plopped it over his head and returned to taunting the king.

"I might not hear you answer me, you sorry excuse for a pea-brained potentate!" Fenzig was especially pleased with that appellation. "But I can listen in on your thoughts with this magical necklace."

The one that belonged to my wife? came the words inside the gnome's head. *The necklace my Carmella was so fond of wearing?*

The gnome's mouth dropped open and he shook his head furiously, as if to clear his senses. It was Duke Rehmir's voice. He recognized it as clearly as if the words had come from the portly man's mouth. There were a few other voices inside his head, other unfortunate people who somehow wronged the duke, but he shoved all of those away and concentrated on Duke Rehmir's thoughts. Fenzig clung to the bars and stared at King Erlgrane. *Had those mental words come from the king?* he wondered.

The necklace that allows you to read another's thoughts? The inaudible voice persisted. *Are you reading my thoughts now, gnome?*

"I'm reading someone's thoughts," the gnome answered as much to himself as to the king. "But I'm not believing what I'm hearing. I don't like to be tricked, your majesty." The last two words came out as a sneer. "I don't like tricks, at all, thank you. And I've decided I don't like kings."

I've never much cared for them, either, the thoughts continued. The words inside Fenzig's head sounded tired and old. *Especially the king who did this to me.*

"Another trick!" the gnome spat. "Another trick of yours, Erlgrane, and I'm not going to listen. You and your wizards and homing spells and emeralds. You're evil!"

But the gnome listened anyway, out of curiosity and because he had nothing else to do at the moment. He listened closely to a very convoluted tale. When it was finished, he tugged free his belt and ruined the clasp, used the prong to worry at the lock on his cell. It was an old lock, and it only presented a challenge because it was so rusted and large, and the gnome's makeshift lockpick, which became terribly bent in the process, was so small and fragile. He cursed himself for leaving his picks inside the duke's vault. It would have made things simpler.

Once free, Fenzig eased open the door, cringing when the iron grated angrily against the stone again. He didn't bother to close the door, not wanting to hear the sound again and not wanting to risk any additional noise that might give any listening guards a reason to come looking. *Not that I didn't give them a reason with all my bellowing at the king,* he thought.

He slipped from the hallway, moving silently and clinging to the darkest shadows and ignoring the slime he brushed up against when he accidentally touched the wall. He glared at the few starving rats he spotted, chasing them away with wild gestures, and he began his long journey up from Duke Rehmir's imposing catacombs.

It wouldn't have been such a long journey, had the gnome been paying more attention when the guards brought him down here, or had he possessed any sense of direction beneath the earth. But eventually—he guessed it must have been an hour or more—he found his way into familiar territory: the hallway outside the duke's treasure chamber. From here, he made his way to the stone steps that wound up to the palace above.

There were two guards perched like attentive birds at the bottom of the steps—not the same two who threw him in that cell. Despite their rigid posture, they looked bored, and likely weren't paying a great deal of attention. But Fenzig wasn't about to leave anything to chance, and certainly didn't want to chance getting thrown back in a cell. This time the guards would make sure he couldn't get out.

The gnome picked a spot a good hundred yards away from the guards, reluctantly removed the leather shoes, and climbed the wall. The stones were old, and the gaps between them where they were mortared together were deep. *Perfect for climbing,* Fenzig thought. His fingers and toes fit neatly in the cracks, and he skittered up like a spider. Clinging to the wall just below the ceiling—which even here was filled with webs and crawling insects—the gnome inched forward, over the heads of the guards and around the corner, up the stairwell and into the lowest level of the palace.

He glanced outside, noting that the dark sky was lightening just a bit, hinting that dawn couldn't be too far off. *The party must be over by now,* the gnome thought happily. *That'll make everything much easier. I'll go find Carmella, and then. . . .*

The strains of the orchestra reached his ears. He concentrated and picked out laughter, the clinking of glasses. Fenzig softly groaned. "They're still at it," he moaned. "Now what am I gonna do? However can I get to Carmella looking like this?"

He crept through the palace, sticking to the darkened passages not used by the guests, until he eventually reached the far corner of the kitchen. Along the way he schemed, discarding each plan as impractical and likely to get him pitched into the dungeon again.

"Fenzig! How'd you get so dirty?" It was Grechen, and he greeted her with a weak smile, put his finger to his lips to keep her voice down.

"Went for a walk," he whispered. "And I . . . I fell down. Practically ruined these fine clothes Elayne got for me. I can't let anyone see me like this. Not even the other cooks, okay?"

She waggled her finger at him scoldingly and quickly ushered him through the pantry and into a room filled with mops, pails, and assorted cleaning supplies. Grechen pointed to a wooden tub. "I'll bring hot water," she said. "You can wash up in that— just yourself. I'll deal with your clothes." She wrinkled her tiny nose when she saw the streak of slime on the back of his shirt, from when he'd sat against the wall in his cell. "Looks like you fell more than once."

He grinned at her sheepishly and shrugged. "Clumsy," he offered. "Too much to drink, I guess."

Grechen plucked up his clothes, gave him a curious glance when she spotted the human-sized woman's necklace dangling about his neck. This time he offered no explanation, and thankfully registered that in her mind she hadn't remembered it as Carmella's. *She thinks I stole it from someone at the party,* he mused disappointedly. *She thinks I'm a thief. But she's not going to tell anyone, thank the gods.*

Grechen, frowning, pointed to a low shelf that held a few folded outfits, gnome size. "The gardener's spare clothes," she said. "Something there will have to do until I can clean these—if I can clean these. Silk. Must've been expensive." She shook her head.

"Yeah, I feel bad about it," he said. Fenzig truly did. "The party," he said, changing the subject. "Should be over soon, huh?"

She closed her eyes, shook her head again, and hurried back to the kitchen, his clothes dragging along behind her.

Several minutes later, he was soaking in warm, soapy water, in a tub that he suspected was used for especially stubborn pots and pans that were too unsightly for the kitchen sink.

"Breakfast?" he groaned as he dipped his head beneath the suds. "The cooks are going to start breakfast soon?" He'd read Grechen's mind via Carmella's necklace when she made her last trip with the hot water. "What kind of party lasts that long? Gnomes never have such parties. At least none I've been invited to." *But then gnomes have more sense,* he thought. *Some gnomes, anyway, gnomes who don't end up stealing from King Erlgrane and wind up in a dishwashing tub.*

Quickly finishing his ablutions, such as he could manage given his surroundings, he padded to the shelf and looked over the gardener's clothes. "Grays, browns, colors that I like," he mused. "But. . . ."

Next to them were a couple of gnome-sized cook's outfits, Grechen's probably, or perhaps the other gnome cook. Sucking in his bottom lip, and settling on a plan that just popped into his head, he selected one of these, and squirmed into the pale yellow dress. It reached to the floor, covering up his hairy bare feet, and the sleeves were long enough to hide his hairy arms. Next, he selected a white apron trimmed in lace that made his neck itch, and a flouncy hat that helped to hide his masculine facial features.

Wouldn't have thought of this if I hadn't spent some time with Carmen the Magnificent, he reflected.

He slipped into the kitchen, and held his breath. Grechen was there, fussing over a tray filled with wine glasses. She looked his way for just a moment, then toddled away with the tray.

Whew! Didn't recognize me as Fenzig, he knew. *Thought I was someone named Helath. And she was too busy to get a close look to learn differently.* The necklace, which he'd hid under the apron, told him as much.

The other cooks paid him no heed either. So he stretched up, grabbed a large plate of chocolate-iced cookies, and hurried into the ballroom—wanting to be out of the kitchen before the real Helath appeared.

He glanced at the swirling, laughing guests, and his teeth began nervously clicking together. He drew a deep breath, and started looking for Carmella.

ENTERING AND BREAKING

"Cookie, Lady Rehmir?" Fenzig squeaked at her in a high voice, which sounded more strangled than feminine.

"No thank you," Carmella replied. She had just finished dancing with that young human again, and her face was flushed, looking only a shade lighter than her sweeping dress. "I couldn't eat another bite. I don't think I can eat for days."

"Then maybe you'd care for some cider? I'm sure there's some in the kitchen. Something to wash down all that food? Something to keep you going?"

"Well, tea will be served soon."

"But it is not so sweet as cider."

"Yes, you're right. Cider would be lovely. Bring a tray, why don't you?"

"Why not follow me into the kitchen, and I'll fill you a tall glass. It would. . . ."

"Another dance, Carm? This song is delightful. And sharing it with you, sweet Carm, would make it. . . ."

Carm? The gnome glared, ignoring the rest of the gushing words. The young man had approached again, was using the nickname Elayne had referred to Carmella by. Fenzig didn't like the familiarity. *No, she doesn't want to dance, you cretin. She's danced plenty with you, thank you very much. I bet you've occupied her all night. No time for her best friend 'cause of you. If she would have had time for me I wouldn't've ended up in the dungeon and. . . .*

"I'd love to dance again, Gregory." She extended her hand and made a move to join him. But Fenzig placed himself between the pair and stepped on the edge of her watermelon skirt.

"You've been dancing quite a bit, Lady Rehmir. That cider would be good for you, give you some more energy. Why don't you follow me into the kitchen for a glass? It definitely would do you some good."

She glared down at the diminutive cook, trying her best to be polite. "In a while, perhaps. The music is. . . ."

"Magnificent?" the gnome finished, trying a new tack and lowering his voice just a bit. "Magnificent as in Carmen the Magnificent?"

Carmella's eyes widened. She tugged her hand free from Gregory's and bent slightly at the waist to get a closer look at the gnome. "Fenzig?"

The flouncy hat bobbed an affirmative.

"What are you doing in that . . . that . . . outfit?"

"Shh! Not so loud. I'm not very popular with some of the sentries around here."

"I don't understand, Fenzig. You're being. . . ."

"Difficult, Carm?" The young man again. "Is the wee-one being difficult and bothering you? We can't have that. The help should not be intrusive. I can escort her back to the kitchen where she belongs. And then you and I shall dance and romance away what's left of the night and. . . ."

"No, she's not bothering me, Gregory," Carmella said, rising and affectionately touching his cheek. "I'm going in the kitchen with her for some cider. But I'll be right back. Please, don't go anywhere."

"I shant, sweet Carm. I shall wait right here patiently for your return."

Gods! His voice is dripping with more sugar than Grechen put in these cookies. The gnome sat the tray on an empty chair, scrunched his face in Gregory's direction, and hurried from the room. The swishing of Carmella's skirt, and the loud angry thoughts issuing from her head, told the gnome she was right behind him.

He scurried past the other cooks, straight into the pantry. "Listen, Carmella. . . ."

"What do you think you're doing! He's nice! Nice to me! He likes me. And I think, maybe, just maybe, that I like him. I was having a good time. At one of these stuffy old affairs of my father's, I was having fun. Whatever possessed you to interrupt me? To . . . to. . . ."

"Not so fast!" the gnome sputtered. "Stop thinking and talking at the same time. You're giving me a horrible headache!" He tugged free the necklace, and she grabbed it from him.

"I forgot all about this!"

No doubt Gregory made you forget a lot of things.

"You've had this for days!" She put it over her head. "Little thief!"

Would've returned it to you earlier but I forgot about it. Good thing I remembered it after I was thrown in your father's dungeon.

"Dungeon?"

"Lady Carmella?" The call came from the kitchen, sounded like Grechen's voice. "Can I help you with anything?"

"No, no. I'm fine. Just need to clear my head, get away from all those people." She returned her attention to the gnome. "Dungeon?"

Fenzig thought quickly, not bothering with vocal words. *She's got the necklace, let her use it.* When he was finished with his little tale, she leaned back against a spice shelf, her flushed face growing instantly pale.

"You stole into my father's treasure chamber." Her voice was sad.

I wasn't going to take anything.

"But you broke in."

I was bored. Sorry. I didn't mean any harm. But your father. . . .

"But my father's in the ballroom. It is *my* father. And he's just proposed to Lady Elsbeth of Genoa Acres. He's going to remarry."

Fenzig closed his eyes, and dejected, shook his head. "A fine mess," he said. "Great family. But he's not what he seems. Hawk-nosed, clumsy. . . . Maybe we should. . . ."

The rest of his words were lost in the swishing of Carmella's skirt, she brushed past him and headed toward the far corner of the palace, toward the steps that led down to the catacombs.

"Wait for me!" Fenzig cried. He gathered up his skirt and apron and hurried after her, his short legs futilely churning away.

It wasn't until she'd reached the bottom of the winding stone steps that he finally caught up with her. She was arguing with the two guards whom he had slipped by earlier. She was standing on the very bottom step, and they were barring her way.

"I'm sorry, Lady Carmella," the taller said. "Orders. You understand. General Ketterhagen said no one was to come down here, except, of course, for the duke himself. We can't let you pass."

From his vantage point higher on the stairway, Fenzig noticed the odd tilt to Carmella's head. He moved closer, until he was practically behind her, though still several steps higher.

"I don't have time for this," she huffed. "Orders are the only things on you fellows' minds right now. And I'm not about to roust Ketterhagen and bring him here to convince you I can go wherever I please."

"Then return to the party," the other guard suggested with a grin. "You look beautiful this evening, Lady Rehmir, like a flower, and you wouldn't want to soil your clothes down here. These dismal surroundings are not for the likes of you."

"I'll do anything I please with my clothes," she snapped back. "And I'll decide my own surroundings." She ran her fingers through her hair in frustration, loosening a strand of beads entwined in her short curls. "I don't have time for this," she repeated with a little more edge to her voice.

Despite her tone, the guards remained nonplussed, like attentive birds. And they refused to move. Fenzig moved to the side so he could see them better, wondered how this standoff was going to end.

"Perhaps I should find Ketterhagen, then," the taller finally proposed. "Or, your father. Either will explain that these chambers are off-limits. Staying away from the catacombs is for your own good, Lady Rehmir."

Fenzig saw Carmella draw her shoulders back and clench her fists. He didn't need her necklace to know what she was thinking about. He squeezed past her, clinging to the stairwell wall. She sharply inhaled, and he managed to skitter past the guards, unseen. Their attention was trained on the very irate Lady Rehmir, the gnome noted with satisfaction, not on their former prisoner in cook's clothing.

Once behind the guards, the gnome stepped back and between them, where Carmella could see him, and where he could see the expression on her face. It wasn't soft, like it had been throughout the evening. It was hard and determined, her eyes narrow, looking like she did as Carmen the Magnificent trying to get away from an angry mob of townsfolk she'd sold worthless concoctions to.

"No. You don't need to get Ketterhagen or—" She stopped in mid-sentence, then smiled, her face softening only slightly. "On second thought, why don't you both go get Ketterhagen. I'll wait here for you."

The taller sentry chuckled and whispered something to his fellow. The latter nodded and started up the stairs, brushing past Carmella, who punched his midsection with her clenched fist and drove her heel down on top of his foot.

The air rushed from his lungs, and he doubled over from the strong, unexpected blow. Fenzig, also surprised, was only a heartbeat behind her in acting. He rushed forward, barreling into the back of the taller sentry's legs. The man pitched forward, straight into Carmella's arms, and she began pummeling him.

"General!" screeched the one who was now grappling with Carmella at the bottom of the stairwell. "Harrold! Go fetch the general!"

Harrold righted himself, while clutching his side, and started up the steps past his companion and Carmella.

"Oh, no you don't!" Fenzig hollered, not bothering to keep his voice down. They were so far below the palace he doubted anyone above could hear them. "You get the general, and I get tossed back in the cell! I'll have none of that!" His short feet carried him up a few steps, then his legs got caught in his skirt and he felt himself flying forward. His arms flailed out to find a purchase—and his hands struck the back of the retreating guard's legs. It would do. He grabbed hold and grimaced. The guard was bounding up the stairs anyway, dragging the gnome with him.

Fenzig's chest and stomach bounced over the sharp edges of the stone steps, each strike sending a jolt of agony into his tiny body. "No . . . you . . . don't!" Fenzig managed. He gritted his teeth in a hopeless attempt to block out the pain. "No . . . you. . . ." And he pulled himself closer to the fleeing sentry. Closer. Closer. "Don't!"

"Ouch!"

The sentry stopped halfway up the steps, Fenzig's teeth dug

firmly into his ankle. The gnome bit down harder, then felt himself being flung backward, kicked down the steps, his skirt flying up, apron ripping, flouncy hat falling away.

"You!" The sentry named Harrold spat at the gnome. "How did you get out of the dungeon?" All thought of summoning Duke Rehmir or General Ketterhagen had vanished. He reached to his belt and tugged free a long knife. "Doesn't matter how you escaped, vermin," he cursed under his breath. "You won't be getting out of anything ever again."

Fenzig struggled with the material of his dress and finally managed to get to his feet and clamber up a few steps just as the sentry reached him. The pair was several steps above Carmella and the other sentry, who from the sounds of it were continuing to wrestle. The gnome planted his feet wide apart and looked up at the charging sentry, gulped when he saw a malicious gleam in the human's eye.

"I didn't hear General Ketterhagen tell you to kill me!" Fenzig tried.

Harrold shook his head. "Doesn't matter. The duke'll reward me well when I bring him your corpse." With that he dropped to a crouch where he could better reach the gnome, and slashed forward with the knife.

Despite the pain in his chest and stomach, the gnome was faster. Fenzig pivoted, and the knife caught only the folds of the long skirt. The material ripped in the same instant the gnome whirled back and flung his hands forward, connecting with the sentry's wrist. He whirled again, tugging with all the strength his small form could muster, and throwing the man off balance. The knife clattered on the steps.

The sentry pitched forward, and Fenzig threw himself flat on the step, sensed the human's body pass over him.

"Carmella! Watch out!" the gnome cried. He turned his head just in time to see Carmella press herself against the stairwell wall. Harrold struck the taller sentry, and both men tumbled into a heap at the bottom of the steps.

Before they could untangle themselves, Carmella leapt on the two men, striking madly at them with her fists. The gnome watched as the men seemed to tolerate the hail of blows, offering no defense as they concentrated on pushing themselves up. Then the tables instantly turned, and the taller sentry threw Carmella to the stone floor and knelt on top of her to keep her from getting up.

"Don't care if you're the duke's daughter," he hissed through clenched teeth, using the weight of his body to keep her struggles to a minimum. "You're to die anyway. Tomorrow or the next. Might as well die now. Stop struggling!" He fumbled at his waist for his knife, tugged it free, and rapped the handle against the side of her head, momentarily stunning her. "I'll make this painless, Lady Rehmir."

"No!" Fenzig bellowed. The gnome grabbed up the other man's long knife, wrapped his short fingers around the handle and hurried down the last several steps.

Harrold was backing away from his comrade and Carmella, catching his breath. Before he could react, Fenzig sped by him and thrust forward with the knife, felt it sink into the back of the tall sentry's right leg.

The man let out a howl and pushed himself off Carmella, jumped to his feet and whirled to face the gnome—who now had both sentries to contend with. Weaponless, as his borrowed knife was firmly lodged in the tall man's leg, the gnome shifted back and forth on the balls of his feet, watching both men and trying to keep out of their reach.

"Wee-one!" the tall sentry swore. "Mine'll be the hand to kill you!" His eyes were narrowed in pain, but he did nothing to remove the offending knife. Instead, he flourished his own weapon. "Harrold! See to Lady Rehmir! Finish her!"

She was moaning, coming around. His companion grunted something in reply, and placed a foot on Carmella's stomach, keeping her pinned to the floor.

"Don't hurt her," Fenzig warned. "Don't you dare hurt her!"

The tall sentry chuckled. "Hurt her? We'll kill her. Earlier than planned. Too bad you won't be able to watch. You'll already be dead." With that he led with his left leg and slashed at the gnome. It was a feint, though Fenzig didn't know it. The gnome moved to the right—into the path of the second jab. The knife bit deep into his shoulder, and he cried out. "Kill you slowly," the sentry hissed. "Wee bit by wee bit. Feed you to the rats."

"I hate rats!" Fenzig spat. The gnome reached up and felt his shoulder, already sodden with blood. The ache raced down from his shoulder to his fingers, which were starting to grow numb. "And I've no intention of filling their bellies! Not to satisfy the likes of you!" This time when the sentry lunged, the gnome was ready. He skittered back a step, then crouched and sprung, leaping at the startled human who was bending down to slash at him again.

Fenzig clutched at the sentry's tabard, just below the man's chin, holding on for his life. The guard used his free hand to tear at the gnome, while his weapon hand moved in for the kill. The gnome saw the blade flash in the lantern light, released the cloth just in time and dropped a few inches. Then he swept his small hands up to grab the man's wrist and drove them forward and down, using his descending weight to angle the blade into the human's stomach.

The sentry's eyes widened in surprise as the blade slid in, and he fell backward, landing near Carmella and driving the blade behind him all the way through his leg. His scream cut through the air, threatening to be heard in the palace above, and Fenzig pushed the knife in his stomach in deeper, ending the man's cries. Then the gnome struggled to his feet only to be sent careening against the stairwell wall.

Harrold had moved off Carmella, was turning his attention to Fenzig now. His eyes gleamed evilly, like the craven cats' eyes had gleamed in the Haunted Woods.

"Murderous thief!" he softly swore. "I'll gut you. I'll. . . ." He stopped, as if standing at attention. Carmella stood behind him, the knife she had pulled free from his companion's stomach was pressed against his back.

"You'll not kill anyone today," she said. The words were ragged, separated by deep breaths. Her struggle with the pair had winded her. "Are you all right, Fenzig?"

The gnome edged away from the wall, keeping his eyes on Harrold, and risking a glance to make sure the other sentry was truly dead. "Not exactly," he said, holding his hand over his bleeding shoulder. He was covered with blood—his own and the dead sentry's. "But I could be worse." He steadied himself, reached out to hold Carmella's skirt for support. The gnome felt faint. Maybe from loss of blood, he thought, or maybe from getting his chest and stomach beat so against the steps, or maybe from getting thrown against the wall a moment ago. Maybe the reason didn't matter. He shook his head to clear it, but that only made matters worse. The back of his head ached terribly, competed with the pain in his shoulder and arm.

Carmella warily bent, pressed the knife into Fenzig's good hand, and instructed the gnome to watch Harrold. Then she ripped strips from her dress and used them to tie the sentry's wrists and ankles. Another strip was stuffed into his mouth as a gag. When she was finished, she shoved him against the wall, made him slide down it until he was sitting. Then she ripped one more strip and turned to the gnome.

"Let me help," she offered, pressing the fabric against his wound.

He cried out from the pressure. "That's not helping," he gasped.

"We've got to stop the blood," she returned. "Here, hold this, press it hard."

The gnome sucked in his bottom lip and complied while she tore more of her dress. The once-beautiful gown was in tatters, filthy from the stone floor, and torn up to her knees. "Didn't like the color anyway," she said, picking up on his thoughts with her necklace. "It was one of Ruthe's castoffs."

She returned to fussing over him, fashioning a makeshift bandage and sling, then prodding him here and there. "I think you've broken a couple of ribs," she said finally. "And that knife cut is pretty deep. One of my father's healers upstairs will mend you." She glanced up the stairs.

"Later," Fenzig croaked. "The healer can look at me later. We've got to figure out what's going on, get to the dungeon."

"You're hurt. Bad."

"I'll be dead, bad. You, too, maybe, if we don't. . . ."

"All right, but let's hurry," she said. "And let's start by quizzing this man."

She tugged the gag free and met Harrold's icy stare. "My father would never condone guards attacking his daughter and a treasured guest."

Treasured guest, Fenzig thought. *I like the sound of that.*

"Ketterhagen? Is he pulling your strings? Is the old general trying some sly move?"

The man sneered at her, worked up a mouthful of saliva and spat it, striking her cheek. She wiped it away and grabbed his throat. "Just because you won't talk doesn't mean you're not telling me anything!" she retorted. "So it's not Ketterhagen and it's not my father giving you directions." The man's eyes grew wide with the understanding that she was pulling the thoughts from his head. "It's a wizard. A stinking wizard. Well, where is this wizard, Harrold? Where?"

Wizard? Fenzig had a bad feeling. *I hate wizards.*

Harrold shook his head furiously, tried to think of anything but the wizard.

"Upstairs? The wizard is upstairs, mingling with the guests, masquerading as a guest. Does he have a name, Harrold? Does he?" She released his throat and moved back to stand next to Fenzig.

"He has a name," she told the gnome. "But the wizard's successfully ensorcelled this man, who used to be one of my father's loyal sentries. He's enspelled his mind, making him do his bidding—and part of that bidding is keeping the wizard's identity secret."

"Do . . . do you think Erlgrane's old wizard isn't really dead? Could have pretended he was dead? Is he working to help Erlgrane even now?"

Carmella shook her head in frustration. "I don't know. It's possible. If the wizard was powerful enough, I suppose he could've fooled us, made us think he was dead."

"Told your father we should have buried him," Fenzig grumbled. "Then he'd be dead for certain."

"The old wizard certainly looked dead to me. But spells can do almost anything if the one who casts them is practiced enough, a true master. I wish I would've put more effort into magic, learned something useful, learned enough to. . . ."

"So what do we do?"

"We leave the guard here. I'm not going to get any more out of him unless I use a spell to break down whatever spell's holding his mind. And I'm not sure that's worth the time or effort. I should save my energy in case. . . ."

Keys?

"Huh?"

Does he have any keys on him?

She knelt before the guard, checked him over carefully, shook her head.

The other one.

Carmella picked through the dead guard's clothes, trying unsuccessfully to keep her hands from getting blood on them. "No keys."

Great. Ketterhagen must have them. And getting them from him is not an option I'll consider. Or maybe the guards from the earlier shift. That's out, too. So what do we do?

"We go to the dungeon anyway, Fenzighan."

With no keys to get in the cells.

"You're a thief. You're good at breaking in places. You'll manage." She shuddered. "The dungeon. It's a place in all my years in my father's palace I never visited."

You didn't miss anything, Fenzig thought.

"He rarely put anyone down there," she continued. "Or so I believed."

Well, he's there himself now . . . or at least a part of him is.

"Can you remember the way?"

I don't think I'll ever forget it.

CARMELLA'S MAGIC

Fenzig retrieved his leather shoes, shaking them to chase out a family of spiders that had moved in during the brief time since he'd abandoned them.

"Thought you didn't like shoes."

Elayne got them for me. Expensive, huh? You were so busy with Gregory all night you didn't notice that I even wore them to dinner.

"There's nothing wrong with Gregory. Jealous?"

Of a human? Never.

"But I thought you didn't like them."

Gregory? Too early to pass judgment. But he seems a little too . . . perfect. Dotes on you too much.

"Not Gregory. The shoes."

I don't like shoes, either. But I like the filth on the floor down here a lot less. Hence, the shoes.

The gnome moved slowly through the catacombs, not because he wasn't sure where he was—which he wasn't entirely, but because he felt so weak. He knew Carmella was chatting with him to keep his mind off his wound. But it wasn't working. He hurt too much—all over—to ignore the pain. He was hurt seriously, he knew it. He knew he was going to need the help of one of the duke's healers in the near future or he wasn't going to have a future. And he knew that Carmella knew her banter wasn't working to ease anything because she was wearing the damnable necklace that allowed no one to have any secrets.

She followed him in silence for a while, walking slow to accommodate his pace and pausing here and there to scoot below a curtain of spiderwebs, which the gnome was short enough to walk under.

"Are we lost, Fenzig?"

We were for a while. I got turned around a bit, but we're back on track. See? The corridor's more traveled here. He gestured with his head toward the ceiling, where the webs were higher up. *People have been walking by, knocked down all the low-hanging ones. Ah, here we are.*

"Fenzig!"

They were in the corridor that led to the duke's treasure chamber, and the gnome was padding toward the ironbound door. The three locks that hung from it had not been relatched. Fenzig noted that General Ketterhagen hadn't bothered with that when he caught the gnome earlier this night.

I need you to unmagic this, he thought to her.

"This isn't why we came down here!" She was fuming, stomping behind the gnome, and huffing. "The dungeon. The cells. The prisoners. My Father!"

We'll get there, he continued to think, knowing that she was still reading his mind. *But I left something in here, something I need. And if you want to get to the prisoners, you'd better help me. Can you unmagic this?* He waggled his fingers at the door.

Still fuming, she stared at the door for several moments. "It has a magical alarm on it," she said finally.

Tell me something I don't know, Fenzig mentally replied. *I set it off, and that's how I got caught.*

Carmella closed her eyes and hummed, a simple human tune that Fenzig guessed had nothing to do with her spell, was just some showman's effect. She traced a pattern in the air, perhaps following the unseen pattern on the door, the gnome continued to speculate. A heartbeat later her tune stopped and she grabbed the handle, tugged the door open.

"I told you I'm best at knocking down other spells." She gestured him inside. "If you steal anything, I'll toss you in the dungeon myself."

The gnome ignored her and moved toward the lantern—which was still burning, though not by much. The oil was nearly used up. *Ketterhagen forgot this, too,* he said to himself. *Forgetful old man.* The gnome grabbed up his thieves' picks, blew out the light, and rejoined Carmella.

"I wasn't going to steal from your father," he said aloud. "I wasn't going to steal from him when I was here earlier." *And if you were paying attention to my thoughts, you'd know that. I might be a thief. But I'm an honorable one.* He held up the tools for her to see. "If you want in the prison cells, these are our keys."

A while later, they were in the corridor that led to the cells.

"We have to hurry," she said. "I've been thinking about those sentries. What if Ketterhagen comes to check on them?"

That's not what I'm worried about, the gnome thought. He leaned against a slimy wall for support, was feeling weaker. *I'm worried about the wizard upstairs at your party—which should be winding down soon, I would guess. What if he comes to check on the sentries? I really hate wizards.*

Without waiting for a reply, he pushed himself away from the wall, headed toward the cell where he'd spotted King Erlgrane.

How many thoughts are you picking up?

"Just yours. Wait. Another thought. Someone just woke up. A prisoner." She touched the gnome's shoulder. "A guard. One of my father's guards is held here."

Fenzig pointed to the king's cell. Carmella looked through the barred doors, at the monarch who, in sleep, looked like a discarded rag doll.

"He's starving," she whispered. "Dying."

The gnome nodded. *And the sentries who put him in here made certain he wasn't going anywhere.*

She took in the thick chains that held his wrists and ankles, and the thick gag stuffed in his mouth. "To treat someone like this is. . . ."

"Barbaric?" Fenzig said. "Political?" He wrapped his foot against the bars until the sound eventually roused the prisoner. "Take a look inside his head, Carm. What do you hear?"

Carmella grasped the cell door, while Fenzig searched through his picks and started on the lock. She stared at the rumpled form, into the eyes that were looking sadly back at her. *"Father,"* she mouthed. *"I don't understand."*

But she listened to the thoughts of the man inside the cell, listened closely as Fenzig continued to work, cursed, and frequently changed picks. She nodded once in a while, and brushed away the tears that were streaming down her face.

"Don't open the door," she said, just as the gnome had finished with the lock.

He looked at her quizzically.

"The wizard cast a spell on the door."

Like on the door to the treasure chamber?

She nodded and nudged the gnome away. "Don't want to set off any alarms, do we?"

Fenzig backed toward the opposite cell, and, exhausted, slid down the barred door and watched Carmella trace invisible patterns in the air. Her gestures were relaxing and hypnotic. So relaxing. His eyes fluttered closed.

Carmella grimaced when she opened the door, and the lowest metal rung rasped angrily against the stone. She opened it just far enough to squeeze inside, took a couple of steps, and stopped before a palely glowing sigil on the floor.

"Lots of precautions," she whispered. "It's a good thing I'm great at knocking apart sand castles."

She knelt before the pattern and studied it. "Masterful," she hushed. "This will be difficult. Curse me for not studying magic longer." She knitted her brow in concentration, slowed the words now, drawing each syllable out.

Again she repeated the words, slower and with more force. This time her hands helped, tracing in the air the pattern she saw in her mind. This time she was rewarded. Bit by bit, the pattern she imagined began to erase itself. She continued with what now sounded like a mantra, a droning of the foreign words that all but shut out the thoughts of the other prisoners, who were now awake, and the thoughts of the very ill man in front of her.

"Please." She focused on what little was left of the pattern now, a complex series of twists and turns that she carefully and slowly undid, as if she were unlacing a favorite blouse. "Yes." Her shoulders sagged, and she wiped at the sweat on her face. She opened her eyes and noted with satisfaction that the symbol was gone.

It was a powerful, well-studied wizard who had crafted such an elaborate sigil. She wasn't sure of its complete intent. But she had gathered that whoever crossed it could very well die. "A very ugly thing you were," she pronounced as she struggled to her feet and gingerly stepped over the stones where the pattern once glowed. Nothing. She breathed a sigh of relief, then glided toward the form of King Erlgrane and gently removed the gag.

Dark eyes looked up at her from deep sockets.

"Father," she said. "Don't talk. We'll have you free in a few moments. Fenzig will pick the locks on these chains, and. . . . Fenzig?" She hadn't felt his thoughts for several minutes. Turning, she saw his crumpled little body across the corridor. "No! Fenzig!"

She hurried to him, cradled him, and gently roused him. "We've got to get you upstairs."

Yeah, he thought to her. *I guess so.* Then he looked beyond her and saw the form of King Erlgrane, and the open cell door. There was no glowing symbol on the floor. *You're a pretty good wizard after all, Carmella the Magnificent.* Mustering his last bit of strength, he grabbed her arm and got to his feet, shuffled into the cell and ignored her protests. *We've come too far to turn around,* he told her. *'Cause once we get out of here, I'm not coming back down. Ever.*

He fumbled with his thieving picks, instinctively selecting the right size to work the locks on the manacles. "You're in about as bad a shape as I am," the gnome told the prisoner. "I'm not sure how Carm's gonna get us both out of here. One more lock. There. That should do it."

The gnome replaced his picks, then promptly sagged, unconscious, against the form of King Erlgrane.

"Lady Rehmir! What happened to you?" Grechen stared slack-jawed at the disheveled form of Carmella.

"Your dress!" exclaimed a doughy human cook behind the gnome.

"And your hair! Those spider webs!" gushed another. "Where have you been?"

Carmella offered them a weak smile and cradled a bundle to her chest. The bundle was wrapped in a large swath of her dress—which was now torn off well above her knees.

"I . . . uh . . . fell," she settled on. "I went for a walk and I fell. Now, if you'll excuse me, I need to sneak up the back stairs and change. Can't have the guests see me like this."

Grechen tsk-tsked at her, and, via her necklace, Carmella picked up all manner of lascivious thoughts from the human cooks—who believed she was the victim of an unfortunate turn of a tryst in the stables.

"The party's winding down," Grechen said, as Carmella brushed by. "We're just about to serve breakfast."

Hours, I was downstairs, Carmella thought.

"Is that blood on your dress?" the doughy cook pried.

She shook her head and continued. "Grechen," she added over her shoulder. "Fix some tea for breakfast, would you please? I'll be down in a moment to help."

"Sweet Carm!" Gregory was surprised to see Carmella in her change of clothes—tight black leggings with a brilliant and billowy orange, purple, and rose tunic over the top. It was one of her more conservative Carmen the Magnificent outfits, and the closest garment within her reach in her room. Her hair was a mass of uncombed curls, all of the beads removed and most of the webs brushed away. "Your dress. . . ."

"Breakfast is about to be served. I wanted to change, get out of all those petticoats. Just too much material."

"Of course," he said, taking her arm and escorting her to the lesser ballroom. "You'd look radiant in anything, Carmella."

"Why thank you, Gregory." *You simpering liar,* she added to herself. The necklace told her he was thinking otherwise, and revealed all manner of thoughts that made her decidedly unhappy. *So I'd be quite a catch because of my father's position? The possibility of him becoming a king?* She inwardly groaned and stood next to him, suffered him pulling out the chair for her and placing the napkin on her lap.

A half-dozen tired servants bustled into the room, bearing trays of shirred eggs, spiced potatoes, bowls of fruit, and pitchers of steaming tea. Carmella took in the remaining guests, who were also obviously tired. Two tables away, the hawk-nosed woman leaned on Duke Rehmir's arm and looked up at him with starry eyes.

Carmella shook her head and ate her meal, drank none of the tea that she helped brew and that slowly and methodically put to sleep every one of the gala event's guests. The cooks in the kitchen would have succumbed by now, too, to her very special tea. Everyone sleeping soundly.

Except one.

Duke Rehmir extricated himself from Elsbeth, stood, and glared across the intervening tables.

"Wasn't sure if it would work on you, Erlgrane," Carmella said evenly. "But I hoped." She rose, carefully concealing a silver-plated knife in the folds of her tunic.

"You know."

"I know some of it. But I'd appreciate if you'd fill in all the details."

He backed away from the table, slowly walked toward her. "Unfortunate that you are not so trusting as your sisters."

"Not so blind," she corrected him, backing away to keep what she considered a safe distance.

"How did you discover my ruse?" He stopped before the last table, leaned forward and brushed his fingers at some crumbs that had spilled on the linen tablecloth. "I had his mannerisms down perfect. And I have his body."

"I found *your* body in the dungeon," she answered. Carmella shivered when she saw the eyes of her father's body narrow, his hands clench the edge of the table until the knuckles turned white. "A few questions, and my father told me what you did, told me that. . . ."

"That when I was dragged down to his cellar and put in chains that I ensorcelled the guards, bade them to fetch Duke Rehmir?"

She nodded and took a deep breath, clutched the knife a little tighter. "That you enspelled him."

"Such a simple term for such an elaborate enchantment," he continued. "I changed bodies with him, left him chained to the wall."

"And stuffed a gag in his mouth so no one would learn what

you did! Wizard!" She spat the words at him, took another step back when she watched him release the table and resume his course toward her.

"And enchanted glyphs and sigils to keep people away from him."

"Except your guards. Just how many of my father's people have you ensorcelled, Wizard-King Erlgrane?"

The portly man stopped a few steps from her, threw back his head and laughed. It was a hollow, haunting laugh, one that her father could never have managed. "Just those I needed," he said, regaining his composure.

"Ketterhagen?"

"The old fool was easy to dominate."

"Guards?"

"Only a handful. Only as many as I needed."

"My sisters?"

"Too weak-minded. It wasn't necessary. They never questioned me. And soon you won't question me, either." The form of Duke Rehmir raised its hands, the fingers of which glowed a sickly green.

Carmella dropped to the floor just as miniature lightning bolts shot from those hands and cut through the air where she'd been standing. The air instantly stank with the smell of sorcery and burnt paint and plaster. Then she rolled to her right, under the table, as another barrage of the magical lightning struck. The marble tiles where she had been a heartbeat before shattered into white and gray fragments, pelting her and biting into her legs. A heartbeat later and the table above her exploded.

"The guests!" she screamed as she rolled away and stood to face the man in her father's body.

"I've killed none of them!" he hissed. "And whatever wounds they have will heal. I only intend to kill you!"

"And my sisters!" She was reading his mind.

"In time," he said evenly, his voice dripping with a malevolence that made her shudder.

"After you've wed, gained more land?"

"Astute."

"After your wife dies. The wealthy, land-owning Elsbeth."

"But not before she produces an heir."

"She's too old!" Carmella spat.

"Magic can do wonders, girl." His hands glowed again, yellow like the sun, mesmerizing.

Carmella felt a force hold her in place, invisible bonds that tightened about her legs and arms, that started to tighten about her throat.

"And when I've my offspring," he continued, "and when my offspring is old enough, I'll let this body die and inhabit the child. It's how I live, Carmella, how I've lived for centuries. And I will have these lands, the lands Erlgrane held, and all of the Northern Reaches."

Carmella struggled futilely, then struggled for breath. He was killing her! She slammed her eyes shut, focused all her energy on undoing his spell. *Concentrate!* she mouthed. *Everything rides on this! Everything!*

She felt herself blacking out, fought it, held onto the last bit of air in her lungs and found the pattern he'd woven in the air. Found it, and began unraveling it. She gasped and dropped to the floor, the magical bands gone.

"How?"

"You're not the only wizard, Erlgrane! And, like you, it's an avocation I don't trumpet to the public!" Using her necklace to anticipate his next spell, she slid across the floor and into the hallway beyond, threw her hands over her ears to cover the deafening noise of the ballroom wall collapsing from the force of his magic.

"Don't want to harm those people? You don't care about

anyone, Erlgrane!" She scampered down the hall past the entrance to the large ballroom, then retraced her steps and hurried inside. The musicians were gone, sent home when breakfast was served. No one to hurt in here except her.

"Erlgrane?" She heard his voice behind her. "Hardly! His was just a convenient body I found at the time my old one was traveling through Erlgrane's lands years ago."

Not Erlgrane? she mouthed. *If he's not Erlgrane, then who is he?* She reached into his mind then, probing his thoughts deeply as she ran. She heard his steps echoing in the hallway, slow because of the bulk and age of her father's body. Taking a deep breath she ran toward the raised dais, dashed behind a curtain and flattened herself against the wall. She forced herself to breathe slowly now, to calm herself and focus on the wizard's thoughts. He was coming nearer, into this room.

"Carmella!" He bellowed in her father's voice. "Come to me and I'll end your life quickly. There'll be no pain. You'll feel nothing. Ah, there you are, girl. Behind the curtain. A scared mouse."

The footsteps came closer, and she concentrated on his mind, determined to discover the spell he was hatching and counter it. *Closer, closer. Now!*

She dropped to her knees and scampered out from behind the curtain just as it was engulfed in ghastly green flames. In the next instant she thrust out with her arm, jabbing the knife into the wizard's stomach.

A look of surprise crossed the man's face, and Carmella sensed his mind churning with another spell, one that would put his consciousness inside her.

"No, you don't!" Tears streamed from her eyes as she jammed the knife in again and again, her mind locked with his thoughts to make sure he didn't spirit his essence into someone else. She felt his pain, every blow she delivered, felt his sinister force seep away, die. Carmella fell across her father's body, sobbed until she hadn't the energy to cry anymore.

Five days later, Carmella sat at the foot of what was to the gnome a very large bed. She was dressed in a plain brown tunic and breeches, very un-Carmen-like, but very functional.

"Feeling better?"

The gnome looked at her from beneath the quilted covers, sighed, and finally offered her a slight smile.

"You'll have to talk," she said, pulling her necklace out of a pocket and quickly replacing it. "I've had enough of reading minds. Gregory was a cad."

"I knew from the first that I didn't like him," Fenzig said. "And, yes, I'm feeling much better. How many hours was I out?"

"Five days, give or take several minutes here and there when the cooks got some broth into you. My father's healers almost lost you."

The gnome paled and his stomach growled loudly. "But I'm gonna be all right?"

She nodded. "Everyone will be all right."

"Your father? I was worried about him, thought you should have carried him up from the dungeon, not me."

"He was safer there, while I dealt with Erlgrane, or rather the wizard who'd been Erlgrane."

Fenzig cocked his head.

"You're right not to trust wizards. A very old and a very powerful one took over Erlgrane's form when the old king of Burlengren died. The real Erlgrane died in the process."

"So the wizard could switch bodies! And that's what he did with your father!"

She frowned and nodded. "So the wizard, in Erlgrane's body, became the new ruler. But Burlengren wasn't enough for him.

He hatched the scheme to marry one of my sisters and take this land, too."

"Didn't work."

"No. And when it didn't, he arranged to fight you on the grounds of my father's estate, knowing you wouldn't kill him, that he'd be imprisoned."

The gnome's eyes grew wide. "So he planned it! Knew your father would visit him in the dungeon!"

"Switched bodies with him then," Carmella finished.

"Wow! And set a plan in motion to take these lands and Burlengren."

"And land to the west by marrying that woman."

The gnome slapped his palm against his head. "No wonder your father had changed, was more ambitious. But everything's all right now."

She rose from the bed and padded to the window, pushed aside the curtain and looked out.

"Everything's all right," he repeated hopefully.

"It will be." She pointed toward a spot that Fenzig couldn't see. "My father's body is buried there. To kill the wizard I had to. . . ." She didn't finish. Drawing the curtain, she returned to Fenzig. "But my father lives on in Erlgrane's body—though the world thinks my father is dead. Younger, healthier, more years ahead of him. And he's a king now."

Fenzig drew his lips into a tight line. "And what about these lands?"

"My sisters and I, we've given these lands to that king, though Elayne is going to manage this estate. It's all for the best. My father is a wise ruler, will make things good for the people of K'Nosha and Burlengren. Though the people of Burlengren will be amazed at the change in their monarch's temperament." She finally smiled. "And he doesn't have to worry about marrying Elsbeth. She was engaged to a different body. She's still mourning my father's death."

The gnome wiped his brow in a mock gesture of being relieved. "And what about you?"

She shrugged. "I'm all right, too, I guess. But I'm not sticking around. Politics, courts, big parties. Not my style. My wagon's hitched, ready to go."

The gnome threw back the covers and gingerly got to his feet, scowled when he saw he was wearing a cutoff and sleeveless Carmen the Magnificent blouse. "I'll join you."

"We've got a stop to make first," she said.

He followed her from the room. "Yeah, to a tailor. I need some clothes. None of your stuff. No cook's dresses, either."

"All right. But another stop after that. To Graespeck."

"You mean what's left of it."

They took a winding staircase downstairs, through a hallway where workmen were busy repairing a wall. Fenzig didn't ask what had happened, figured Carmella would fill him in when she was ready. He poked his head in the small ballroom, saw shattered marble tile, blackened walls, and wished he hadn't been in bed when all the action was going on.

Outside, the Carmen the Magnificent wagon waited, with Summer tied behind it. Carmella somehow knew he'd want to go with her. Nearby were a dozen larger wagons, all filled with lumber and various building supplies.

"For Graespeck?" the gnome asked happily.

"Father insisted you receive a reward for helping put everything in order. If it hadn't been for you, we might have never learned that the wizard had switched bodies with him."

"A reward?"

"Well, I knew you'd refuse, of course. Especially since you said you'd never go below the palace again. And that's where the treasure room is."

"But. . . ."

"So I accepted the reward for you."

"But I might have. . . ."

"I took enough gems to cover all of this." She swept her arm to indicate the caravan. "And the dozen wagons loaded with supplies that left yesterday."

"Another dozen?"

"Well, twenty actually. Eight carried all the gnomes who'd been staying in K'Nosha."

"Twenty?"

"The builders I hired had their own wagons."

"Builders?"

"From the Northern Reaches. Nothing but the best."

Fenzig swallowed hard. "That . . . all of that . . . cost a fortune."

"No small fortune to be sure. I bought the best material available, too, with your reward. Your friends are very happy. And your father and Apple-Pie Annie are supervising everything. Leonard Smithson. . . ."

"Smithsward," he corrected her.

"Is helping, too. So you should be very proud. Your fortune was very well spent. I even got something out of it."

Fenzig didn't ask. He stared at the wagons. *My fortune,* he mouthed.

"Recipes, formulas. Hundreds. Your gnome friends gave me everything they'd committed to memory. Hand creams, skin moisturizers, cold remedies, hair tonics, wart removers, toothache soothers, toenail strengtheners, flu cures, snakebite antidotes, fixes for diseases and rashes I've never heard of. Fenzig, you and I will be rich."

My fortune, he mouthed again. *The prosperity I'd coveted. My prosperity!*

"I kept just enough gems to cover the cost of all the ingredients, some new clothes—we'll have to get something flashy for you, some traveling expenses."

He numbly climbed onto the wagon, still favoring his sore shoulder.

"I've just enough magical paint left to add your name to the wagon." She beamed and climbed up beside him and grabbed the reins, flicked the wrists and set the caravan into motion. "I was thinking about calling you Fenzig the Fantastic."

"It'll do," the gnome replied. "Nothing too flashy to wear, okay?" He jiggled the lapel of his shirt. "I don't like to stand out."

"Some purples and reds?"

"Grays."

"How about dark blue with some beads sewn on?"

"Blacks."

"We'll see." She gently nudged him in the side and grinned broadly.

He smiled back. *Fenzig the Fantastic?* he thought to himself. *Yes, indeed. I kind of like the sound of that.*

ABOUT THE AUTHOR

Jean Rabe has written twenty fantasy novels and more than three dozen short stories in the fantasy, science fiction, military, and mystery genres. In addition, she has edited several anthologies and magazines. When not writing (which isn't often), Jean tugs on old socks with her two dogs, reads by her goldfish pond, attempts to garden, and dabbles in war, board, and role-playing games. She shares her Wisconsin home with her husband, the aforementioned dogs, a cantankerous parrot, a variety of fish, and growing stacks of to-be-read books. Visit her Web site at www.jeanrabe.com.